Jessie's Hope

To Brenda
May God bless you
richly with peace
and joy!

Jennifer
Hallmark

by

JENNIFER HALLMARK

FIREFLY
SOUTHERN FICTION
LIGHTHOUSE PUBLISHING OF THE CAROLINAS

JESSIE'S HOPE BY JENNIFER HALLMARK
Published by Firefly Southern Fiction
an imprint of Lighthouse Publishing of the Carolinas
2333 Barton Oaks Dr., Raleigh, NC 27614

ISBN: 978-1-946016-86-7
Copyright © 2019 by Jennifer Hallmark
Cover design by Elaina Lee
Interior design by Karthick Srinivasan

Available in print from your local bookstore, online, or from the publisher at:
ShopLPC.com

For more information on this book and the author visit: JenniferHallmark.com

Brought to you by the creative team at Lighthouse Publishing of the Carolinas:
Eva Marie Everson, Sue Fairchild, and Eddie Jones.

Library of Congress Cataloging-in-Publication Data
Hallmark, Jennifer
Jessie's Hope / Jennifer Hallmark 1st ed.

Printed in the United States of America

PRAISE FOR *JESSIE'S HOPE*

Jessie's Hope is a slice of southern life, served up with all the love anyone could wish. Author Jennifer Hallmark is a master storyteller who engages us from the start with true-to-life characters and a story that pulls us in and won't let us go. This author is one to watch and I look forward to more stories from her.

~ Edie Melson
Award-winning Author & Speaker
Director of Blue Ridge Mountains Christian Writers Conference
Life-long Southerner

Jessie's Hope will have you flying through the pages to find out if Jessie will receive her dream wedding and happy ending. Every character is incredibly complex and sympathetic, flaws and all, with each granted the opportunity for a redemption, whether they choose to accept it or not. As for Jessie's dream wedding, just about every obstacle attempts to disrupt the plans from bad weather, to wedding dress mishaps, to family members who walked out only to return at inopportune moments. You'll cry, laugh, and smile with the characters as they endure one trial after another and seek to overcome past ghosts to embrace a glorious future. Written in poignant language that touches the heart and mind, Jessie's Hope is the next story you should put on your TBR list.

~ Hope Bolinger
Author of *Blaze*

Jennifer Hallmark's writing is clearly an extension of herself. With her debut novel, *Jessie's Hope,* she brings to life her zeal for life and her love for individuals. She draws you into the romance of not only young love, but the romance of what being a family means. Jennifer's characters triumph over adversity and warm your heart.

~ Fay Lamb
Author of *Storms in Serenity*

Jessie's Hope by Jennifer Hallmark is an amazing book. Filled with tragedy, redemption, forgiveness and threads of faith and love, this story set in a small southern town will hold your heart to the very last word. Jesse is a strong character. Unable to walk after a tragic accident as a child, Jessie is now about to be married to the man of her dreams. But past hurts and new revelations keep getting in the way of her big day.

After beating all the odds and finding her strength in God's grace, Jessie's life turns around and she now looks toward the future, not the past. The slow, steady weave of words in this story are pieced together like a beautiful, patterned quilt that shines brightly with the power of faith. Find a porch swing and a chenille throw and spend an afternoon with *Jessie's Hope*. Your life will be the better for it.

~ **Lenora Worth**
Bestselling Author
Their Amish Reunion

Jessie's Hope is a heart-tugging story of the forgiveness that we all need. It is a triumphant reminder that, even when everything seems to be wrong, God is working our lives out for His good.

~ **Jodie Bailey**
Award-winning author of *Quilted by Christmas* and *Fatal Response*

In Jennifer Hallmark's debut novel, *Jessie's Hope*, the title character doubts whether she can have a normal life, while her grandfather grapples with his inability to provide the wedding she desires. Small acts of kindness blend together with a common thread of hope to bring Jessie's and her grandfather's dreams to fruition. This is an inspiring story that catches hold of your emotions from the beginning.

~ **Betty Thomason Owens**
Author of *Rebecca's Legacy*

Jennifer Hallmark depicts southern culture in a way that makes one want to sit on their neighbor's porch swing sipping sweet tea. In our rushed and often disconnected culture, it's refreshing to encounter, through the story Hallmark creates, enduring community, family, and faith.

~ **Jennifer Slattery**
Award-winning author of *Restoring Her Faith*

ACKNOWLEDGMENTS

Wow. I've dreamed of this day since I stepped out of my comfort zone and took my first writing class in 2006. I owe so much to so many.

The Lawrence County Writers Guild. Jane, who taught that first class, thank you for stepping out. My friends in the guild—your encouragement never ceases to amaze me.

North Alabama Writers. Another group of friends who keep me grounded.

Fay Lamb and the ACFW Scribes 218. Fay, you believed in me before anyone else. Shirley and the group—you read my simple prose and reassured me I'd get better.

Tracy Ruckman. You gave me my first chance in a book compilation. Thank you.

Word Weavers and the members of Page 11 and Page 20. You've helped me further develop my critiquing and computer skills. I can't wait to read your books.

Lighthouse Publishing of the Carolinas. Eddie, Cindy, Marcie and everyone else. You helped me brainstorm at a conference, then later bought my book. I am thankful and truly blessed.

Eva Marie Everson—my editor and mentor. Your time and patience took me and my writing to a new level. I appreciate you and am humbled. Cyle Young—agent extraordinaire.

Inspired Prompt bloggers. It started with Betty Thomason Owens, Christina Rich, and myself: the editor, tech master, and guru. Look how we've grown. I've made so many friends. Love y'all.

Vera Rutherford and Mary's Bridal and Formal Wear. Thanks for all the advice.

Betty Thomason Owens and Jennifer Slattery. My closest writing friends and critique partners. Betty, we've got to go to another conference together soon. Jennifer, we could be sisters.

My church family and friends at New Life and The Bridge. You've made me a better person. (Patty, Jennifer, Christina, Debbie, Debbie,

Tina, Meleah, Valerie, and all the rest) I'm blessed to know you.

Steve and Kathy. You're my sounding boards and pick me up when I'm low. I'm forever grateful.

Joyce. My best friend. I get tears in my eyes trying to think of how to thank you. I love you.

Rose. We had so many plans of what we'd do when I sold my first book. I know you're cheering me on. I miss you. Save a place for me.

My extended family. The Disons, Swets, and Gautneys. The Hallmarks and Landers. I'm proud to be a part of you.

My brother, Jesse, and his family: Rita, Jessica, Ben, Jeffrey, and Lura. My sister-in-law, Kay, and her family: Charlotte, Thomas, Elijah, Nate, and Colt. My daughter-in-law, Kristie. Love y'all.

Mom and Dad. For all your support. My stepdad, Thomas in heaven. You helped take care of Mom. My stepsister Michelle and her family.

My grandchildren: Ava, Sadie, Zeke, Cohen, Phoebe, and Rozlyn. So much of my world revolves around you. Love you to the moon and back.

My children: Mandy and Jonathan. You've put up with so much over the years for me to write, from quick meals to listening to me read parts aloud. Can you believe I made it? No. We made it.

My husband, Danny. You love me anyway. I can't think of anyone I love more on this earth. Thank you for supporting me in everything I've done and still do. You're the best!

God. We wrote this book together and You held me when I cried and high-fived me when we formed a great sentence. I couldn't have done it without You. You are truly my everything.

DEDICATION

For My Parents
Mom—you're my biggest cheerleader and encourager.
Dad—you loved to write and understood me. Wish you were here.

Chapter One

April 28, 2008

Homer watched the enormous four-wheel-drive tractor as it crawled down the gravel road in front of his house, then released a sigh. That machine could do in a few hours what he'd been working at all day. Would it ever get any better? He only wanted to care for his household, but life threw more at him than he could deal with. What if he failed? His granddaughter Jessie deserved more. Better. How could he help her deal with the emotional blow of their family torn apart by the divorce?

The forest green glider outlined in dirty white creaked in protest as he shifted to a more comfortable position. He had to sit a minute and cool off. Straightening his long legs, he winced as his arthritic knee stiffened. *Why'd we put off buying cushions to pad this cold metal antiquity?*

He pulled off his cap and ran his fingers through his hair, leaning forward. Too much work to do, too many bills to pay. Why'd Wayne have to leave?

Homer opened his eyes to the sound of a vehicle rambling up the driveway. One glance at the Chevrolet Beretta initiated a slight smile. His girls. Elizabeth had barely parked the car between his old truck and Martha's Ford when ten-year-old Jessie bounded from the car.

"Hey, Papaw!" She scampered up the porch steps. Her brown hair, the color of molasses, was tucked into a blue baseball cap, the same color as her Riverview Bulldogs jersey. "We need your truck."

She flung herself on the seat beside him. "Can I have a dollar for a candy bar? You know I'll need it when the game's over." Jessie was a miniature version of her mother. Same color hair, same deep brown eyes.

The screen door to the old house swung open and Martha padded across the porch. "Why, Jessie. I thought you had a ballgame." She pushed back the gray streaked bob from her face, then hugged her granddaughter.

"I do, Mamaw. And we're in a hurry."

"Let me see what I've got." Homer dug the faded wallet from his jeans pocket. Thirty dollars left. He produced two one-dollar bills. Anything for his only grandchild. "Here's enough for a candy bar and a coke."

By now Elizabeth—their only child and one they'd had a little later than most of the folks they knew—joined them on the porch. "Dad, you don't have to do that."

"You know I don't mind. Something wrong with your car?"

"Tammie's bringing me an old rocking chair she doesn't want. I thought I'd stain it to sit on the front porch. And I'm about out of gas and really don't have time to stop." She bent to kiss his cheek. "You do have gas, don't you?"

"Of course." He furrowed his brows and poked around in his pocket until he found the truck key. "A vehicle runs better if you keep it topped off. Here you go."

"I know. There just doesn't seem to be enough hours in the day." She glanced at her phone. "Wow. Ten 'til six." She waved Jessie to her. "We've gotta go." She smiled in appreciation, her brown eyes looking almost apologetic. "Love y'all."

As they trotted to his truck, Homer readjusted his cap. Was Elizabeth overwhelmed or just tired? Or maybe she's coming down with something. He'd ask her about it when she brought the truck back.

"Be careful," Martha called after them. "They're calling for a downpour this evening."

"We'll be fine." Elizabeth slid into the old truck and waved as she cranked it. She shifted into reverse and lumbered back down the driveway.

"You know, Homer, you need to go ahead and buy new tires for that pickup." Martha plopped down on the nearby porch swing and it creaked with her weight. "And maybe clean it up."

"We've been over this." He shook his head. She just didn't understand a man's farm truck. And the fact that the money just wasn't there. "When the cotton's in, I'll get 'em. And it's clean enough for me."

In the distance, the vehicle turned from their gravel road onto the pavement. The dust stirred on their driveway making an eerie filter for the sunlight peeking out behind thickening clouds.

"Yep," Homer muttered. "Looks like we're in for a storm."

***

The last flecks of light faded as fat splashes of rain stirred the dust below his feet. Homer stood outside the barn door and grinned up at the sky, happy to see the rain. The cotton sure needed it, and he needed all the extra money he could lay his hands on to help Elizabeth and Jessie. But how long could he keep robbing Peter to pay Paul? As long as he had to.

He set off at a trot from the barn. The cows and chickens fed, time now for a late supper. And his girls should be back soon.

He stopped on the back stoop and knocked the wet from his ball cap. He inhaled. Something smelled good. Cornbread and beans. Maybe a pie. He pushed through the door and into the small kitchen. Bright yellow curtains were stirred by the breeze through the window.

But no Martha. He opened his mouth to call for her when the phone rang.

"Homer, can you get that?" Martha's voice sounded from their bedroom.

He trudged into the living room and picked up the landline on the end table by his recliner. "Hello?"

"Homer? It's Bill."

"Yeah, Bill. What's up?"

"Look … it's Elizabeth and Jessie." The tension in Bill's voice ran fingers of fear up Homer's spine. "You gotta get to Hodge's Corner. There's been a bad wreck." He paused but only for a second. "Hurry."

The receiver slipped from Homer's hand. Not his girls.

"Homer, what is it?" Martha's face blanched as she stared at the fallen receiver.

"We gotta go."

As they raced toward Martha's car, a wicked flash of lightning split the sky right before the deluge began.

***

Ten years later...

Jessie glanced around, her fingers loosely clasped in her lap. Was something wrong? Matt's silence created emptiness in the pit of her stomach. She leaned back and snuggled closer to him on the dark-green porch swing.

"What is it?" She pushed back her brown bangs, then giggled a bit too loud. "You've been acting awfully weird. Not remembering what day it is and misplacing your keys. Now we've been sitting here for ten minutes, and you haven't said a word."

"Nothing." Matt grinned and jingled the keys in his right front pocket. "Had a lot on my mind, I guess." He stretched his arm along the porch swing, shifting away from her.

Jessie squinted. "Like what?" He'd been reserved all week, so unlike his easygoing ways. The cool breeze picked up and wafted across the porch, causing her to shiver. He wrapped an arm around her shoulder.

"Jessie, can I ask you something?"

"Of course. Anything." She looked up to the light-blue eyes that captured her long ago. They were nearly buried under the rim of his ballcap, but they still managed to make her heart leap. He gently swung the swing with his foot. Her heart rate increased as his tender smile met hers. She reached up and grasped the hand around her shoulder.

His mouth drew to a line as he stared in the direction of the barn. A lone cow mooed in the distance as darkness swallowed up the farms on Blue Ridge Road. From the nearby pond, frogs sang their raspy songs as a few fireflies floated nearby. The dusk threw wide shadows from the tall oaks that inhabited the front yard. From inside the house, someone flipped on the porch light.

"Jessie?" Matt straightened, removing his arm from around her.

She fidgeted, then rested her elbow on his shoulder. "Yes?"

Why was he taking so long?

He pushed back his ballcap and continued to survey the barn. Scant light illuminated his smooth features. "How long have we known each other? Since I moved here in the fifth grade, right?"

"Of course." Her mind drifted back to elementary school. "We met in the lunchroom, after your mama brought you in. You had to eat with us little kids. I felt so sorry for you."

He turned his head to smile at her. "You never told me that. How come?"

She grasped his hand again and traced her finger over the rough skin. "How come I never told you that or how come I felt sorry for you?"

"The second one."

"You were petrified. And I know what it's like to be stared at."

"Do you know what I remember about that day?" He smiled once more and his teeth shone against his farmer's tan. "The teacher guided me to the only available seat at the end of the table by you. You had your lunch perfectly laid out. The Salisbury steak was cut in uniform pieces, peas lined up around the square tray and the potatoes were smashed into a neat square. I'd never seen a kid organize their food before."

Heat crept up Jessie's neck. She stiffened, releasing his hand. Why did he have to mention her OCD tendencies? "Well, I guess I've always been a bit of a perfectionist."

"A *bit*?"

"Okay, a lot." Jessie crossed her arms. "But isn't that what you love about me?"

His smile faded. He stood and walked to the edge of the porch. He pushed his hand in one of his pants pockets, then drew it out in a fist.

She licked trembling lips, knowing that what she'd feared had come to life. Matt was breaking up with her. He didn't love her. A minute ago, she'd asked him if her OCD was one of the things he loved about her and he'd not answered.

She drew in a breath, but it only strangled her.

But then, with a quick movement, he perched on one knee beside the porch swing. "I think I've loved you since the first day I saw you." His left hand gripped hers while he opened his other hand, revealing a ring, the diamonds small, round, and perfect. "I don't ever want us to be apart. I want us to get married."

She gasped as he slid the cool metal onto her finger. "Oh, Matt." She stared at the white gold circle with the small cluster of diamonds. Every ounce of fear dissipated as she relaxed. "It's beautiful."

He shifted, but didn't rise. "Well?"

She held the ring toward the porch light, and twirled it on her finger. "Well, what?"

"Yes or no?"

Marriage. She couldn't help but wonder how Mamaw and Papaw would react. Would they be happy or would they ask her to wait a while longer?

If only her mother were alive.

Jessie patted the seat beside her. Her smile widened as he pushed from his knee and slid in by her. Her arms encircled his neck. "I love you, Matt Jansen, more than anything in the world. Yes, I'll marry you." She pressed her lips against his for a long moment.

In the fading light, she snuggled against his chest as he pushed the swing back into a gentle motion. She could stay here, just like this, forever. With the crickets singing their praises of the momentous occasion, joined by an occasional hoot of an owl. Her old dog, Bear, toddled up the steps and plopped down on the worn welcome mat by the front door. The rest of her life faded in the perfection of the moment. Except that ...

She glanced at Matt. He loved her. That much she knew. But would he stay when things got tough?

Matt gestured toward the hound. The dog's short grizzled hair and floppy ears revealed a sprinkling of basset in his heritage. "Lazy dog. We'll have to get us one, you know. Bear will never want to leave your papaw."

"That's true." She sighed. "Our own dog." She took a moment to allow everything to settle. "Mrs. Matt Jansen," she said. The words tickled her ears as she glanced at the ring. "How am I going to tell Mamaw and Papaw?"

"Don't you think they know how we feel about each other?"

Jessie released a deep breath as she glanced at the front door. "Mamaw does for sure, but Papaw, he still thinks I'm his baby girl. Ever since Mama died, they've raised me like their own. It'll be a shock."

Matt brightened. "I've got an idea. I'll come over for breakfast in the morning, so we can tell them together."

She poked his shoulder as she grinned. "Any excuse for Mamaw's cooking."

"Jessie." Mamaw's voice rang from inside the house. "It's late. And it's getting cool out there."

Jessie straightened. Her grandparents worried too much. "I sure hope they understand. Mamaw still treats me like I'm ten instead of twenty. Some things will probably never change."

Matt kissed her cheek before standing. "I'm glad your grandparents are protective. Gives me less to worry about." He ambled near the door and pulled the self-propelled wheelchair toward the swing. Matt parked it as close to the swing as he could, then locked the wheels. With a practiced hand, he bent over to swing the foot pedals up and out of the way.

"I don't know why you worry about me." Jessie huffed. "I'm as able-bodied as anyone you know. You're starting to sound like Mamaw." She gripped the armrest and carefully maneuvered herself into the chair, straightening her useless legs. He flipped the foot pedals down as she picked up each leg to set it on the pedal.

He crouched beside her. "You are the most capable person I know. I'll be back in the morning, and we'll tell them together."

She leaned over and kissed him. "I can't wait."

"Bear," he commanded the old dog. "Out of the way."

The short-legged hound heaved to all fours and shuffled toward the steps before he collapsed again. Matt pulled the screen open and swung the old wooden door inward as Jessie pushed against the lightweight wheels to maneuver into the house. "See you in the morning," Matt said, closing the door.

Jessie only nodded as she glanced over one shoulder. Once fully inside, she slipped the ring from her finger and shoved it into her jeans pocket.

"Is Matt gone?" Mamaw wandered into the living room, turned off the television, and picked up an empty glass from the end table. She peered out the window. "I reckon so. I hear his noisy truck now."

"He'll be back for breakfast." Jessie turned her wheelchair and reached for her book, which was propped on the floral print couch. Mamaw's expression at the sight of the ring would be priceless, but it could wait until morning.

"That young man sure likes to eat." Mamaw narrowed her eyes. "Are you feeling okay? You look flushed."

"I'm in love." She flashed a small grin. Hopelessly, extremely in love. "I'll see you in the morning."

"Goodnight, dear." She brushed a kiss on Jessie's cheek before disappearing into the kitchen.

Jessie stared at her grandmother's retreating form. Her grandparents' bedroom rested on the other side of the kitchen where Papaw had long ago retired for the night. *Homer always goes to bed with the chickens*, Mamaw would say.

Got up with them too.

Some things never changed.

She maneuvered between the chair and the recliner, pushed into her bedroom, and carefully pulled the ring from her pocket. She flipped on her bedside lamp and admired it under the light.

"Mrs. Matt Jansen." She couldn't say those words enough. The small diamonds sparkled, and Jessie slipped it back on her finger.

She couldn't wipe off her smile as she brushed her teeth, combed through her baby-fine hair, and changed into her gown. As always, the extended time it took to complete the simplest tasks wore on her.

"No wonder Mamaw always pushes me to bed early. She knows how slow I am," Jessie whispered at her reflection in the low-hung mirror. But at least she didn't fuss as much as she used to.

She found her phone and sent a text to Matt. *I love you. Goodnight.* She cradled the phone close, waiting for his reply.

In a moment, her doorbell-text ring sounded. She read the message aloud as if it were the first time he'd ever texted her. *Love you!*

She drew her journal off the nightstand and tossed it on the pillow before moving herself onto the bed.

What am I thankful for today? She penned the words at the top of the journal page. Pastor Allen had preached last Sunday morning on learning to be grateful and on keeping a thirty-day journal. She was now at Day Five. *I'm thankful to be alive and to know that Matt loves me. He wants to marry me. Wheelchair and all. What more could I ask for?*

Jessie blinked back tears. She could have told him she'd loved him from the first time he spoke to her. He was the first of the students who hadn't gawked at her wheelchair as if she were an alien from another planet instead of the same classmate as she'd been before the accident. He later shared that his grandma was wheelchair-bound also.

I think that's what means the most to me, she wrote. *Matt knows the struggles, the aggravation of dealing with a chair. He proposed anyway. I've always hoped he would. I was so afraid he wouldn't ...*

Jessie laid the journal on the nightstand and flipped off the lamp. Her light pink curtains and white chenille bedspread faded as darkness, except for a slight glow from her phone, hugged her.

She squeezed her eyes shut. It was almost like being whole. When the room was dark and the covers surrounded her, she was like everyone else. When she sat beside Matt on the swing, she was not crippled. The movement belonged to her, rising inside her chest until she was pushing the swing with her own foot.

She stared in the direction of the chair near her bed. How could she hate and love something at the same time? An unwelcomed tear trickled down her cheek. The church had purchased the lightweight modern wheelchair, so much better than the clunky ancient one she had before. With this one, she could go almost anywhere. Do almost anything.

Except pretend to be whole.

Jessie shook her head again. Why did she have to be crippled in the wreck? Why did her mother have to die? She forced the questions from her mind. Don't go there, she told herself. Not tonight. Not tonight of all nights.

She could easily vent her anger on everyone around her, but what good would that do?

Concentrate on the blessings. If she could focus on the good, maybe for a moment, she could forget the bad. The wreck. The pain. The blessings were her grandparents. God. Church. Life. Matt. She covered her face with her hands.

Matt.

Did he really know what he was in for?

Chapter Two

Jeff Claremore pedaled down the dirt road, then stopped when he reached the driveway. Man, was it hot. And barely daylight. A bead of sweat rolled down his cheek. He pulled up the tail of his faded t-shirt and wiped his brow.

A rickety building sat a good piece back, facing him. Long tendrils of carpet grass broke through the fescue in clumps. No trees for shade, but a brisk breeze kept the heat bearable. The hue of hunter-green paint contrasted with the age and dilapidation of the building.

He dismounted and pushed his bike close to the faded door, leaning it against the shed. He gazed at the monstrosity. What a weird building. And why *green*?

Two large doors, with an opening wide enough to admit a car, remained closed with two padlocks gleaming in the early morning sunshine. A small side door, almost hidden from view, displayed another padlock and proved surprisingly sturdy.

He tugged at the lock for good measure, as he did each time he came. Three padlocks. What could be inside? Stolen goods, he'd bet.

Didn't matter. He had a lawn to mow.

He shrugged and trudged toward the red push mower concealed beneath a moldy tarp. Three bricks stacked atop each other stood behind the machine. He pushed them with the toe of his sneaker, then stepped back. He didn't mind creepy-crawlies, but snakes were another thing altogether. The black racer hidden there last week could've been a rattler.

He bent over and picked up the sealed sandwich bag. He pulled out a ten and two fives. Twenty dollars, same as always. The old man never forgot. He shoved the money into his jeans pocket, tossed the bag into a nearby burn barrel, and checked the oil and gas.

A high-pitched creak rolled shivers up his spine, and he jumped as he looked up. Only the loose tin on top shuffling in the wind. Nothing to fear. He turned and scoped out the place. He'd watched one too many horror flicks. So, what if he was in the middle of nowhere?

Still … why would the old man want his yard around the old shed mowed every week? He stared at the two stone lions nearby. Creepy. One of the four-foot high statues waited by the shed while the other stood like a sentry near the end of the driveway. Their concrete snarl fixed in his mind.

He glanced around the yard for any trash and flinched as the tin screeched again. Stop it, he told himself. It's money and it would provide gas for Saturday night and a date with Brittany. Like all his other mowing jobs that were close enough to ride the bike.

He grinned as he pulled the rope. The mower coughed to life.

***

Homer stood at the edge of the porch and sipped his lukewarm coffee. Should go get a refill, but the sense of peace that rolled over the farm this morning refreshed him and he was loath to leave.

He leaned against one of the timber posts. The weather-beaten porch was much like other porches on the other wood-sided houses in the small town of Riverview. Comfortable. Three steps led to the front of it and the front door while a small ramp worked its way off the left side toward the driveway. A fresh coat of paint would do it good, as would a few well-placed nails.

Yeah … it was time to get to that fix-it list Martha made him. A movement near the barn caught his eye. The old cow blinked at him as she stood by the feed trough. The quiet of a Saturday morning never lasted long enough. He inhaled. Bacon.

Okay. First breakfast, then chores and the to-do list.

"Bear." The dog, lying under the porch swing, never lifted his head. "I need to work on Martha's list, and I think I'll start with the glider."

He turned back to the porch, running his hand over the cool metal arm of the long seat. A fleck of dark green stuck to his hand, and he flicked it away. "The bacon sure smells good," he said to the dog. "Hope it's crispy."

Homer opened the screen door, then shut it quickly behind him to keep out the flies, a constant battle on a farm. Might need to spray again. As he crossed the living room into the kitchen, he walked slowly, not wanting to wake Jessie. Saturday was her only day to sleep in since she worked in the office at the elementary school. She even worked during summer school for extra money.

"Didn't want her to get a job," Homer mumbled. "I'd have taken care of her." He would do anything for her, but she had wanted to work. Yes, keeping busy had been good for her, learning to do things for herself, but he still worried …

He stepped into the kitchen. The small walnut table was covered with a checked tablecloth and a vase of day lilies graced its center. Jessie was already at the table, setting out plates and silverware. She stacked napkins by the salt and pepper shaker.

"You're up early." Homer added coffee to his cup. "Today is Saturday, isn't it?"

"Yes, it's Saturday." She grinned, then wheeled to the hutch and drew another fork from the drawer. "Matt's coming to breakfast."

"Well, I'm almost finished cooking." Martha stood over the well-used stove, scrambling eggs. She tucked a loose strand of dark gray hair back into the relaxed bun she often wore. "I hope he gets here soon."

"Matt's here." A voice erupted from the living room. The tall, sparse young man loped into the kitchen, planting a kiss on Martha's cheek. He removed his ball cap, exposing his chestnut brown hair. "I smelled the bacon when I stepped out of my truck, so I raced inside before your husband ate it all."

"Oh, Matt. You won't ever need to do that." Martha shooed him with her fork. "Get a cup of coffee."

He picked a cup and poured his coffee.

"Where's *my* kiss?" Jessie pursed her lips.

Matt bent to kiss her, then pulled up a chair next to Homer as he heaped sugar into his cup.

"Mornin', Mr. Smith."

"Mornin'." Homer approved of the young man next to him. A fine boy from a good farming family. He had a decent job at the Tool and Die plant, but the best thing about him was the way he treated Jessie. Like the princess she surely was.

Matt turned to Homer. "When are you going to plant your soybean patch? It's supposed to be dry all next week."

"That's when I aim to do it." Homer eyed the plates of food Martha placed on the table. Over forty years of marriage and her cooking still made his mouth water. "I've got to do a little work on the tractor before I can finish the plowing."

"Ready to bless the food?" Martha nodded toward Jessie as she set her own mug on the table.

Everyone bowed their heads. "Dear Lord, thank you for this lovely day," Jessie said. "You've done so much for me—" Her voice broke and Homer peeked at her. A tear ran down her cheek. Something was wrong ...

"Bless this food for the nourishment of our bodies," she continued, the words rushed. "Amen." She wiped her eyes. "Please pass the eggs, Mamaw."

Still watching Jessie, Homer grasped a couple of pieces of toast. Why had she gotten so choked up? Matt passed him the plate of bacon as Martha refilled Homer's cup.

"Need more coffee, Matt?" Martha eyed the mug, half empty already.

"No, ma'am. I'm good." He winked at Jessie and she blushed.

What was wrong with them? Homer frowned. Acting like schoolchildren.

Martha set the coffeepot back on its base and sat. Jessie giggled as she reached for the salt.

"Jessica Rose Smith." Martha jumped up from her chair, hands clutching her cheeks. "What is on your finger?"

Homer stared at Jessie's ring. A diamond. Small, but still a diamond.

Jessie held out her hand. "Matt won it in one of those machines at the dollar store."

"That's no quarter trinket." Martha stepped around Homer and seized Jessie's hand. "It's beautiful. Oh, Matt. Oh, *Jessie*." Her ample arms surrounded both of them. "Homer, can you believe it? Our Jessie is going to get married."

Homer stared. Jessie married? The girl that meant so much to him? To Matt? Of course, to Matt. He'd always been there for her.

"Well, Papaw, are you happy for us?" Jessie grasped his hand. "You are, aren't you?"

"Course I am." He grunted. "You couldn't have picked a finer girl, Matt."

"Have you made any plans yet?" Martha still stood by them. "Or set a date?"

"Matt only asked me last night." Jessie released Homer's hand. "I've always loved a fall wedding. With warm days and cool nights. Orange and brown colors."

"Anything's okay with me." Matt refilled his plate with eggs and two more biscuits. "After we eat, we're going to tell my folks. We'll figure out a date later."

Homer moved his fork around, but couldn't manage to swallow much of Martha's fine breakfast. Could Jessie make it without them? Sure, Matt would be there, but where would they live so he could be close enough to help?

Of course. The spot of land where Wayne and Elizabeth had their trailer. Right next to them. It would be the perfect place. He wondered then if Summerton's Mobile Home World would have something he could reasonably afford.

Homer picked up his mug and gulped his coffee.

A "doorbell" chimed and Jessie snatched her phone from her front jeans pocket and read the screen. "It's Millie," she said to her grandfather. "I called her earlier. She's already volunteered to help organize the wedding."

Millie. Homer rubbed his nose. Jessie's overly-energetic friend … the kindergarten teacher … bounced instead of walked. Well, beggars couldn't be choosers. Besides, they'd need all the help they could get.

Martha pushed back from the table and raked the rest of her breakfast into the scrap bucket. "I still can't get over the thought of you two getting married. Seems like yesterday, you were riding your bike to see Jessie, Matt. And now, look." She smiled. "I'd hoped it would be you."

"I'm glad to soon be a part of this family, Mrs. Smith." Matt stood and handed her his plate. "Seems like I already am."

"Of course, you are. We all think the world of you." Martha turned on the water and squirted dish soap. "Now you go on." She said over her shoulder. "Jessie and I will have these dishes done in a minute."

Homer motioned to Matt, and the young man followed him out on the front porch where Bear perched near the steps. Homer cleared his throat. He needed to know how much of the future Matt had planned for. "Well, son, I guess you've thought this through. How you're going to take care of Jessie. She's special, you know."

"Yes, sir." Matt stood at the edge of the porch staring at a dirty white pick-up rumbling by, kicking up dust. "I've got a good job and insurance. First, we'll have to find a place to live."

"You'll stay here," Homer interrupted, waving his hand to his left. "I mean, we've got a place right over there, on the corner of this land. Septic tank and everything."

The tall wiregrass past the barn swayed in the breeze. Beyond the boxwood shrubs and a driveway, the skeletal remains of a once-used house trailer spot lay dormant, in wait of someone to come along and possibly love it back to life.

A whiff of honeysuckle from the nearby woods made its way to Homer's nostrils.

Normally he found the aroma soothing, but the trailer spot always riled him, being the place where Wayne and Elizabeth made a home, before the good for nothing goat ran off. Homer clenched his teeth. Always drinking, that boy was. Why Elizabeth couldn't see it …

"Mr. Smith? I'd like to walk over there. Take a look."

Homer unclenched his teeth. "Oh, sure." He lowered his shoulders. "You know, son, all this will be Jessie's when Martha and I are gone, so y'all might as well live here."

Homer led the way to the barn. Matt unlatched the gate enclosing the cow pasture and corner trailer spot. Bear tagged along, sniffing everything along the way. Avoiding the cow piles, they passed the small catfish pond that provided water for Homer's few cows. Sage grass mingling with fescue grew thick. Almost time for the first cutting of hay. Would he make enough extra hay to sell part of the crop? With a wedding to pay for now, they'd need the extra cash.

"Right here is where the house trailer used to sit. And the septic tank is buried there." Homer traipsed toward the sparse area of grass. "You could get a double-wide home. Jessie will need the extra room to maneuver around inside."

"That's my idea." Matt moved down the driveway. A field with cows roaming and a muddy pond surrounded by weeping willows and thistle bushes lay across the road. "This is a good piece of land. Maybe they'll even pave this dirt trail one of these days," he said, pointing.

Homer nodded, but closed his eyes. Scenes, ten years gone by, flashed through his mind.

The wreck in his truck. The tires he should have replaced.

The trip to the hospital.

His daughter's lifeless body.

Jessie, crippled.

And no-good Wayne … gone. He'd left the state and never came back. Leaving was probably a good thing, because Homer wanted to show him what happened to anyone who would hurt his Jessie.

That girl had cried and cried for a mommy and daddy who were never coming back—

"Matt!" Jessie hollered from the porch.

"I've gotta go." Matt thrust his hands in his pockets and gave a wistful smile. "My mama will cry, you know. I hate to see her cry."

"We'll talk later, son."

Matt crossed the field to the barn. Bear slumped down at Homer's feet and he reached down to rub the dog's coarse hair. "Well, old boy, I guess we'll need to take this electric fence down and put it back like it used to be. Shouldn't be too much trouble." He took a breath. Sighed. "A wedding? Now there will be some labor involved with that."

He studied the spot for another moment, then trudged back to the porch. Martha stood near the door, arms crossed. He stopped beside the steps. "What?"

"Homer, we're going to have a wedding and Jessie wants to get married at the church, have the reception right there in the fellowship hall." She placed her hands on her hips. "That's not going to be a problem, is it?" Her voice raised an octave.

Homer glared and thrust out his chin. She needn't start nagging. "No, it won't. I can go there one time to see Jessie happy. You know I'd do anything for her."

"It wouldn't hurt you to go back." Martha's voice softened. "It's been ten years."

"Yep. God changed his mind about me and I changed mine about him." His body tensed. "Enough said."

Martha turned and pulled open the screen door. "You know better. Someday you're going to have to let it all go."

"Well, that day's not today." He stomped off toward the barn. She was always in his business. "I've got work to do."

Martha should forget about church.

He had.

The wooden barn housed everything from the old Ford tractor, to cow feed, and baled hay in the loft. Homer walked through the big open doorway and into one of the stalls which lined the left side. He picked up a pair of pliers and a screwdriver sitting on his workbench and hung them in the tool holder on the wall. He grasped a rake and carried it to another stall, which housed his timeworn riding mower and chainsaw.

Two cans of paint—the labels long past recognition—lined the wall. Dark green paint frozen along their sides. Homer drew back to kick the closest can, then stopped. Instead he picked up the can, grabbed a paint brush, and started toward the glider. No use being angry today. His Jessie was getting married. He would be happy.

No matter what.

Chapter Three

Jessie leaned back in her wheelchair at the kitchen table, sipping the hot chocolate Mamaw had fixed her. She breathed deep, and allowed the rich aroma to tickle her nose. The perfect way to end a perfect day. Why had she worried about telling Matt's parents? His mom—Pam—hugged her while Matt's younger sister, Sarah, snapped a picture with her phone. Soon the news of their engagement would be all over Riverview.

Papaw stood by the sink. He reached for the brown pill bottle on the window sill, brushing the yellow curtains with his hand. After dumping a large tablet into his palm, he popped it in his mouth and swallowed it down with his coffee.

Jessie set the mug next to her open laptop as he turned toward her. "Are you going to bed?"

Papaw nodded and squeezed her shoulder as he did every night. "My guess is you and Martha will be up until all hours talking. Goodnight."

"Night."

Mamaw wandered into the kitchen, her pale pink robe cinched at the waist. Jessie moved the laptop where they both could see the screen as Mamaw pulled up a chair. Jessie had been planning on marrying and moving out since she was fifteen. Not that she didn't love her grandparents. They were her *parents*, as it were. But as they grew older, their smothering attention grew, too. Marriage would be a fresh start, a move toward more independence.

"See?" Jessie pointed toward the computer. A gorgeous display of autumn and wedding filled the screen. "Here is the way the church might look decorated with orange and brown."

"And you said this is called Pinterest?" Mamaw tugged on her ear.

"Now how does it work?"

"It's like a computerized scrapbook. People pin pictures or website addresses to their board and other people look at them and gain ideas. This is one I pinned from a fall wedding board."

Most of the decorations could be gathered from nearby woods and fields to save money. They'd already decided on a date acceptable to everyone, the third of November, a Saturday afternoon. They would have the summer to plan and prepare. Maybe save a little more money.

"And here are some dresses I like." She clicked on her wedding dress boards and pointed to her favorite. "See, it has a long train to flow behind. It'll almost hide my wheelchair."

"It's lovely," Mamaw said. "Can you buy it like that to fit?"

"No. This dress would have to be custom-designed." Jessie frowned as she considered her meager savings. And Mamaw and Papaw lived on a limited income. Even a simple wedding would stretch their budgets. There could be no designer dress.

"Why, the model wearing it is lovely." Mamaw grasped her handkerchief and wiped a tear.

"Now, Mamaw. Don't start crying again. Matt and I are going to be living right next door."

Jessie swallowed a sigh. Sometimes she needed extra assistance, whether she wanted it or not. With Mamaw and Papaw close by, she and Matt could make it. His parents would help, but as independent farmers, their time and income were limited. The dry weather they'd been having would cost them needed crops and meant more work.

Now to tackle the guest list. And time to bring up the taboo subject. She drew in a breath. "What about my father?"

Mamaw shifted in her chair, then lowered her voice. "Don't let Homer hear you ask that, Jessie."

"Do you know where he is?"

"I honestly don't. Elizabeth didn't want the divorce, but when he abandoned you and your mother, even before the wreck, she had no choice. They ran the ad in the paper with no reply. So, the judge granted the divorce. He came back to this area for a short time … but after the wreck he ran ..." She shrugged. "We tried to find him after you got better but—"

Jessie's heart tightened in her chest. "I know. And I know I shouldn't care. I want *Papaw* to walk me down the aisle. Sometimes, though ... it's just that ... I feel incomplete, wondering what it would be like, if my father hadn't left ..."

Mamaw closed her eyes; her chin trembled.

Jessie stopped. She couldn't cause her grandparents any more pain than they'd already been through.

Mamaw's eyes opened, her mouth drew in a tight line. "Now show me those flowers again." The subject was closed, at least as far as Mamaw was concerned.

But not for Jessie. What *would* it be like to find her father? Surely, he'd changed ... but maybe not for the better.

If she looked ... if she *dared* look for him, she couldn't tell Mamaw or Papaw. Absolutely not. *That* would have to be her secret.

***

Homer stretched out in the bed, shifting to his left side. Maybe it would ease the pain in his hip. From the kitchen, Jessie's soft voice mingled with Martha's.

A wedding. He closed his eyes. Faded memories of Elizabeth's wedding danced in the recesses of his mind. Farming had been good to him, back then.

She'd been so excited to marry Wayne. Martha rode with Elizabeth to purchase an expensive gown, as up-to-date as anyone's around. Martha decorated the church with white carnations and candles, all with the help of friends and family. Heck, he'd even provided a sit-down dinner alongside the wedding cake and paid for the honeymoon to the beach.

But now ...

He drew in a breath and turned over, pushing the covers away. How could he provide for *this* wedding? Four years of dry summers had depleted their savings. It'd been all he could do to pay for what Jessie needed during her senior year of high school. And there always seemed to be more medical expenses. Not her fault, but the bills still came.

He punched his pillow into shape and turned on his back. At Elizabeth's wedding, the moment they'd stepped into the church, she latched onto his arm. Her trembling didn't surprise him. He was sure shook up. And time stopped when he spotted Martha on the front row, dabbing at her face with a tissue. His eyes misted over, making it hard for him to see.

Elizabeth tugged on his arm. "Come on, Dad. It's okay."

She gave him that sweet smile. The same one Jessie shared with him so many times over the years since.

Homer pulled himself to a sitting position and crossed his arms. He had to stop this wallowing in self-pity. Jessie needed him. She would have a beautiful wedding like her mama and a fancy dress to boot. She deserved that much and more. Somehow, someway, he would make up for all she'd lost with the wedding. She would be happy. He'd see to it.

***

Jessie breathed in the aroma of chocolate chip cookies fresh out of the oven. When it came to cookies, Mamaw always outdid herself. She laid aside the bridal magazine she had been skimming through and pushed to her feet, then hurried to the kitchen. As she reached for one of the gooey confections, her phone rang.

And rang. And rang.

She willed her eyes to open as she grasped the phone to shut off her alarm. Six a.m. She lay back on her pillow and closed her eyes again, trying to recapture the dream. But it had fled, back to a time that no longer was hers.

She sighed. Time to enter the real world. There was a lot to do before church.

"Why do you get up so early on Sunday?" Matt had asked one day as they sat on the front porch.

"It takes a little longer to get ready for church," she'd told him. "And I don't like to rush."

Jessie stretched her arms and then reached for her laptop, notebook, and the journal that lay beside her pillow where she placed them each night. She breathed deeply.

Routine. The only way she knew how to exist, to not flounder in self-pity and depression. As much as possible, she took life one moment at a time—had her checklist, so to speak. If she could bring her way of order into their marriage, life would be easier for her and Matt.

Her routine proved more difficult than the average woman. She'd been able to discuss her special needs from bladder maintenance to preventing bed sores with Matt. No one else knew those details beside Mamaw and Papaw. No one else needed to.

The time he spent assisting his grandmother had proved invaluable. He really understood.

Jessie propped her pillows and pulled herself to a sitting position before pushing the power button. One day she'd have a smart phone, she decided, so she wouldn't have to boot up the computer to check every little thing.

A new phone would help her quest for even more independence. So far, she'd purchased her own clothes, this phone, and computer accessories. She would contribute in every way, even financially, to their marriage. Matt deserved that.

Jessie pulled out her journal and turned to the last page. A faded photo slipped out, revealing a young couple in wedding attire. The bride's champagne gown was ahead of its time. Her hair color was similar to Jessie's as well as the same chocolate brown eyes. But Jessie's features, her nose and the cleft in her chin, resembled the man.

Why couldn't she remember him?

Sure, she had been only seven when he left. And the wreck had impaired so much of her memory. Distinct images of her mom dwindled at times, but her remembrances of her dad were basically gone, as if he never existed.

And to Papaw, he didn't.

He and Mamaw had adopted her, given her their name so she wouldn't have to hear the name Riggs. But they couldn't understand; even without the name, that's who she was. Wayne Riggs' daughter.

She tucked the photo back in the journal, then placed the computer on her lap. The blank space of the search engine flashed before her and she typed in her father's name. The screen glowered as her heart hammered within her chest, with a warning not to push the enter key.

What if she found him? He obviously wanted nothing to do with her. He never returned after she came home from the hospital. She'd lived in the same home as her grandparents, a home he knew well. So, why hadn't he come by? Called? Written so much as a Get Well Soon card?

Then again … what if … Wayne Riggs could be dead. If he was, did she want to know?

Her finger wavered over the enter key, but with one push, she closed the search engine. She couldn't face the emotion bound to surface, no matter what she learned. Not now. She had all of her life ahead and a wedding to plan.

Routine. Stick to the routine. Jessie opened a file labeled Names and Addresses. Just focus on the guest list for now. This she could control.

***

Matt readjusted his cap after loading Jessie's wheelchair in the back of his truck. A crow cawed at him from the powerline swaying above in the breeze. A smattering of clouds dotted the pale blue sky, just enough to cool the full onslaught of the sun. What a beautiful afternoon to ride around. He jogged to the driver's side of his blue Dodge truck, climbed in, then cranked the engine. "Where to?"

"It doesn't matter." Jessie tucked her hand in Matt's as he steered with the other from her driveway. "It's gorgeous out. Let's go look at open houses on the market. I know we're going to live in a doublewide for now, but maybe one day we'll get to build our dream home."

A little dust swirled around the open window as he chugged down their road. "Whatever you want, Mrs. Jansen," he said, then laughed as Jessie blushed. Matt rubbed the flat of his stomach. "Your grandmother sure fries up a mean chicken. I don't know about you, but I may not eat again for a week."

For as long as Matt could remember, Jessie's Mamaw always cooked lunch after church. As a kid, he would ride there on his bike, just in time for dessert. Now, he was there every Sunday for the entire meal.

He slowed to avoid a pothole. Would things change after they married? Or would they continue to head over to the house after church for Sunday dinner? He hoped so. Life was good.

"How 'bout we go east around Sycamore Corners and look in that area? I'll cut through the back roads and we can look at houses on the way into Riverview." Matt came to the end of Blue Ridge Road and turned left. Soon they approached a crossroads.

Jeff Claymore pedaled toward them. His long-limbed frame was almost too much for the bicycle. He moved to the side of the road. The bike skidded on the thick blanket of rocks.

"Look out," Jessie screeched. "He's going to crash."

Boy and bicycle tumbled into the ditch near the stop sign. Matt slammed on his brakes. He jumped from the truck, leaving his door open. Was the kid all right?

He stopped in front of the fallen teen, reaching a hand to help. "Hey, Jeff, are you hurt?"

The boy grabbed his hand, stood, and brushed dirt from his jeans. He squinted as he looked at the bike, then at a tear in his pants.

Matt picked up Jeff's ball cap and handed it to him. "Are you okay?"

"Yeah. Thanks." Jeff stooped to lift his bike. "Man, I twisted the frame. And I've got to finish trimming the yard I started yesterday."

Matt released a breath. "Where you going? We can load the bike and I'll take you."

"Could you? Just a piece down that way." He pointed east as he half-carried the mangled bike.

"Is there a house down there?" Matt shielded his eyes as the sun dipped from behind a cloud. "I didn't know anyone lived on that road."

"They don't. I get paid by this old man to mow around a shed and keep it clean. I was supposed to already be done, but I had a ball game. So, I was trying to hurry."

Matt lowered the tailgate. Jeff's eyes widened as he spied the wheelchair. Why did everyone have to act so weird about it? Jeff climbed in. Matt hefted the bike to him. "Have a seat and I'll have you there in a few minutes."

Jeff hunkered down in the left corner of the bed. "Just don't drive too fast," he teased.

Matt grinned. "You got it."

"Who is that?" Jessie peered through the window at Jeff while Matt climbed back into the driver's seat and turned east.

"Jeff Claymore. He lives on Cross Creek Road, not far from here. His mom fixes my mom's hair."

"Oh."

They returned to easy conversation until a few minutes later when Matt swung the truck into the driveway.

In front of them a faded hunter green shed and a pair of lion statues stood, adorning a vacant spot of land. They stared straight ahead as the truck bobbed under Jeff's jumping from the bed.

A gust of wind pulled at a loose piece of tin, releasing a high-pitched squeal. Matt frowned. "Weird. And creepy."

"Out of a horror movie maybe. But something seems familiar about this place." Jessie rolled down her window and leaned out. "Why would someone keep this yard mowed?"

"I have no idea." Matt stepped from the truck, but Jeff had unloaded his bike before he reached him. "Do you need anything else?"

"No, thanks. My phone's okay, so I'll call Mom to pick me up. I appreciate the ride."

Matt shut the tailgate. "No problem, man."

Matt climbed back in the truck and turned to Jessie. "He's going to call his mom to pick him up when he's done mowing."

"Oh, good. I hate to leave him." Jessie glanced out the window as they backed out of the driveway. "Those lions really bug me. What's so familiar about them?"

"No telling. You'll think of it later." Matt pulled onto the road. "Back to house-hunting."

Heat waves shimmered from the road as he drove toward Main Street in Riverview. They rode through the square in the old part of town, passing the ancient courthouse where massive oak trees surrounded the limestone structure, partially shading the street.

"Hey, look over there." Jessie pointed toward the intersection ahead. The brick sign at the entrance to the subdivision read Sycamore Corners. Balloons adorned a large realty sign posted nearby. *Open House Today.*

"Cool." Matt slowed to turn in. "Looks like there are some beautiful homes in this neighborhood. Good bit of traffic."

Jessie tightened her grip on his hand. "Let's drive through."

He leaned back, straightening his shoulders. Somehow, house-hunting cemented the fact that they were getting married. "Let the dreaming begin."

Two- and three-story brick homes decorated both sides of the street. Perfectly manicured lawns complete with shrubs and small trees. Flowerbeds brightened the dull brick.

"Oh, look." Jessie pointed out the elaborate display of the brilliantly colored blossoms beside one small mansion. "I love those roses."

He touched his brakes and started to turn in.

"Oh, don't stop, Matt." Her lips quivered as he pulled up to the "Open House" sign in front of the gorgeous home. A young couple stood in front, admiring the flowers.

He furrowed his brow. "Why not? I thought you wanted to look."

"From the road. Not go in. It's too much trouble." Jessie stared out her window as he pulled away. "Just go to the next street."

Matt chewed on his lip. He understood. The chair always drew attention. People might not know Jessie in this upper-class community. Or then again, they might. To them, she was the crippled girl. And either way, people always treated her like a child or they gawked. Why couldn't they see her for the wonderful woman she had grown up to be?

He pulled out of the gated community and drove toward the next street of attached townhomes. "A townhouse would be something different."

"Such tiny yards." Jessie wrinkled her nose. "I'd rather live in the country."

As they passed one residence, a young woman stepped out, holding a pot of flowers and puffing on a cigarette. Ebony hair and well-tanned skin complemented her curvy figure. As she turned, he sucked in a breath. Angeline Springer.

She placed the pot on a small bench beside the petite front door area.

Jessie touched a finger to her chin. "Hey, don't I know her?"

"I think it's Angeline Springer." He cleared his throat. "She was a cheerleader at school."

"Oh, I remember. You should remember her from playing football."

"Yeah, that's it." He had to be careful here. No use upsetting Jessie. "She acted too good for everybody. Flirted with a lot of the guys."

Jessie twisted in the seat. "Did she flirt with you? She's awful pretty."

"Hey, Little Miss Insecure, I've only had eyes for you." He paused at the stop sign and leaned over, placing a kiss on her lips. He then held up her hand, flashing the diamond in the sun. "Forget this?"

She glanced at the ring, then the corners of her mouth turned up. "No, I haven't forgotten." She snuggled closer.

He pulled away from the townhouses and glanced into his mirror. Had Angeline seen into the truck and recognized him? Probably not. He'd driven a different truck back in high school.

He turned the air conditioner up a notch. One thing was for sure. Jessie could *never know* about Angeline.

Chapter Four

Homer pulled into the parking lot at Bentley's on Tuesday morning. The pristine pink brick building with its lavish window displays and flawlessly shaped landscaping glowed in the morning sun, daring him to enter. He rubbed his hands on the pant legs of his overalls as the truck continued to idle. Boy, was he out of his league.

He finally switched off the key. Martha said the dress Jessie liked needed a designer. Gotta go inside for Jessie, he figured.

He pulled on the door handle of his old truck, stepping out before he could change his mind. He walked up to the building, which stood on the outskirts of Riverview. How in the world could a wedding boutique exist so far from other businesses?

The shop was a Bentley enterprise, of course. The Bentleys owned a good portion of the town and when Mrs. Olivia Bentley decided she wanted to open a wedding shop, she purchased a stately old home and had it converted. More money than was good for anyone, that family.

Homer shook his head as he mounted the five steps to the door then looked to the right and to the left. No ramp in front? Maybe this was a mistake.

Tiny taps clattered behind him. A slender young woman in heels raced up the steps past Homer and jerked open the door.

She turned up her nose at him. "You coming, Pops?"

He shuddered, but couldn't back down now. Homer followed her inside and removed his soiled cap, clutching it in his hands as the aromas of coffee and vanilla reached his nostrils. Racks of poofy white dresses lined the large room with the high ceiling. Through another doorway he spied dresses splashed with color, like the ones girls wore to a prom. Fluff, ruffles … and *pink*. He'd never seen so much pink.

"Angeline." The slender woman's nasal voice screeched. "Someone to see you." She turned to Homer. "Hold on. Angeline will help you."

A seamstress knelt nearby, placing a pin in the hemline of a dress containing Mrs. Leonard Upton's daughter. Cecile Upton had graduated with Jessie, and was in a class of her own.

The mayor's daughter buying a dress here? Homer was most definitely in the wrong place. He turned to leave, twisting his cap, when another young lady approached him, nodding to the woman who'd held the door for him. "Thank you, Glenda."

Glenda sashayed to a nearby coffee station. Several ladies were gathered there, staring in his direction.

A bead of sweat ran down the back of his neck. Time to go.

"Is there something I can do for you?" Her tone rang flat, her appearance impeccable, from her fitted black pantsuit to her matching jewelry. She pushed back dark bangs from a suntanned face.

He rotated the cap in his hands. "Well, ma'am, it's like this. I'm needing a wedding dress designer for my granddaughter Jessie ... and this being Bentley's, I thought—I mean—that is to say—"

He stared at the shiny tiled floor. Why had he come here? Did he really think they could afford this?

The saleswoman plastered on a smile. "We specialize in all types of ready-made dresses, from our special sales rack"—she gestured toward a handful of dresses adorning a metal rack in one corner of the store—"to top of the line. I'm sure we can find something for Jessie. What style is she looking for?"

Style? Homer had no idea. Maybe the photo he always carried would help. She was dressed up in it. "Ma'am, me and Martha have raised Jessie from a child after her mama died in the car wreck." He fumbled in his overall pocket, finally producing a small photo of Jessie and Matt. They were sitting on the porch swing, laughing. "Here."

Angeline glanced at the picture, and then took a second, longer look. "Oh. Jessie Smith."

Her controlled tone didn't match her trembling lips. She continued to stare at the photo. How did *she* know Jessie?

"All I know is"—Homer rubbed his hand up and down his pant leg—"I need a dress with a long train." He motioned to the sales rack. "Those dresses all look too short."

"They probably are." Angeline handed the photo back. "I really don't think we can help you."

"But a designer might be able to sew—"

"When is this wedding? I'll look at the calendar."

"November third. On a Saturday." Homer crossed his arms as she moved toward a desk. She looked like she might cry. Had it been the wheelchair?

Angeline glanced at her computer. "Sorry. All of our designers are booked through the rest of the year. If you'll excuse me—" And with that, she walked out.

Homer turned to leave. He'd been right. Coming here was a mistake.

"Wait." Glenda sashayed back across the tile floor until she stood in front of him, clutching a note pad. "There's a *wonderful* wedding shop in Central City called The Dress Boutique. I'm sure they'd love to help you. They have tons of gown designers. Let me give you their address."

Glenda scribbled on the pad, ripped out the page, then tucked it in Homer's overall bib pocket. His face heated as she winked. "There you go, Pops." She cast her chin over her shoulder and raised her voice as she said, "I'm surprised you didn't think of this, Angeline."

"Thank you, ma'am." He fumbled toward the door, cap still in hand. "Jessie will appreciate this."

"Don't mention it." Glenda's snicker followed him outside. Homer cringed when Angeline's words pursued him. "Glenda, how could you? He obviously can't afford—"

He shut the door and shuffled down the steps. Maybe there was a chance. This Dress Boutique could have a designer.

He glanced toward the clouds. The sun passed into them, and a blast of wind tugged at his cap.

No. God wouldn't help.

Homer remained on his own. As he cranked the truck and put

it into reverse, his shoulders slumped against the seat. How could he give Jessie what she deserved? A perfect dress and a wonderful wedding might help her to forget, if only for a day, the hell she lived in day in and day out.

No mother, no mobility. What could be worse?

He closed his eyes. If she knew the truth.

***

Angeline watched Homer drive away from a nearby window, then turned to Glenda. "Are you crazy?"

"For what?"

She clenched her hands. Glenda always caused trouble. "Why in the world did you encourage that old man? He can't afford a dress designer."

Glenda laughed and she moved toward the back room. "Hey, I did it for kicks. Imagine the looks on those women's faces at The Dress Boutique when Pops walks in. Lighten up."

Angeline let go of the breath she was holding and walked over to her desk. Matt Jansen, getting married. A shiver ran through her.

Why did it have to be him? The starting tight end on the football team. They'd gone out on a couple of dates. She liked his easygoing nature and good looks, but he didn't seem interested in her. Nor in her social order. Angeline had grown up in an upper-middle-class life … and Matt? Well, he hadn't.

Yet, somehow, she couldn't quite forget him. Or forgive what he'd done.

She stared at a dress rack, unseeing, as the memory washed over her…

"Hey, Matt, wait up." She'd tugged at her cheerleading skirt, smoothing it, on her way to the pep rally. She skipped down the hallway, having gathered the nerve to renew the relationship between the two of them. She grabbed his arm and held on tight. "What are you doing tonight? My folks are out of town, and I'm having a few friends over."

His eyes widened. "Tonight? No, I can't."

She grinned. He was flustered, probably over her new perfume and stunning outfit. Angeline leaned against him, almost pinning him to the wall near the lockers. She tugged at his shirt collar. "Please. I want us to date again, so I can get to know you better."

Matt looked away. "Sorry, Angeline. I-I've got a date with Jessie."

"Jessie *Smith*? The cripple?"

Matt's eyes narrowed, and his nostrils flared. He opened his mouth, but then clamped it shut. Shaking free of Angeline's hold, he stormed away, leaving her standing alone.

Jessie Smith. Sure, she'd seen them talking, but they were neighbors, and Matt was a good guy. Good guys talked to everybody. But Matt and Jessie? Why would he shrug off another chance to be with *her* for a girl in a wheelchair?

No worries. She'd just have to try harder.

Her chance came at the next ballgame, the last of the season. She'd put her duffle bag in the football gear trailer before stepping onto the bus. Riding back from the game, the cheerleaders sat up front, football players in the rear. As the kids moved around in the dark, Angeline spied Matt sitting alone. Using her tight cheerleading uniform with its short skirt to her advantage, she sashayed toward the back seat, drawing several glances from the team.

"Hey, Matt." She plopped beside him. "Scoot over."

He didn't move, so she nestled close, placing her hand on his thigh and whispering in his ear. "I'm going to be lonely tonight with my parents partying at the country club. Why don't you come over?"

For a moment, he didn't move, and she brushed her lips against his cheek. He wouldn't reject her this time. "Real lonely."

He turned toward her. She slid her arms around his neck, pressed her lips against his as she pushed her body against his. Unwillingly, he kissed her back. But after a moment, he held her at arm's length. "Leave me alone." He untangled her arms from his neck. "I love Jessie."

Leave him alone? Her hands fisted. How dare he kiss her back only to reject her a minute later.

Fine. If he wanted to play that game, she could dish it out. A little gossip here, doubt planted there. Teasing came easy for her and her friends, and it appeased her pain to know she could bring misery to perfect little Jessie's life.

Jessie caused their breakup. Matt obviously felt sorry for her. She could taunt Jessie. Nice girls didn't say anything back …

Two ladies pushed through the door at Bentley's, drawing Angeline's attention. She tapped her fingers on her desk. And then there had been her father's death. If it hadn't been for that farm girl … Angeline shook the thought aside.

The recollections piled on, but she couldn't rake up the memory. Not at work.

She slapped her hand on the table and swore under her breath. Help Matt and Jessie? Not a chance.

***

The end table in the farmhouse living room gleamed as Jessie wiped the last of the dusting spray from the antique wood. She pushed the accent lamp back in its spot, setting the coaster where Papaw could easily place his tea glass.

The nearby fireplace with gas logs was the focal point of the living room. Against the walls, an overstuffed couch, a tawny mismatched chair, Papaw's recliner, and a television crowded the small room. Photos of family stood or hung everywhere—on the hearth over the fireplace, the walls and on top of the two end tables. All needed to be dusted.

Her housework would be done early, since summer school had been canceled due to electrical issues. No power, no school.

She wheeled to the other table across the room, but paused as a television commercial caught her attention. She grasped the remote off the couch and turned up the volume. "Prom Dresses. Wedding Dresses. Our biggest sale—this weekend only."

Stunning models paraded luxurious gowns across a runway,

advertising the top of the fashion world. Jessie muted the volume. If only, but one of those gowns would likely take a large chunk of her yearly salary.

She pressed her lips together and resumed dusting. How could she and Matt ever afford this wedding? Maybe Millie would have an idea.

The screen door banged behind Jessie, startling her.

"Working hard?"

She turned as Papaw crossed the room. "You scared me."

"Sorry." A grin graced his face. "I tried to catch it before it slammed."

"You've been gone all morning." He worked too hard for his age. After the wedding, maybe Matt could help more.

"I had things to do." He wiped his brow. "In fact, I need to get feed for the chickens. I wonder if Matt wants to go to Central City with me to the new feed store when he gets off work. Could you text him and ask?"

"Okay. He's probably at lunch now." Her fingers flew over the phone. In a moment, she looked up. "He said he could."

"Good." Papaw turned and trudged toward the kitchen. Jessie maneuvered into her room to finish dusting then stopped. Wait. He'd purchased feed yesterday. She'd watched him unload the truck from the porch.

She frowned. Was Papaw getting senile? Or was he hiding something? He'd acted odd ever since Matt proposed. He liked Matt, didn't he? Or could it be the wedding that bothered him?

***

Mmm. The rich, meaty aroma in the kitchen reminded Homer of the diner at lunch. Full-flavored. Beef stew steamed in the crockpot, a cake cooled on the counter, and a fresh pot brewed in the coffeemaker. He glanced through the back-screen door. Martha stood in the yard, hanging quilts out to air.

Homer opened the refrigerator. He pulled out several slices of American cheese, unwrapped each and folded them twice before taking a large bite.

Matt could go with him to this bridal store in Central City. He could keep this visit from Jessie. Homer sure wasn't going to get her hopes up to see them dashed again. She'd had enough trouble in her life already.

Martha pushed through the door with a basket full of sheets. "Homer Smith, where have you been? I was getting nervous."

"I needed more seed to plant." He shoved his hands in his pockets.

"You fret too much. You need to remember your blood pressure."

"I can't help it. I just worry. Anyway, lunch is almost ready." She moved toward the living room. "Don't run off."

He poured a cup of coffee and shoved through the back door. He glanced at the pump house. A five-gallon bucket had dumped, spilling its contents.

Bear.

Where was that dog? Homer set his coffee on the nearby bench and stooped to scoop the odds and ends back into the bucket. Screws, nails, an old hammer, a paintbrush, its bristles stiff with green paint. He finished picking up the supplies and then headed toward the old barrel he burned trash in, tossing the brush inside.

"I know it's almost lunchtime," he muttered. "But I need to go to the shed."

Homer shuffled toward the front of the house where he always parked his truck. He passed the porch, laying his cell phone on the handrail of the ramp.

Now nobody would bother him. Didn't know why he needed a phone that traveled anyway. He'd spent all the years before without one. Truth be told, he had a phone because Martha and Jessie fretted and he didn't want that.

Opening the door, he scooted into the seat and shook his head, then cranked the truck and crept down the driveway. He hadn't meant to sound grouchy, especially not to Martha. She'd stood with him all these years. But she worried way too much.

Trees dressed in their summer foliage greeted him, so close to the edge of the dirt road, leading to the land left to him by his great-uncle, Seth. Uncle Seth never married and had lived on the five-acre plot for as long as Homer could remember. The house had long ago fallen in and been cleared away, leaving only the shed.

Uncle Seth had lived alone.

Died alone.

He pulled into the driveway. Stopped the truck and got out then trudged to the door of the building, and glanced both ways before digging the old key from his pocket and inserting it into the lock. With a twist, it clicked and he forced the creaking door open. One more glimpse toward the dirt road and he stepped inside.

***

Jessie pushed her chair into the widened utility room to replace her dust rag on the lower shelf, setting the can of dusting spray beside it. Papaw had worked hard to redo the house to accommodate her wheelchair. She owed him and Mamaw so much.

Mamaw stood by the dryer, folding the clothes and placing them in a basket.

"Let me get those." Jessie patted the low bench and Mamaw set the basket there. "Where is Papaw off to now?"

"Don't know. He purposely leaves his phone on the porch. He *forgets* it when he thinks I'm worrying him." Mamaw shook her head, then tossed towels into the open washing machine before starting it. "I told him lunch would be ready in an hour."

"He's acting odd, don't you think?" Jessie raised her voice over the whoosh of the water filling the washer. "Is Papaw bothered about the wedding? I thought he really liked Matt."

"He does." Mamaw brushed her hand in the air. "I gave up a long time ago trying to figure out your grandfather. He's proud you're marrying and you're going to live on the spot where you were before."

Jessie shrugged. "Oh, okay then."

"I'm going to fix sandwiches for lunch. The stew should be ready for an early supper." Mamaw patted Jessie's shoulder. "Don't worry about your papaw. He's fine. But I am going to have to talk with him about his phone. *Again.*"

Jessie carefully sorted the clothes in two piles—hers and theirs—her mind more on the situation than the clothes. Papaw could be grouchy at times. Maybe worry made him like that. Or maybe the fact that he still hated Wayne. Unforgiveness would harden any heart, even someone as giving as Papaw.

She bunched together a pair of her grandfather's socks. *Please God, help Papaw to forgive my father. He never says much, but I see the look on his face.* Jessie then folded her favorite gown. *And God, if it's what You want, please bring my daddy back into my life.*

Jessie quenched tears threatening to flow as she laid both small piles of clothes on her lap. She pushed through the kitchen and into her grandparents' bedroom, placing the pile on their bed. Jessie put up what she could and left the shirts for Mamaw to hang in the closet.

A clothes hanger had fallen onto the floor nearby. Jessie pushed her chair close and stretched but couldn't quite reach it. She overbalanced and grasped the closet door. It had been a while since she'd fallen from the chair. The last time, Mamaw had fretted over her for days. She tried again, but couldn't quite grasp the hanger.

Out of reach.

Why was everything out of reach in her life?

She huffed and wheeled her chair through the living room, and placed her own clothes where they belonged.

Her laptop sat on the desk at the far side of her bed. Jessie flipped it open and went to her favorite search engine. She typed in WAYNE RIGGS. Her father's name both fascinated and repelled her. She pushed ENTER and scanned the information that pulled up, then found a site she hoped would help in her search. But was she ready for what her efforts might uncover? Her finger pushed ENTER again.

Today. She would know something today.

Chapter Five

Homer peered out the living room window as Matt's blue truck eased up the driveway. He picked up his house key from the table. Jessie and Martha had taken an afternoon trip into Riverview to buy groceries.

No need to get their hopes up about the dress. As he reached for the remote to turn off the television, he scowled at the news and the report as to whether or not gas prices would climb. The wedding already seemed out of reach, and prices could go up. Well, wasn't that just another possible nail in the coffin …

Homer opened the door, turned the lock and stepped outside. He crossed the porch, glancing at the sky. *God, I know I haven't talked to You in a long time, but could You help me find Jessie a dress? Not asking for me, but for her sake?* He mouthed the prayer before climbing into Matt's truck. "Hello, son. Glad you could go with me to Central City."

"No problem." Matt's grin put Homer at ease. "I don't always enjoy going to work so early, but I like being home by three o'clock. I've wanted to check out the new feed store anyway."

Twenty minutes lapsed as topics of planting corn and soybeans, a possible gas price hike, and the new road commissioner passed between them. The drive to Central City consisted of long stretches of plowed fields mingled with patches of pinewoods. Homer leaned his elbow on the open window of Matt's pickup as they approached a gas station on the right.

He wouldn't be stopping there anymore. During his last visit, he complained about them not being wheelchair-friendly. By golly, it wouldn't take much for them to fix a better ramp.

He shook his head. Not his fight today.

"We'll be at the hardware store in a few minutes." Matt pointed west. "It's only a couple of blocks away."

"Matt, I need to go somewhere else first." Homer reached into the bib pocket of his overall and frowned. That forward lady at Bentley's had shocked him, but surely this shop wouldn't be a repeat performance. "The Dress Boutique. The address is 311 Ashton Drive."

Matt tilted his head to the side. "You picking up something for Martha?"

"No. Martha doesn't know. Jessie either. I'm looking for a wedding dress designer to make Jessie a special dress."

Matt slowed and said nothing, then turned left on Ashton Drive. He pulled into a parking space on the right. "Here we are."

Homer stared at the brick building nestled between the bakery and the thrift store and swallowed. The sophisticated window dressings and expensive gowns could be described with one word. Money.

"This is it." Matt turned to Homer. "But won't a designer be expensive? I mean, I know it's Jessie, but ... well ..."

"I have to try." Homer pulled the handle and stepped from the truck. He dusted his overalls off, more from habit and nerves than anything. Maybe he should've dressed different this time.

Homer led the way through the lavender-painted doorway. Two women were seated on a white leather couch, thumbing through thick catalogs. Could be a mother and daughter. A middle-aged lady scanned a rack of gowns near the cash register.

"May I help you?" An efficient young associate stared from the counter. "Are you here to pick up an order?"

Homer crossed the room, removing his cap on the way. He pushed his gnarled hand through his coarse gray hair. Just say it. "Yes, ma'am. I mean, no, ma'am. I'm needing the services of a wedding dress designer."

The blonde's eyes scanned him while the middle-aged lady focused her attention on the men. "We have designers on staff."

"Good." Homer straightened. "My granddaughter, Jessie, needs a special dress." He pulled the photo from his pocket and smoothed it before handing it to her. The middle-aged lady stretched to glance over the associate's shoulder.

"She's a beautiful young lady. Your bride-to-be?" She favored Matt with a big smile.

"Yes, ma'am," Matt said. "We're getting married in November."

"November?" The associate handed the photo back. "Sorry, sir, but I don't believe anyone here would have time to work on a project like this. We only have two designers."

Homer's shoulders slumped. Failed again. He shoved the photo in his pocket, mumbled a "thank you," stumbled out the door and walked straight for Matt's vehicle. He leaned against the hood of the truck as a lump rose in his throat. The designers were probably too expensive anyway. Jessie wouldn't get the dress he wanted her to have.

Matt joined him. "I'm sorry they couldn't help. But these stores are so high priced and all. Like Bentley's. They acted so busy, making my sister wait when she wanted a dress for the Riverview beauty walk."

The tinkling of a bell sounded as someone exited the store. The middle-aged lady stepped over to where they stood, clutching her purse. Her sandy hair hung in loose curls, glasses hanging from an eyeglass chain. "Excuse me, I don't mean to interfere or anything, but are you looking for a wedding dress designer?"

Homer blinked. Maybe this lady could work the miracle he needed. "Yes, ma'am. Do you know one?"

"Well, actually, I sew custom-made dresses and I've designed wedding dresses before. I work over at the dollar store, but I sew in my spare time." The lady extended her hand. "My name is Estelle Granger."

Homer wiped his hand on his overalls before gripping hers. "Homer Smith. And this is Jessie's fiancé, Matt Jansen."

Estelle's mouth flew open. "Matt Jansen. You're not Irene's boy, are you?"

"No, ma'am. That's Ben. My mom is Irene's sister-in-law, Pam."

"Pam's son? And all grown up. I didn't realize." She clucked like a hen. "It's a small world, isn't it? Anyway, I heard you say you need a special dress."

"Well, you see, Jessie is in a wheelchair. And she really needs a special dress with the chair and all—"

"I understand perfectly." Estelle fumbled through her purse and came out with a pad and pencil. She slipped her glasses onto the end of her nose. "You need a custom design to fit her *and* the chair," she said, jotting notes. "It sounds like a challenge." She smiled at them both. "And I love challenges."

"You do?" Homer held his breath. This might work. "It would mean so much to Martha—that's my wife—and me if you could try."

"Homer Smith." Estelle spoke aloud as she wrote. "Address?"

"Eight-six-seven-two Blue Ridge Road outside of Riverview."

"Blue Ridge Road. Do you live nearby, Matt? I've been down that way, but it was years ago."

"Yes, ma'am," Matt said. "They're less than a mile past our farm on the left."

Estelle stuck the pad into her oversized purse. "Wonderful. I believe I know where it is. And I've looked over the new shipment of dresses that have arrived here and I'm simply brimming over with ideas. I'll get together with Jessie and I'm sure we can work out something."

"Thank you." Homer shook her hand again. "So much."

"May I come over tomorrow? Say around three-thirty? It will give me time to get home from work, change, and drive on over there."

Homer nodded. "That'll be just fine."

"I'll see you then." Estelle waved, then marched toward a small red SUV.

Homer turned toward the truck, his grin reflecting in the window. How long had it been since he'd smiled like that?

He opened the truck door and slid in as a thought struck him. Estelle had not quoted a price. "I can't believe it worked out. But what if she's real expensive? I didn't think to ask."

"I'm sure it'll be all right." Matt cranked the truck. "She acted like normal folk and she knows my family. Do you still want to check out the feed store?"

"Yes, I do." Homer breathed out as the hundred-pound load lifted off his chest. The lady acted so kind. Martha would like her. A quick stop for another bag of feed and then home so he could tell the good news to her and Jessie. He readjusted his cap.

His Jessie would get her special wedding after all.

Maybe God *did* hear him. Probably not for his sake, but for hers.

Yep. No doubt about it. God did this for Jessie.

***

Plastic bags of groceries lined the kitchen table. Jessie pulled each item out, and then gathered the ones that belonged in the pantry. Canned goods. Rice and beans. Honey buns for Papaw. She placed them on the shelves while Mamaw stocked the refrigerator with the milk, butter, and mayonnaise.

"I've put up the pantry items. Here's the bread." Jessie passed it to her grandmother, who set the loaf near the coffeepot.

"Good. That's all done." Mamaw wiped her hands on the kitchen towel. "I'm going to the porch to work on the bibs I'm crocheting for Ruthie's granddaughter. You want to join me?"

"No. I think I'll go to my room for a while." She had to get back to her computer. When she'd searched for her father's name earlier, it said there were fifty-two men by that name in the United States. Five of them lived in Mississippi, which is where Mamaw thought he'd moved. His family resided there and he'd worked in Tupelo before he married her mother.

Once in the safety of her room, Jessie pulled up the white pages and glanced again at the one name whose age was listed in the early forties. She clicked on the link and a name and address came on the screen. Wayne Riggs, 355 Indian Circle Drive, Alden, Mississippi.

Her hand trembled. She moved the mouse over the icon VIEW PROFILE. No picture. Only Wayne L. Riggs, age 43. Under possible relatives, two names were listed: Joy and Shay Riggs. Who could they be?

Mother? Sister? Wife? Jessie selected the icon for complete details only to see it would cost $29.95 to find out. She shook her head. Too much money for her to waste on a dream.

Especially one that would probably lead her nowhere.

"Jessie, Matt and your papaw are here." Mamaw's voice carried from the porch.

Jessie cut off her computer, hand still trembling. How much further should she search? Did she honestly want to know?

Chapter Six

J essie rolled onto the front porch, narrowing her eyes in the bright sunshine. *Just act normal.* She had to forget about her father attending the wedding. No use upsetting everyone.

Mamaw's crocheting lay on the newly painted glider. She now watered the two planters of impatiens perched on the edge of the porch.

Bear toddled toward her chair and pushed his head near her hand. She scratched right behind his ears, and his tail thumped against the glider. Jessie loved the dog Papaw had given her when she finally returned home after the wreck. Funny how that tiny bundle of long ears and short legs gave her such hope.

Bear yawned, then lumbered down the steps and crawled under the ramp to escape the afternoon heat.

Papaw and Matt stepped onto the porch. Papaw scooted the crocheting over, then plopped on the glider. It protested with a series of creaks while Matt brushed a kiss on her cheek. His musky cologne tickled her nose. Her favorite. His grin widened.

"Something's up." She glanced from Papaw to Matt. "What is it?"

Matt motioned to her grandfather. "You tell her."

"Well, Jessie, we've found someone to design a special wedding dress for you." Papaw pulled the name from his pocket. "Estelle Granger."

Jessie gasped. A designer. He'd been out looking for one? "Papaw, we can't afford that."

Mamaw dropped her watering can. "Where did you find one? I thought you said Bentley's couldn't help."

"They couldn't." Matt joined in. "We drove to The Dress Boutique in Central City."

"You went to Bentley's and The Dress Boutique?" Jessie laid her hand on Papaw's arm. She couldn't let them do that. "Won't that cost a lot?"

"Their designers couldn't help." Papaw handed the paper to Mamaw. "This lady, Estelle Granger, was in the store, and she sews for the public. She's coming tomorrow at three-thirty to talk to you, Jessie. Matt thinks she'll charge real reasonable."

"Oh, Papaw. You're the greatest." Jessie strained to reach and then hugged him. He took such good care of her. A sudden thought tickled her bones. "Didn't you feel a bit out of place at The Dress Boutique? And Bentley's?"

"You should have seen us," Matt said. "Or you should have seen the look the ladies in the shop gave us."

"The important thing is Jessie's going to get her dress." Mamaw picked up the can. "And my pot of beef stew is almost done. I'll make a pan of biscuits, then I have a lot of cleaning to do before Ms. Granger arrives tomorrow. I don't want her to think we're heathens."

"As if anyone would," Jessie called after her grandmother.

The evening rushed by. After supper, Matt left for home and Jessie sought the shelter of her room. Everything was happening so fast. She pulled up her Pinterest site and scrolled to the board featuring wedding dresses. She read the description again for the dress:

"This fitted wedding dress made of dreams and tulle and lace is detailed by a belted waist. The classic sweetheart neckline is the perfect frame to show off the bride's shoulders and her slender curve is accentuated by the fitted, full-length skirt. Enticing beads and pearls embellish the center bodice and the charming, detachable tulle train complements the elegance of the dress."

Such a beautiful dress. Shouldn't she be happier? An ache started somewhere deep inside and over the past few days had worked its way into her heart. No one could see it, but whenever she closed her eyes, the cry rose.

Pain. So much pain.

Matt's proposal had forced her to face so much. She needed her independence. She missed having her real father in her life. It pushed against her heart like a wave pushing against the seashore as she drowned in the water.

With everything he had done for her, why couldn't she accept the fact that Papaw was a father to her and she needed no other?

Jessie logged onto her Facebook page and read the newsfeed. She glanced at the search box, then typed in Wayne Riggs. Would she ever find the man in the faded wedding photo?

Different faces popped up. She frowned. Not him. Not this one. Too old … too young. Tired, she logged out of Facebook and shoved the laptop to the back of her desk.

Why did she even care? He'd left his family, deserted her and her mom. Sure, he made a few visits again right before the wreck. But that had only made it worse when his coming around stopped afterward. He never even came to see her at the hospital. No wonder Papaw hated him.

If only there were someone who could understand how she felt. Matt had never dealt with anything like the rejection pushed upon her. But Millie's parents divorced when she was a teenager. Maybe she could talk to her.

Later that night, Jessie pulled the comforter to her chin, and whispered the twenty-third psalm. *The Lord is my shepherd; I shall not want.*

Only one problem. She did want.

The pressure of not being able to share her deepest feelings, even with Matt or Millie, needed to be released. Her jaw clenched. Could this tension be freed without blowing up like an unregulated pressure cooker? She willed her body to relax. Her family and friends didn't deserve the messiness of her life erupting all over them. Bottling everything up inside had seemed like the best way to deal. Now, it threatened to undo her control.

Maybe she should talk to God more, cast her cares. It sounded easy, but letting go proved beyond her. *God, help me.*

Chapter Seven

Homer pressed his fork through his stack of pancakes, then placed a bite of buttery goodness into his mouth, savoring the maple syrup. He swiped at a falling drop, but it landed on his pant leg. No matter.

The sun, shining through the kitchen window, warmed his heart. Or was it finding Estelle to make the dress? Jessie would get her wedding. Today the world was good, as it should be.

"What're you doing today, Homer?" Martha cradled her coffee cup, sipping the steamy beverage. "I hope you're going to be around when Ms. Granger gets here."

"I will." Wasn't he *always* there for Jessie? "There's a lot going on. I'm picking up the last of the seed at the co-op. Going to try and get it in the ground tomorrow. Got to keep up with the farm, wedding or not."

"I think Jessie will want us both here. We're all she's got."

Homer pushed back his chair as the kitchen darkened by a passing cloud. "Don't you think I know? Remember, she has Matt now, too. And he'll be there to take care of her when we're gone."

He traipsed into the living room before Martha could answer. Her words had pushed the heavy load back on his old shoulders. He tried to do all he could for Jessie. He puffed a breath. Couldn't they see?

Homer pushed through the screen door and cranked the old truck. The black Ford had as many dents as years, but it fit him as comfortably as his overalls. It turned over once, and stalled. He turned the key again and revved the motor, then pulled onto Blue Ridge Road. Freshly plowed fields on one side of the road with pastures loaded with cows, houses here and there, greeted him until he reached Highway 198, which led into Riverview.

The Riverview Co-op carried all the supplies a farmer could use, plus things for the garden and a repair shop next door. Andy Dolin managed the co-op. Homer entered the small metal building and Andy waved at him from the counter.

"Hey, Homer, 'bout time you came to pick up the rest of your seed." He reached out a large paw and his handshake shook Homer's entire body. "So glad to see you. Heard Jessie and Matt are getting married." When Homer raised his brow, he added, "John was in here yesterday."

"Yep, John's got a good boy. We're glad to have Matt as a grandson-in-law." He leaned his elbows on the counter.

Andy wrote up the order, then punched it in the computer. "Should I put it on your account?"

"Yeah. I'll be in at the end of the month to make good on it." He calculated the time in his head; should have time to plant quite a bit of the place.

"Here you go." Andy handed Homer his bill. "Pull the truck around back and we'll load up the seed."

Homer trudged back to the truck, slid inside, and turned the key. Nothing. He tried again. He didn't have time for this. After a few more attempts, Andy came around from the back of the building. "You comin'?"

He turned the key one more time, then stepped from the truck and raised the hood. Andy walked over. Homer stared at the motor. Looked okay.

Andy peered under the raised hood. "Maybe it's the battery."

"Bought a new one last month." Together they jiggled wires and the spark plugs. Homer attempted to crank the truck again but it was no use. A shiver ran down his spine. Not now.

"Let me call Bill at the garage. He'll tell you what's wrong." Andy pulled his phone from the holster and, after a short conversation, turned back to Homer. "Bill said he'd walk over in a couple of minutes. What do you want me to do with the soybean seed?"

"If we can't get the truck running, I'll see if Matt can pick it up after work." He patted the truck, felt the heat of it from the sun against the dryness of his hand. "I don't know what could be wrong with the old thing. I had a tune-up and the oil changed when I got the new battery." Homer wiped his brow. "I sure hope it's nothing serious."

It couldn't be. Not with a wedding to pay for.

Homer squinted. A skinny man with raven-black hair sticking out from under a greasy ball cap crossed the parking lot. "Hey, Bill."

"Homer." He wiped his hand on a rag before gripping Homer's. "What can I do you for?"

"The truck won't crank. What do you think?"

Bill bent into the truck and after several minutes of inspection turned to Homer, his mouth drawn in a tight line.

"I hate to tell you this, Homer, but I believe it's the timing chain. Can't be sure until I get it to the shop." He dropped the hood and it slammed in place.

"Timing chain?" Homer leaned against the truck, all energy gone. A major repair.

"If you want, I'll get it towed to the garage, and let you know."

"Okay." Homer straightened, and pulled his phone from its case. "You know I only want *you* working on my vehicles. Martha can pick me up, and you call me at home when you know something."

In a few moments, Bill was back. Homer stared at the wrecker as it pulled his truck and his livelihood away. How could he farm without it? Martha's economy car was no help when it came to picking up supplies and taking them to the field. This couldn't have happened at a worse time.

His stomach rolled. What could they do? There'd be no extra money until the beans and cotton came in.

Homer wrenched his cap off and ran his fingers through his hair. Normally he tucked away a little extra money, but they'd planned to use it for the wedding expenses. Not on the truck. The winter wheat would go in after the cotton and soybeans, but it wouldn't help him now. The few calves he raised weren't big enough to sell either. Hope slipped away…

… and back into the canyon created long ago by the accident.

***

Jessie followed her grandmother into the house and set her purse on the end table. Another hectic day. "They let me leave a few minutes early, thank goodness. Seems like everyone needs something near the end of the day. Mr. Atwater said he'd listen for calls."

"He's the best principal Riverview Elementary has ever had." Mamaw wrapped her stained apron around her generous waist. "Now you'll have time to eat a snack before Ms. Granger gets here."

"I think I'll just have an apple." Jessie reached for a Golden Delicious in the bowl on the counter. "At least I was able to fill Millie in on some of our thoughts for the wedding. How she's going to teach kindergarten this fall and direct my wedding is beyond me. I'm putting all ideas in a file in my computer to help her." Millie was a peach.

Mamaw's cell phone rang and she dug through her purse until she located it. "Yes, Homer … what happened?" Mamaw rolled her eyes toward the ceiling. "All right. I'll be there as quick as I can."

Jessie studied her grandmother's troubled countenance. Not good. "What is it?"

"Homer said the truck won't start. He needs me to pick him up at the co-op. And could you ask Matt to pick up the seed for him?" She untied the apron, laid it on the counter and picked up her purse. "I'll be back in a minute. If you don't mind, set the pork chops out of the freezer so they can start thawing."

"I will." Jessie sent Matt a text. She then moved to the refrigerator-style deep freezer and pulled out a package of pork chops. The front door slammed. Corn on the cob would be good too.

She set the bag of corn in the sink beside the pork chops. Why not look over her wedding plans while she waited for them to return? Then everything would be ready for Ms. Granger.

She pushed to her room, then booted up the laptop. Millie had a dozen ideas of how to make a fall wedding lovely, yet inexpensive. She started scanning other wedding sites when the phone rang in the living room.

The landline. Why they even kept it when they each had a cell phone was beyond her.

She hurried, but the phone stopped ringing before she reached it, the answering machine kicking in. After the beep, a voice chimed in.

"Homer, this is Bill Lyles at the garage. Sorry to say, the problem is the timing chain. You're looking at six- to eight-hundred dollars to fix it. Call me and let me know what to do." The machine beeped again.

No. Jessie clenched her fists and squeezed her eyes shut. Her grandparents didn't have that amount of money. She hugged herself as she sat in her chair, tears oozing.

Why? Papaw tries so hard, God. Do You even care?

She swiped at the tears that dripped from her chin. Papaw and Mamaw had done so much. They couldn't bear the burden of a fancy gown and wedding. No matter what they wanted for her. Maybe she could borrow Millie's wedding dress. They were about the same size, except for Millie's height. Factor in the wheelchair and it might work.

Jessie straightened. She would have a simple ceremony at the church. The dress and all the frills didn't matter. Mamaw and Papaw couldn't be allowed to sacrifice any more. Lots of women had borrowed gowns and she could too.

She gritted her teeth and stared down at her useless legs. Why did her parents have to divorce? If her father had stayed, would the wreck have happened? Her mother might still be alive. If she could only walk, she'd be more of a help on the farm.

Jessie glanced around for something she could throw.

At her father. Once again, the anger of being deserted boiled close to the top.

She pushed back to her room. Mamaw and Papaw would be back in a moment and Mrs. Granger would arrive soon. They couldn't catch her crying. Or angry.

How could she hide her pain from everyone, when she couldn't bury the truth from herself?

***

A lone coffee cup perched on the end table near Homer's recliner. From his usual spot, he commanded the corner of the room, with a good view of the television and the front door. A lot of good it would do for Ms. Granger to come now. Bill had called his cell phone, telling him the bad news. He should let Jessie know about the expense but he didn't want to worry her.

Martha swooped in like a hawk, grasping the cup with her left hand as she dusted the table with the rag in her right. "Homer. I'm trying to clean."

"Martha, give me back my coffee. I'm not finished. And the house is clean." He grumbled, pushing himself from the chair before banging through the screen door. Soon as Matt arrived with the seed, he'd have to start planting. "Maybe I can think out here."

In the distance, a red SUV crept down the road, stirring a little dust. "Must be her. About that time." Homer reached into his pocket and pulled out his father's pocket watch. "Yep. Three-thirty already."

Bear lifted his head and let out a couple of low barks. He stood, and barked again at the car creeping down the driveway.

Homer licked his dry lips. They couldn't commit to anything today. How would he do this without Jessie becoming suspicious? He hollered through the screen door. "Jessie, Martha. She's here."

Estelle Granger exited her car and started toward the steps, neat in her blue slacks and summer sweater. She halted. Bear sat by the ramp. "Is he friendly?"

"Who? Bear? He won't hurt nobody." Homer motioned her up the steps. "Way too lazy," he added and she smiled. "Come on in. Martha and Jessie are waiting." He held the screen door and she entered, clutching a large carry-all bag.

"What a lovely home." Estelle said when she stepped inside.

Homer lifted his head. It was a nice place, one they'd worked hard to build. The room reflected who they were. Simple country folk.

"Ms. Granger, come in." Martha grasped her hand. "I'm Martha. Jessie will join us in a moment. Won't you sit down?" She pointed to the couch and they both sat. Homer plunked in his recliner. He muted the television, but left it on the weather.

Jessie wheeled herself from the bedroom, a weak smile on her face and her laptop on her lap. She extended a hand. "How are you, Ms. Granger? It was so good of you to come."

"Glad to." Estelle shook Jessie's hand. "Well, when I heard your grandfather's story, I knew there must be something I could do to help. Do you have an idea about the dress?"

"Yes, ma'am." She opened the laptop and pulled up her Pinterest page. "Here's my wedding dress board."

Estelle scooted closer to Jessie. "So, this is Pinterest. I can see by these pictures, I need to be a member of this. Look at all the ideas."

Jessie pointed at the screen. "This is it."

"Oh, my. It is gorgeous."

Homer glanced at Jessie. Her hand trembled while steadying the laptop. What was wrong?

Estelle glanced through the pages, eyeing them with care. "I don't think this will be too hard, except for the train. But I'll put it to thought and we'll pull off the perfect wedding for you."

Homer closed his eyes. No perfect wedding.

"I appreciate it," Jessie said. "But I've decided to borrow a dress."

"What?" Homer and Martha's voices blended.

Jessie straightened. "Papaw, I know about the truck. There's no way you can pay to have it repaired and buy a gown. I called Millie about borrowing her dress, and she didn't mind. And maybe we could get married here."

"Jessie, you'll do no such thing." Martha stood, hands on hips. "You want a church wedding, and you'll get one. It's not until November. Homer and I talked and we believe we can put enough money back."

Homer gripped the arms of the chair. "Martha's right. We'll think of something."

"I'm sorry to hear there's a problem." Estelle said. "I'll do whatever I can to help. Why don't I at least draw up the sketches of this dress and get a firm price? In case you change your mind."

She stood, and clasped Jessie's hand. "I'm sure we can remedy this. The Lord works in mysterious ways, you know.

"He does." Jessie cleared her throat. "I'm sorry you drove all the way out here."

"Don't apologize. I'm going to join Pinterest and get right to work on this." Estelle walked to the door. "I'll return Monday with the sketches if you'd like."

"Yes, ma'am." Homer stood, but could find no other words. Borrow a dress? No excuse for it. He couldn't even provide the one thing his granddaughter should have.

As the screen door slammed, Martha clutched her hands. "How did you know about the truck?"

"Bill left a message on the answering machine." Jessie shut the laptop, then looked from one grandparent to the other. "I would never want this wedding to be a burden."

"We know you wouldn't. Let Ms. Granger get us a price and we'll see."

Homer walked out on the porch, staring at Ms. Granger's retreating car. He gripped the porch post until his knuckles hurt, then heaved a sigh and plodded to the barn. How could they raise the money? There had to be a way. He had to figure it out. And soon.

***

Angeline stretched her back and readjusted the desk chair. Another too-long day. The sunlight, which splashed through the large front windows, had faded along with her energy. She sat alone in the main room at Bentley's, an hour after closing time, going over the day's sales.

Just finish.

She entered each ticket into the desktop computer, double-checking the price with her calculator.

"Angeline."

She glanced up to see the manager, Francine Davis, sweep into the room. Francine had been gone for a week to New York on a purchasing run, a gloriously relaxing week for everyone at Bentley's. Her Gucci pumps clicked as she crossed the shiny tiled floor. Her Max Mara silk suit must have set her back a thousand dollars easy. Did she really make enough to afford those clothes?

"Yes, ma'am?" Angeline stood at attention.

"Before Glenda left a few minutes ago, she stopped by my office. She said a rather shabby old man came in the other day, and you entertained him." Francine thumbed through the sales tickets. "I hope that isn't true."

Angeline's eyes narrowed. "An *elderly* man came in looking for someone to design a wedding dress for his granddaughter. I told him plainly we couldn't help him and sent him to The Dress Boutique."

"Oh." She laid the receipts back on the desk. "You did the right thing. We don't do charity. Sales have been good since I've been gone, making Olivia Bentley happy. And we do want her to be happy."

"Yes, ma'am." Angeline tugged at her skirt. Inwardly, she rolled her eyes. "I'm entering the last of the day's sales."

"When you're done, you can go." Francine turned, her shoes click-clacking as she disappeared into the back room.

Angeline sighed, the tickets all out of order. She'd have to start over.

She went back over the figures, then filed the receipts. Three years at Bentley's and Francine still terrified her. What a week. First the reminder of Matt and his rejection, right in the middle of a Francine-less week, and now Glenda tried to sabotage her. She entered the final totals on the computer, shut it down, and shouldered her purse.

"Well, it didn't work, Glenda." She shook her head and exited Bentley's. "I'm Francine's favorite employee. I still have my Lexus and townhouse. And what do you have? A beat-up SUV and a divorce."

Glenda only had the job because Olivia Bentley was her cousin. Angeline unlocked the car and slid into the gray beauty. "I have this job because I'm good at what I do. Manage."

Too bad you can't manage your love life. Her mother's biting words echoed in her ears. *If so, I'd have a grandchild by now. Your father might have lived to be a grandfather.*

Tears blurred her vision as she pulled from the parking lot. *Don't think about it.* But a day didn't go by without her dad in her thoughts. His heart attack three years ago still devastated her. After his death, her mother grew bitter. With her own life and her only child. If not for the accident …

She focused as she crossed the four-lane highway that led to her neighborhood.

The Lexus LS 460 her dad willed her and the townhouse kept her far from her mother and more rejection. She couldn't do anything right as far as her mother was concerned so why try? The effort was not worth the pain. She turned the volume up on the radio and focused on the music.

"Has anyone seen my broken heart?" the country band crooned. She punched the knob, turning it off. Not today. She had cemented her heart back together by herself and wouldn't soften it for anyone. Especially not her mother.

***

Homer peered through the screen door, the damp gray of Sunday morning squeezing every drop of emotion from his heart. He turned and paced the length of the living room. The chain hanging from the ceiling fan clicked in rhythm with his footfalls as its blades rotated on low speed above his head.

Earlier, he'd paused on the back porch after feeding the animals, hearing the sound of muffled weeping. Martha. He crept inside but she wasn't in the kitchen. The calendar hanging on the side of the refrigerator caught his attention. June twenty-fourth.

Elizabeth's birthday.

And he'd almost forgotten.

Slipping back outside, he wandered to the small vegetable garden they kept, pulling a random weed here and there, reining in any stray tear that might try to fall. By the time he went back inside, Martha had her church clothes on, her sorrow hidden once again. She and Jessie then left for church, leaving him alone to sort out the week.

How could so much happen in so few days? The day after Estelle Granger had visited, Martha's back tooth crown split and then Friday his best cow died, trying to birth her calf. He was relying on the calf to fatten up and sell for the extra money. Now he'd lost the cow and the calf would have to be bottle-fed to live. The sick gnawing in his stomach wouldn't leave. A decent wedding for Jessie? Not going to happen.

Jessie told him it would be okay. Of course, she did. That's the kind of girl she was, willing to sacrifice for the good of the family. She'd overlook his failure. But he couldn't.

An invisible mist, thick and unyielding, hung over the house and his heart. He had to do something. But what? He'd exhausted every avenue he knew.

But one. He looked out the screen door once more to make sure no one was around, then lowered himself to his knees on the living room floor by the recliner.

He closed his eyes. *God, are You still there? Would You work a miracle? Not for me but for my Jessie?*

Homer strained his ears and his mind to hear a voice. A thought. Anything. The fan continued to click above him joined by the ticking of the wall clock.

His chest tightened. No answers.

He grasped the arm of the recliner and pulled himself up. He reached over and lifted the photograph of Elizabeth in her wedding gown from the shelf it occupied. "I tried. I'm so sorry, baby girl."

His sobs joined the fan and clock.

Chapter Eight

Jessie picked up a pretzel and bit into it, the salty tang drying her mouth. She took a sip from her bottle of water and set it back on her desk. She needed to get some sleep. Her mid-length fingernails made little noise as they tapped the keyboard. Normally, she had no take-home work during summer school, but how could she turn down the opportunity to help Millie organize a fundraiser for Devin Luke, the fourth-grader suffering from pediatric Crohn's disease? Not when she understood how it felt to struggle.

The clock above the desk read 11:30. Almost Monday. The preparations had been going on for the last month, but the final details of the summer carnival in the school gymnasium had to be on paper before the event tomorrow night. At least her mind was occupied with something besides their financial struggles.

Jessie typed the last-minute supply sheet, attached it to an email to Millie and sent the detailed packet on its way. Everything should be in place. Latoya Cower of Channel 7 News would be broadcasting from the event to bring awareness to the disease and young Devin's plight. Ms. Cower would arrive around six, an hour after the carnival opened, for the live newscast.

Jessie stretched and rubbed the back of her neck after shutting the laptop down for the night. Tomorrow she would have to inform Ms. Granger they couldn't afford the dress. She swallowed more water to combat a bitter taste that rose in her throat.

Forget the wedding. It would be small and informal. She needed a way to make more money to help, especially since the cow died. But how?

Jessie had barely closed her eyes before it was time to get up. She dressed and arrived at the school early. After a day which lasted forever, she left the school office at two o'clock. She needed to see Ms. Granger and change into jeans to keep with the western theme that meant so much to Devin.

Papaw waited for her near the door of the elementary building. Mamaw must still be cleaning. He said little on the way home. How could she comfort the man who was her world?

"Papaw, it'll be okay." Jessie patted his arm as he parked the car. "Millie's dress is beautiful. And since I'll be sitting, the extra length won't matter. Matt's mom and aunts are going to help with the food. Everything will be simple and pretty. Millie will help decorate with bundles of fall leaves and pumpkins. She's so creative. It'll be lovely."

Papaw brought the chair around for her. She maneuvered into it, then started for the house.

"Only wish I could do more." He followed her up the ramp. "Are you sure you'll be happy?"

"Of course." She had to convince him somehow. "I'm happy because I'm marrying Matt. My family will be there."

"If you say so." He looked around, then trudged back down the ramp. "I'll be back in a minute. I forgot to buy me a newspaper at the store."

He crawled into the truck and pulled away. She shook her head. Did he believe her?

Mamaw pushed open the screen door. "Where's your grandfather going?"

"He said he forgot the newspaper."

"But I bought one."

"That's strange." Jessie wheeled into the house and to her room. Life was beyond bizarre. Her heart cried from its shattered condition, working in opposition to her need to be healed. If only she could get it repaired.

She picked up her journal. It was a struggle to find something to be thankful for with so much going wrong. At least Matt had his job. She had a job. And they would be married.

Jessie penned those thankful thoughts, then laid the journal back on the desk. She should concentrate on the good, but the *what ifs* never went away.

What if she hadn't played ball? What if it hadn't rained that night? What if?

Why was she unable to walk? Could it have been the man who stopped to help, moving them from the car? Mamaw said the doctor couldn't say whether moving her mattered or not. That man probably ruined her life.

Stop it. Her double-mindedness was worsening. Could God hear her prayers when she kept going from hopelessness to faith then back to hopelessness?

She crossed her arms. The biggest question had no answer: Why did her father leave and never come back? Did her very presence repulse him? A real father—no, a real *man*—wouldn't turn his back on a crippled child. Papaw didn't.

She wiped sweaty palms on her jeans, then stared into the mirror. Matt wasn't thinking. Why would he want her, a cripple, for a wife? Her brave façade had begun to crumble under the pressure and stress of life. Could she stop the snowball effect? Independence was slipping from her grasp.

A knock sounded from outside the house. Probably Ms. Granger. No wonder Papaw left.

"Come in." Mamaw's voice permeated her room.

Jessie drew a deep breath, then went to meet her. Estelle sat on the sofa beside Mamaw, clutching a thin folder and a bag in her lap. "Jessie, Martha told me things haven't changed, but let me show you the gown."

"Okay."

Estelle passed the folder and a swatch of fabric to Jessie. "Here are the sketches, and the way we can work the train with the wheelchair. What do you think?"

Jesse looked down at the sketch and her breath caught. "The gown is simply beautiful." Jessie fingered the silky material. It was strong and lightweight at the same time. Perfect.

"I created front and side sketches of the dress and how it will work with the chair. The best way to design this gown is with a hemline that allows the dress to be floor length in the front but shorter in the back behind the wheelchair's footplate. I'll make a removable train and we'll attach it to the back of the chair so it will flow. Two young ladies will follow behind and direct the train so it won't get tangled." Estelle couldn't sit still. "And I could make it for only four hundred and fifty dollars."

"I'm sorry. It's so lovely." Jessie handed the folder back to her. "But it just won't work."

Estelle's smile wavered. "I could let you make payments to me, or maybe find a way to save money on the material."

"No, Ms. Granger," Mamaw said. "You've been more than kind, and I'm sure your price is beyond reasonable. We're still praying something will change. How long could you wait before you had to start making it?"

Estelle pulled a small calendar from her purse. "I would have to know something by the first week of October. The material would have to be ordered, and there'll be several fittings. No later than that."

Mamaw clutched her hands. "And if we can't think of something, you'll still be paid for your trouble, I promise."

"That's not necessary." Estelle gathered her things as she stood. "It's been worth it to me to meet your family. I'll definitely be trying to think of a way to help you. Here, let me leave you the sketches. I'm a little disorganized and they'll be safer here."

Jessie took the folder. "Thank you for everything."

"You're welcome, dear."

Mamaw walked Ms. Granger out to her car. Jessie gathered the sketches and pushed to her room. Would life ever get easier? She stopped and bowed her head. *God, all this trouble has knocked my faith to the ground. Can You help me? I can't see very far.*

She lifted her head. Now she would wait for an answer. No time for pity. She had a carnival to attend. Jessie placed the folder in her desk drawer along with her emotions. There was nothing more she could do about their finances, no matter how badly she wanted life to change. Nothing.

***

Jessie paused by the last game, the dunking booth, and taped the price sign to the table. Two dollars was nothing for what was sure to be the carnival's favorite attraction. With the head football coach, Matt, and Mr. Atwater among the dunkees, the benefit carnival was sure to prove a success.

Teachers and students in western wear scurried around, completing last minute decorations. Jessie hadn't had a chance to talk to Millie about her pre-wedding struggles, and wasn't sure if she really wanted to open up like that. Anyway, Millie was surrounded by several teachers, probably handing out last-minute instructions.

The transformation of the gym still caught her breath. Ring toss, a duck pond, face painting, and a fish booth would provide children with loads of fun. Each area was decorated with imaginative posters drawn by other fourth graders. Hay bales and cowboy gear lay scattered among the booths, adding to the festive theme. Food was plentiful: caramel apples, popcorn, cotton candy, hamburgers, and hot dogs were set up in the corner with chairs and tables for seating.

"Isn't it just wonderful?" Millie sprinted over to where she was, waving a clipboard. Her new do, short and spiked up, made her look more like a student than a teacher. "I mean, it doesn't even look like the gym, huh?"

"You've outdone yourself." Jessie grinned at her close friend, in her blue jean skirt and pink cowgirl blouse. If you could be blessed with a gift of decoration, Millie had it, overabundant and running over.

"Everyone helped, of course." Millie checked the clipboard, made a mark with her pink pen, then trotted toward the duck pond. "Ellen! Do you have your prizes?"

Jessie pushed across the gymnasium to the donated-items booth, her responsibility for the night. Floral arrangements, Alabama and Auburn football memorabilia, and a nice set of cookware were among the many items displayed.

Everyone who paid admission to the carnival would be entered in the drawing for donated prizes at the end of the evening. She glanced at her list, noting one unchecked item. The gift certificate promised by Olivia Bentley hadn't been delivered.

Heels clacking on the wooden gym floor drew Jessie's attention. She glanced up to see a well-dressed young woman in a black jumper and designer heels crossing the gym floor.

Angeline.

Her mind flashed from the townhouse back to high school. She cringed. The not-so-subtle way Angeline picked at her. *Why did she seem to have it in for me?*

The worst part of being in a wheelchair is you can't run.

Angeline paused mid-floor. Even from that distance, Jessie saw her downturned lips, attitude spilling over. Angeline beat the envelope in her hand for a moment before a smile lit her face and she took the last steps to stand before Jessie.

"Here's the gift certificate from Olivia Bentley." She shoved it into Jessie's hand. "I'm surprised you'd be helping at a benefit."

"Why wouldn't I? I work here at the school." She crossed her arms to stop the trembling. Why did she let Angeline get to her?

"With a wedding to plan, or so I hear." Angeline tapped her foot. "Or has Matt dumped you already?"

"What is your problem, Angeline?" Jessie gripped the armrests of her wheelchair. "What have I ever done to you?"

Angeline leaned close as a young man passed by, clutching a bale of hay. "You think Matt's always been yours? Well, he should have been with me. He *wanted* to be with me. But it was his pity for you that kept us apart. Ask him about the summer before his junior year and the bus ride back from the Monroeville football game. I can still taste his lips and feel his body against mine." She paused long enough for the words to register. "Go ahead. Ask him."

Angeline's last words came out as a snarl. Jessie recoiled against the brunt of the blow. That was the summer she and Mamaw spent three weeks at Aunt Darlene's house in Birmingham. But she and Matt were going steady then. Or so she thought.

"And—and if it wasn't for you"—Angeline's words choked—"my *father* would still be alive."

Angeline whirled around, sashayed across the gymnasium and back through the double doors.

Jessie shut her open mouth. Why in the world would Angeline blame her for her father's death? She didn't even know Angeline's parents.

Her other words, though, hurt the most.

Her greatest fear stared her in the face, taunting her. Matt would marry her because he felt sorry for her. He was noble enough to do that. But she couldn't let him throw his life away.

Jessie's eyes closed as the last of her hopes dissolved. If he wanted Angeline or someone else, she would free him.

Tonight.

***

The next hour reeled by as Jessie pasted on an artificial smile. *Follow the routine. Don't think. Don't feel. Just do.*

She straightened each item in her booth, placing all prizes according to type, then checked over her list. A shadow fell across the clipboard. Was Angeline back? A quick peek released some of her trepidation. Latoya Cower stood in front of her.

"Jessie Smith?" Latoya's bright yellow pantsuit contrasted with her dark skin in a pleasing fashion.

"Yes. I'm Jessie." Jessie grasped Latoya's extended hand. "We're so thankful you're able to give our benefit air time."

"We're glad to. Mr. Atwater said you helped organize the event and had an information sheet about Devin."

"I do. Let me get my folder." Jessie rolled to her large tote bag and removed a sheet from inside, then handed it to her. "Here it is."

"Thank you. And I see congratulations are in order. What a lovely diamond ring."

"Thank you." Jessie held her hand steady while Latoya examined the ring.

"Who's the lucky groom?"

Jessie barely kept from clenching her eyes. "Matt Jansen." She looked across the floor in time to see him trotting toward them from the dunking booth. "Speak of the devil."

Matt came to Jessie's side and kissed her cheek, the muskiness of his cologne teasing her as always. She swallowed hard. He looked so good in his boot-cut jeans and plaid Wrangler shirt. How could she let him go?

"Matt, this is Latoya Cower."

Matt pushed back his cowboy hat. "Glad to meet you. We always watch Channel 7 News at home."

"Good to hear. And congratulations. Jessie was telling me you two are getting married." Latoya waved to a man who peeked in the doorway laden down with a large camera.

Matt grinned. "Yes, ma'am. In November."

"Planning a large wedding?"

Matt flushed as the heat rose in Jessie's face. She had to say something.

"No, ma'am." Jessie finally got the words out. "Something simple."

"Well, simple is best. Hey, we have a series of reports on local weddings coming up. Maybe I'll contact you, Jessie, and showcase a simple fall wedding."

"Are you ready, Ms. Cower?" The cameraman scanned the room before Jessie had a chance to reply. "We go live in five minutes."

"Just about." She turned back to them. "You'll have to excuse me. Nice meeting you, Jessie, Matt."

Jessie pulled away from Matt when he reached for her hand. Angeline's words rang in her head. *He wanted me.*

She retreated to the corner by the concession stand knowing full well she had to hold it together. Couldn't cry.

Matt followed. "I'm sorry. I wish we could afford to spend more on the wedding. There's no overtime at the plant. Maybe a second job—"

Jessie stopped him with a motion of her hand. "It's not that. You already work so much. I—I don't want to talk about the wedding now. Let me focus on this fundraiser. I need to help Millie." She looked at him quickly, then away again as if she were concentrating on something else right then. "We can talk on the way home."

"Are you sure?"

"Yes. I'm fine." Not really, but he could think that she was for now.

She glanced behind him. Angeline flitted toward them in tight jeans and red western shirt. How had she changed so fast? "Matt," she said, practically cooing his name. "The coach wants you to take your turn in the dunking booth like you promised. I told him I'd get you."

"Oh, okay." He turned to Jessie. "I'll be back."

Angeline grabbed his arm and led him away. Jessie hugged herself to stop the shaking.

The time had come to let him go. He needed someone he could walk through life with. Not someone wheeling beside him, holding him back.

Chapter Nine

Jessie sat beside Matt in the truck, battling a throbbing pain over her right eye. Classic migraine symptoms. At least for her. Her nausea had grown through the evening, probably due to Angeline sashaying by the donated-items booth far too often. Finally, she'd ended up in the gym restroom, throwing her guts up. Millie stayed with her until she felt well enough to leave.

"I'll have you home in a few minutes." Matt reached for her hand, and held it gently. "You should have told me you were hurting. I would've taken you home earlier."

"I wanted to do my part." She rested her other hand over her eyes. Why did the approaching headlights have to be so bright?

Matt turned onto their road. The vehicle bounced over a dip in the gravel surface. She groaned.

"Sorry."

"It's not your fault." No. It was her fault for believing anyone could look past her deficiencies. She was a liability and if he couldn't see it, well, she'd have to take care of that. But not tonight. Even the sound of his soft voice pounded away at her aching head.

Tomorrow. She'd break up with him then.

***

Homer lifted the pile of manure with his pitchfork, and tossed it into the wheelbarrow. Flies buzzed around his head, and he flinched at the stench invading his nose. Not a fun chore after breakfast, but the last stall was cleaned.

Had to be done.

He then cut the twine and broke apart a bale of hay, filling each trough, then grabbed a scoop from against the wall. Two shovels of pine shavings to freshen each stall and he was finished. The wheelbarrow weighed little, as he pushed it toward the compost pile near their small vegetable garden, but his shoulders sagged as if it contained boulders.

Not being able to provide for Jessie was the hardest thing he'd ever had to face. Except for burying Elizabeth. The pain was the same, for again he failed.

Ms. Granger had cut corners as much as she could and she would have let them make payments—which he wouldn't hear of—but it would still be too much. With all the new bills, he could never raise it. And no charity. He should be able to support his own family.

He lifted the wheelbarrow and dumped the cow piles into the compost, stirring it in to lessen the smell. The small tomato plants nearby caught his attention and he reached over and plucked a weed.

The garden needed hoeing. So much to do and a wedding on top of it. Even without the dress, he would be hard-pressed to save enough for the simplest of events.

Martha waited by the barn as he turned the corner to return the wheelbarrow.

"Homer." She twisted her apron in her hands. "I've racked my brain 'til I can't think anymore. Isn't there a way to raise more money for Jessie's special day?"

He parked the wheelbarrow outside the barn, then turned to Martha. "I laid awake half the night trying to figure out one. I just can't see it."

"Well, we could sell that land your Uncle Seth left you."

Homer grunted and trudged toward the house. Martha didn't know about the shed. And if it were up to him, she never would. "You know I don't want to sell that land. What if Jessie needs it someday?"

She followed him up the back steps. "But she needs money for a wedding *now*."

He held the screen door open and followed her inside. "I'll think of another way. Just give me time." He reached for the coffeepot.

Cold.

"I'll make a fresh pot." Martha reached for the carafe. "If Wayne wouldn't have left, Jessie might have more money."

"We don't need him. Besides, I hate Wayne Riggs and everything connected to him." Homer sat at the kitchen table, burying his head in his hands. "I'm her father now and I'll pay for it. I'm responsible for everything."

Martha worked to prepare a fresh pot of coffee. "I'm sorry. You're right. Wayne is in the past. But what do you mean by responsible for everything?"

He lifted his head, then turned toward her. "Don't you see? It's my fault. I should've replaced those tires sooner. I'm sure Elizabeth and Jessie would have never wrecked with good tires. I was so wrapped up in the farm, not taking care of you girls like I should, and anyway—it's my fault."

"Homer Smith. You were wrapped up in trying to live." Martha's voice cracked. She laid her hand on his shoulder. "You've always been a good provider. You aren't to blame."

Homer scratched his chin. Not responsible? Was it even a possibility? He didn't know.

Time to change the subject. "Is Jessie still in the bed? Have you checked on her?"

"Yes. She's asleep. The migraine is better." The coffee finished brewing and Martha poured a cup and set it in front of him. "She hasn't had one in a long time. I don't know what brought it on."

Homer sipped the beverage, then lowered the cup. "It's all this worrying about the wedding and our finances."

"You can't help her not worry. Matt's coming over right after work." Martha rubbed his shoulder. "If anyone can help her work through this, it's Matt."

Homer stood, walked into the living room and turned on the television. Could Martha be right? He couldn't control everything, though he wanted to. He had done everything he could to make Jessie happy. Perhaps it was time to quit blaming himself.

Maybe even tell Martha and Jessie about the shed. He gripped the cup tighter as his stomach churned. But what would they think of him?

***

Jessie woke to the sound of Bear's barks. She forced one eye open, then the other. A small amount of sunlight leaked through the blinds in the window. Was the headache gone? She squinted in the darkened room, then relaxed. No pain so far.

She pushed herself to a sitting position, inch by inch, propping on both pillows. Still no pain. Her phone peeked out from under the comforter. She pushed the home button. Eleven o'clock. Time to get awake and coherent before Matt's workday ended. She had to talk to him. Before she lost her nerve.

Her bedroom door opened a little and Mamaw peeked in.

"You feeling better, honey?" Mamaw opened the door a little wider. "I thought I heard you moving, so I brought you a cup of hot tea with a touch of honey if you're up to it."

"Thank you, Mamaw. You know what helps." Jessie rearranged her pillow. "I think you can raise the lights."

Her grandmother lightened the room with the dimmer switch, then stepped inside. She set the steamy beverage on her nightstand. "Here you go."

Jessie reached for the cup. "Let me sip this and lie here a while. My head's okay. I'm weak though. You might have to help me dress before Matt gets here."

"Just let me know. I'll fix you something to eat first." Mamaw paused at the door. "How about chicken and dumplings? I'm stewing a chicken for supper."

"That'll be good."

Jessie lay back against the pillows and sipped the tea. A trickle of dizziness still remained. Nothing unusual.

She released a breath. Too weak to dress herself. Once again, she struggled to do the simplest tasks on her own. Not that it mattered anymore. If she didn't marry Matt, there would be no one else.

She laid the cup aside and listened to a bird warble outside her window. Its sweet sound brought a tear to her eye. She'd always believed a sparrow didn't fall without God knowing it. Did He know what she was wrestling with? The Bible said yes.

But she wasn't so sure anymore.

Jessie glanced at her cell phone to see if it were time to take her meds and it was. She grasped the bottle of water she kept on her nightstand along with the pill bottle. She twisted the cap, dropped one in her hand, then swallowed. Bitter.

The aroma of chicken soon wafted into her room and she thanked God. It didn't nauseate her. The empty feeling in her stomach wasn't all the result of no food. Matt would soon arrive and life as she'd known it would end. She closed her eyes against the thought.

Her door opened. She rubbed her eyes, realizing she'd dozed off again.

"Here's the dumplings." Mamaw carried in a lap tray balancing a bowl. "Try to eat some. Is it time for another dose of medicine?"

"I already took it."

"Good. Now call me if you need me." Mamaw exited the room.

Jessie forced the first bites down, then settled enough to finish the rest. When Mamaw came back, she could get dressed.

And then she'd wait.

Three hours later, Jessie sat in the living room, trying to concentrate on the cooking show on television. Anything but what lay ahead.

"You coming, Martha?" Papaw's voice carried from the porch where he sat. "Going to be late if you don't hurry."

"You sure you're okay with us leaving?" Mamaw asked for the third time.

"I haven't been sick all day." Jessie waved her hand. "Go before Papaw leaves you."

"I wouldn't leave if my crown wasn't ready. I'll have to be there." She opened the door. "We'll be back as soon as we can."

Jessie wheeled to the window and watched their truck head down the driveway. The finality of what she had to do burned in the pit of her stomach. Would Mamaw and Papaw understand? It didn't matter. She had to do what was best for Matt.

She gritted her teeth. If she really loved him, she would want him happy. And how could he be happy with her? He didn't need a liability for a wife.

God, I love Matt so much. But I don't want him to marry me from pity. I thought he loved me, but now I'm not sure. Help me to make the right decision. I need Your wisdom now. You say You have a plan and purpose for me, even like I am. Is Matt in that plan and purpose?

She glanced out the window. Matt's truck trailed dust as he coasted down their driveway.

Her heart beat faster. *I need to know now.*

The heavy thumping of his boots on the ramp tore at her heart afresh. How could she bear not hearing or seeing him again? He looked in through the screen door. "Jessie?"

"Come in." Her voice trembled. Weak. That's what she was.

God, help me.

"Hey," he said with a broad smile as he pulled his work boots off and left them by the door. His work uniform had a smudge of grease below the pocket, right below his name emblem. "You feeling better? You worried me last night."

"I'm tired, but I'll be okay." She allowed his kiss and joined him at the couch where he helped her to move beside him.

He glanced toward the kitchen. "Where are your grandparents?"

"They went to pick up Mamaw's new crown." She grimaced. Small talk. She couldn't do that. She had to end it now. But how could she go through life without him?

"You never told me last night what was wrong." He grasped her hand. "Tell me now."

She shook her head to try and stop the forming tears, but it was no use. She laid her other hand on top of his. "I—I want to release you from our engagement."

"*What?*" His grip on her hand tightened as his mouth drew in a line and he turned more fully toward her. "*Why?* What have I done?"

"*You* haven't done anything." She couldn't let him blame himself. "I know there's a better woman out there for you, Matt. Someone you won't have to care for all your life. I don't want to hold you back."

The color drained from his face. He dropped her hand and stood, then walked to the screen door to peer outside.

The clock ticked, the only sound breaking the silence.

"How shallow do you think I am?" Matt's words cut as he turned to her. "Do you think I didn't think about that long and hard before I proposed? I counted the cost, Jessie."

She swallowed hard. "But I have so many issues."

"I'm not perfect myself, you know." He crossed his arms. "Have you considered that?"

She hadn't. "No." Her focus had only been on herself. "I—I'm sorry if I upset you. I just don't want you to marry me because you feel sorry for me."

"I wouldn't do that." He walked back to her, sat again and pulled her close. "You're the woman I want. There is no one I could love more, or who could make me any happier. Wheelchair or not."

"I love you too." She leaned against his shoulder. Why had she doubted him?

Oh, yeah. Angeline.

***

Matt held Jessie as she dabbed at her eyes with a tissue. What had made her try to call off their engagement? He sure didn't understand women. "Tell me what put such a crazy idea in your mind. And I want the whole truth. You and your grandfather have both been acting strange. If this marriage is going to work, we can't keep secrets from each other."

"Then don't," Jessie blurted. "Tell me about the night of the Monroeville football game. And what happened the summer I was at Aunt Darlene's house."

His throat tightened. How had she found out? "I'm not sure—"

"Did you date Angeline? And what about you and her on—on the back seat of the—the bus." She hiccupped. "Did you make love to her? We were serious then."

Matt's face grew hot. "Did Angeline tell you that last night? I thought she was acting all weird."

"She did. But you haven't answered my question." Jessie clutched her hands. "You said no secrets." She stared at him. "So? Did you?"

Matt stared toward the window. He didn't want to hurt Jessie. But lying wouldn't help. "I dated her a few times while you were gone. And I will admit I was tempted on the bus when she sashayed back to where I was sitting in her skimpy outfit and threw herself on me. I did kiss her back. But only for a moment."

Jessie pulled away. "She said you did."

"But only for a moment." He reached for her hand, but she shook it off. He reached again; he had to make her see. "All I could see was *your* face, feel *your* kiss. You make me crazy in love, not her. I pushed her away, even when she wanted me to start dating her again. She's hated me ever since, far as I know. I don't think a guy ever told her no before."

Jessie released a pent-up breath. "How could you cheat on me? You dated *her* while I was gone. If it were only a kiss, why did you hide it? And how can I trust you now?"

Matt stood and paced across the floor again. He'd been such a fool. "I was stupid. And young. And wrong. After it was over, I just tried to pretend it didn't happen."

She lifted her chin. "Well, it did." She cocked a brow at him. "Is there anything else I should know? Any other girl? I can't take finding out anything else from someone like I did Angeline."

"Nothing or no one else. I promise. No more secrets. I'll come clean about everything from now on." He sat beside her. "And I'm really, really sorry."

There wasn't anything more he could say. He rubbed the back of his neck and stared at the floor.

She reached for his hand. "I forgive you."

He tilted his head. "What?"

"You made a mistake." She sighed. "We all do."

"There's been no one else."

"I believe you." A flush crept across her cheeks. "I have a secret too."

He straightened. What could it possibly be? "You do?"

"It's just—well, I keep thinking about my father. The wedding has brought up so many lingering issues. Like this chair and my mom and da—Wayne. What I missed. I think I want to try and find him."

Whoa. He hadn't seen that coming. Still— "That's not unusual. Have you looked on the internet?"

"I did. I found a name and address in Mississippi in the White Pages that I believe belongs to him." She leaned forward, glancing in the direction of her room. "I thought about looking on Facebook but I haven't had the nerve."

He breathed out slowly. There was more, of course. "What will your grandparents think?"

She glanced at the front door, then back to him. "They can't know. Not now, anyway."

"All right. Let's look then." He stood. "I'll get your laptop."

In a few minutes, they found the Facebook page of Wayne Riggs. "There's not much here. Looks like he started this page a few weeks ago." Matt pointed to the bio. "No photo."

"The age is right. It might be him. Only a couple of posts about work and no replies. A few friends." Jessie's hand trembled as she maneuvered the mouse. "Should I friend him?"

"It's the only way you'll know." Matt laid his hand over hers and together they slid the cursor over the "add friend" button and clicked. "Now regardless of what happens, you've done something you thought you should do. Right?"

"Right."

She agreed but her tone spoke defeat. He cupped her cheeks and kissed her lightly. "I'm glad you told me. It'll work out."

Tears brimmed in her eyes. "I shouldn't keep things from you or you from me. For this marriage to work, we need to trust each other. I'm sorry I haven't already told you about looking for Wayne."

"Don't worry." Matt pulled another tissue from the box on the end table and handed it to Jessie. "Now how about you brighten up before your grandparents get back? They'll think we've been fighting or something."

"We don't want that." She pushed back her hair. "I'm glad we talked it out."

"Me too."

Being engaged was more difficult than he imagined. But they had survived their first real argument.

"Together, Jessie." He brushed another kiss on her lips. "We'll face life together."

Chapter Ten

The coffee shop perched between Elliot's Jewelers and Salon Divas across from the Riverview courthouse and boasted the best coffee in town. Angeline pushed the door open, the aroma of freshly baked pastries mixing with espresso and chocolate. A working woman's paradise after a long day.

She'd promised to meet her cousin Elaine for dinner. Tuesdays at Bentley's tended to be slow, and that frustrated Francine. Was anything worse than a frustrated Francine?

Elaine waved from a booth in the back corner. "Over here." She fit the mold of a classic sanguine: talkative and friendly. Her hair was dark like Angeline's but Elaine had several inches on her and was marathon-runner thin.

"Hey, Ang, have a seat. I ordered your usual."

Angeline nodded. She always ordered the same thing here: Grande vanilla latte, hold the whipped cream, a chicken salad sandwich, and baked chips.

"Thanks." Angeline slid into the seat across from her perky cousin, chucking her purse beside her. She kicked her shoes off under the table, the tile floor cool to her feet. "Whew."

"Let me guess. Francine didn't have a good day. *As* usual."

Angeline leaned back against the booth. "You got it. Francine never has good days."

A waitress approached with two cups and set down the steaming beverages, with extra napkins between them. "Be right back with your order."

Elaine nodded. "Thank you."

A few minutes later, their food arrived as Angeline stifled a yawn.

Nothing a twelve-hour nap wouldn't help. She munched on her sandwich while Elaine chatted about her day working as a hygienist at Longley's Dental Clinic.

Elaine finally wound up her long discourse. "And this is only Tuesday."

Angeline set her half-empty cup on the table and finished her chips. Her cousin had few problems compared to hers. If Elaine really wanted something to gripe about, she should work for Francine. "At least your business isn't owned by Olivia Bentley." She lowered her voice. "She probably has spies in this shop just waiting for me to slip up."

Elaine tilted her head. "You do look kind of stressed and paranoid." Her eyes narrowed knowingly. "Or is this *all* about work? Your dad again?"

"I'd *rather* not talk about Dad." Her voice quivered. Why did they all want to bring up her father?

"I'm just saying that when your father died, you changed. You've gone into a shell."

Angeline crumpled one of her napkins. How could Elaine understand? Her dad was still living. "It's called survival. Listen. It's all I can do so don't try to force me to face anything more. I can't handle it. Not on top of everything else."

"What else?" Elaine pushed her empty plate away. "The job?"

"No, not the job. You don't know what it's like to be *me.*"

"Meaning?"

"Meaning your mother doesn't berate you for being single and childless." Angeline leaned closer. "And now everywhere I turn I run into Jessie Smith and Matt Jansen." Her voice hit a shrill tone. "That crippled girl who stole Matt from me."

Elaine shook her head as the people nearby stared. "*Stole* Matt? I thought she was dating him first."

"Yes, but I wanted him and she messed all that up. He quit dating me and went back to her because he felt sorry for her." She glared at Elaine. Was she siding with Jessie? "And she was the reason my father died. Dad blamed himself for her being crippled."

"How was that his fault? He stopped to help them, not hurt them."

Angeline blinked back tears. Her cousin didn't know the truth. The whole truth, wrapped up like one horrible story. Perhaps the time had come. "His car was about to meet theirs in the pouring rain when a large dog ran between them. Dad ran off the road in a small ditch, but they hit a concrete barrier. The truck was smoldering and he panicked and moved them both from the vehicle."

Elaine's eyes widened. "I knew about the wreck, of course, but I didn't realize he moved them."

Angeline rubbed her chin. "Mother said the doctors couldn't say for sure that's what paralyzed that girl, but Dad blamed himself. He already had a weak heart and well, you know …" Angeline swiped at a stray tear.

"But you can't blame Jessie for that, Angeline. She was a kid when that happened." Elaine said, then shook her head. "Angeline, you have to let it go."

Angeline shifted. Why should she? "My father is dead. Give me one reason."

"I'll give you two," Elaine said. "It was nobody's fault, all the way around, and the girl has nothing but Matt. You have a nice car, a townhouse you have no trouble paying for, a good albeit stressful job, and … and you can walk. Do you really want *him*, too? Or did he hurt your pride?"

Angeline closed her eyes. Someone needed to pay for ruining her life. Jessie was handy. But her stomach ached, something it did a lot these days.

Could it be from tormenting a crippled girl?

Elaine was right; Angeline didn't really *need* Matt. He treated her with respect when all the other guys seemed to only want one thing. And he intrigued her. She placed her face in her hands and rubbed her forehead. Were there other guys out there like him?

"Ang?" Elaine reached across the table and laid her hand on Angeline's. "Just think about what I said. Okay?"

"I will." She sighed and picked up her cup of now tepid coffee. Her life couldn't continue at this stress level. Something had to give. Why did it have to be her pride?

***

Jessie rummaged through her purse, pulling out items and laying them on her lap. Where was her key to open the office? Surely, she hadn't forgotten it.

Packet of tissue, wallet, phone, mini photo album. There. She pulled the key ring from the side pocket where it nestled. Next to the house key and office key was Mamaw's car key. She shook her head. Why Mamaw wanted her to have a car key was beyond her. Matt had even offered to mount hand controls and teach her to drive. No way, no how would she ever try to drive.

She wanted her independence but the thought of getting behind the wheel of a car pushed her to the point of a panic attack. The doctor said her reaction wasn't abnormal considering the trauma she'd gone through, so she left it at that.

She opened the door and moved inside with a growing list on her mind. Make the coffee and check email. Jessie would need the extra caffeine after yesterday. She opened the gallon of water beside the coffee maker and added the right amount, then set the pot to brew.

She flipped through a folder on the desk. Oh yes. The information packets she received at the Central City bridal fair. She shoved them into the bottom desk drawer.

No time to look now.

She turned on her computer and pulled up the school's email account, and busied herself organizing each piece of mail into its correct folder when Mr. Atwater entered with Latoya Cower and Millie trailing behind.

"Hello, Jessie." Latoya extended her hand. "So good to see you again."

Jessie shook her hand. "Good to see you. Did you hear that the fundraiser raised two thousand dollars for pediatric Crohn's research?"

"That's what Mr. Atwater said. I'm thrilled we could help."

Millie smiled. "I can't believe it did so well."

Mr. Atwater unlocked his inner office, then turned. "Jessie, can you join us in my office? We need to have a quick meeting."

"Yes, sir." She pushed away from her desk wondering if this had something to do with Devin and the fundraiser. "Do I need to take any notes?"

He shook his head. "Not today."

Millie giggled. "*Notes.*"

Jessie cut her eyes at Millie. What was wrong with her?

They entered the midsize office, a large desk the central point with bookcases on each side and a view of the ball field through the large window behind. Mr. Atwater took his place behind the desk while Millie and Latoya stood by the bookcase.

"Jessie." Latoya smoothed her paisley jacket. "The event was a great success and I know you worked hard. But after you left with a migraine, I was concerned and asked Millie about you. She told me how anxious you were about your wedding."

Jessie gasped. "Millie. My goodness." Did they know about Angeline?

"Financial woes can happen to anyone." Millie crossed her arms. "Well, *someone* had to help you. You and Matt are so stubborn."

Latoya continued. "Anyway, I mentioned it to my producer at Channel 7 and we decided to do a piece on your wedding in our upcoming bridal series. We want to ask Estelle Granger to create the dress she designed for you. Several local businesses have offered to donate supplies. It's free advertising for them and good for the community. We're going to tie it in with our monthly installments that feature small acts of kindness."

Jessie's mouth opened, and then closed. Help with the wedding. The community would do this for her and Matt? "I—I don't know what to say."

Millie grasped Jessie's arm. "Just say yes."

Jessie couldn't contain her smile. "Yes. Of course. Thank you so much."

"You're very welcome." Latoya pulled a notepad and pen from her shoulder bag. "The dress will be featured in the piece. The sketches anyway. We'll be doing a story about Bentley's on Monday and follow with your story on Tuesday."

Millie crossed her arms. "*Bentley's* is the shop that treated Jessie's grandpa so shamefully. They wouldn't give him the time of day."

"You're kidding." Latoya had a new gleam in her eye. "How interesting. Not the first negative remark I've heard about Bentley's."

Millie threw up her hands. "They *carefully* select their customers."

Latoya jotted something down. "Jessie, how about we meet next Tuesday afternoon at four o'clock at your house? We would like Matt to be there if possible. We'll air the interview on the six o'clock news."

"That would be wonderful." Joy bubbled through her smile. "Thank you again."

I'll see you then." Latoya bent to hug Jessie, then left.

"I can't believe it." Jessie grasped Millie's hand. "You're the best friend anyone could have." She looked up at her boss. "May I take a half-day vacation on Tuesday, Mr. Atwater?"

"Of course," he said. "It isn't every day one of our staff is on the news. I guess I can answer my own phone for one more afternoon."

Millie followed Jessie to the outer office. "I've got to get my grocery shopping done. We'll talk more later."

"Okay." Jessie reached for her phone. She had to call everyone. "I have to tell Mamaw and Papaw. But I'll wait until I see Matt to tell him."

She dialed Mamaw's number. As she waited for it to ring, she breathed a silent prayer. *Thank You, God.*

***

Sunlight danced on the porch floor, creating flower shadows from Mamaw's planters. Jessie waited, breathing the sweet floral scent of the numerous pots and flowerbeds scattered around the farmhouse. The swing moved to a slow rhythm in the breeze. What a lovely moment.

Mamaw was inside cooking a special supper while Papaw watched the weather on television. The news about the dress brightened his countenance, but there was still sadness in his eyes.

Why?

Matt pulled in the driveway and parked beside Papaw's truck. He jumped out and trotted to the porch. She couldn't wait to see his face when she shared the news.

"Hey, Jessie." Matt took the ramp in two bounds, his face anxious. "You said in your text you had something important to tell me. What is it?" He scooted beside her on the swing.

She grasped his hand, entwining their fingers. "Latoya Cower came to the school today and she's going to interview us next Tuesday about our wedding."

Matt paled. "On television? Why?"

"Millie told her about the dress Estelle designed for me, and Channel 7 News is working with the community so she can make it. Different businesses are going to contribute whatever she needs to finish the gown. Can you believe it?"

"Wow. That's great." Matt tightened his grip on her hand. "But I don't think I want to be on the news. The guys at the plant would never stop ribbing me."

Jessie poked him in the side. "They're only jealous. Don't worry. You need to be here a little before four if you can."

"All right. I'll do it." He reached his arm around her and pulled her close. "For you."

The swing rocked to the tempo of life. She had Matt and now God opened a door for even more. She'd have a beautiful dress for her wedding day. And everyone would be there. Everyone but …

Jessie stiffened. "I need to check my Facebook. I forgot to see if there's been a reply."

"Sit still and I'll grab your laptop."

She chewed on her bottom lip. Did her father check his Facebook often like everyone else? The enormity of the moment weighed on her.

What if her father *had* answered her?

What if he hadn't? Or never did?

The screen door creaked. Matt came out of the house and sat beside her. After Facebook booted up, she saw that she had no answered friend request.

Jessie released a breath, hardly realizing she'd been holding it. Had he added anything to his page? She typed in Wayne Riggs, to go there. Wayne Riddle and Wayne Rhodes came up, but his name had been removed.

Within, her blood ran from the top of her head and pooled in the feet. "He's deleted his page." Jessie ran the search again before shutting the laptop. Her stomach went from flutters to knots as she closed her eyes. "He doesn't want anything to do with me."

"You don't know." Matt's voice betrayed him. "It could be anything."

She shook her head. "But it's not. My own father wants nothing to do with me. Can't you see?" Her voice cracked as it rose. "He barely visited me when I could walk, but after that ..." Jessie handed the laptop to Matt.

"Don't go there." Matt set the laptop over onto her wheelchair, then clasped her hands.

"Why not?" She dug her nails into her palms, and stared at the porch floor. "What does it mean if your own father avoids you? That you're worthless. That's all I am to him. All I'll ever be."

Matt lifted her chin. "Only to him. You're *everything* to me. And to so many others. Look at how people offered to help you with the wedding dress."

She strained to smile. "I appreciate your words, but they can never take my father's place. Even with Papaw, I still feel a void."

Matt pulled her close again, and Jessie tried to relax in the warmth of his embrace. She had no tears, though the hurt pierced deep into her soul. There was nothing else she could do. Life would go on, with or without her father. She so wished life could be different, but it wasn't. What had Pastor Allen said that Sunday? To focus on your blessings. Leave the past behind.

The screen door opened and Mamaw peeked out. "Supper will be ready in thirty minutes."

Jessie nodded. Well, there was one pot of gold at the end of the rainbow: Mamaw didn't have a clue at what had just transpired. And she never would.

"Thirty minutes?" Papaw emerged from behind her. "I think I'll go to the store and get a newspaper."

"Okay." Jessie turned as Papaw got in his truck, puttered down the driveway and turned left onto the road. "Wait a minute. The store's not that way."

"No, it's not." Matt adjusted his cap. "Maybe he's taking the long way around."

Jessie wrinkled her brow. But why? What was wrong with Papaw? Yes, he was growing older, but his health was pretty good. Was it his mind?

She straightened. Time to stop worrying about what she couldn't fix and concentrate on what she had. Her family, the wedding, and a new life.

Okay. So, her father didn't care. That was a fact. Her grandparents needed her. Especially Papaw.

That was also a fact.

***

The door banged behind Angeline as she pushed her way into Bentley's. She marched to her desk, plopped down, and punched the start button on the computer. *Just let someone irritate me today.*

"Oh, Angeline, dearie," Glenda called from across the room. "Francine said for you to report to her office as soon as you arrived. I guess you're in trouble."

"Over what?" Angeline stood, straightening her skirt. If she could *only* straighten out Glenda.

The troublemaker pointed to the door. "The old man you threw out the other day, I guess."

"Francine commended me, thank you." She huffed and pushed by Glenda. "And *I* took credit for sending him to The Dress Boutique."

Angeline gained a moment's satisfaction from Glenda's open mouth and entered the hallway to Francine's office. What could her boss want now?

"Oh good. You're *finally* here." Francine tapped her pen against her desk.

Angeline eyed her watch. "I'm a half hour early."

"That's true, but remember, not only is this a Monday, but Channel 7 News is coming here for our part of their wedding series today." She splayed her fingers on the desk, leaning forward. "And I want everything perfect. Olivia Bentley will be here also."

Angeline's heart sank. Olivia Bentley was even more demanding than Francine. And less patient. "Yes, ma'am. I went over the checklist before I left on Saturday. There's only a couple of things left to do."

"Well do them." Francine reached for a mirror and dug a tube of lipstick from her purse. She glanced up, eyebrows knit together. "Now."

"Yes, ma'am." She slunk back to her desk and grabbed her list of reminders. *This job is worth it. The townhouse is worth it.*

She scanned the list, mumbling under her breath. "Check on the dressing rooms, prom gown display, and of course, everything to do with weddings. Dust all counters and check display cases."

Angeline spotted Glenda wiping up the coffee station. She thrust the list toward her. "What have you gotten done?"

Glenda glanced at the paper. "I've dusted and checked for fingerprints on all the glass cases. But I didn't check the dressing rooms. You'll have to, because Francine asked *me* to re-straighten the wedding jewelry."

Angeline pursed her lips and trudged toward dressing room one. Did Channel 7 know the hassle they were causing? A quick scan revealed the room to be adequate, so she stepped to the next room. Angeline pushed the stool back into the corner, then stifled a scream which threatened to erupt from within.

A dead mouse.

She backed up a few feet. What if Francine had found *that* disgusting wad of fur?

She stepped across the hallway to the bathroom and grabbed a handful of paper towels. If only she could pick it up without touching it. Angeline bent, scooped up the mouse, and shuddered.

Ew.

She tossed it into the garbage can, pulled the plastic bag out and hurried it through the back door. She tossed the bag inside the small dumpster, then slapped her hands together as if to clear them from any disgusting diseases.

It was always something. Francine proved harder to work for each day. Everything was smiles and compliments when she was first hired, but it only lasted a week before Francine's true character expressed itself. If Angeline was to keep her sanity she'd have to keep focusing on the money she made.

A brisk breeze tangled Angeline's hair. Colorful leaves lay strewn along the walk and blooming begonias lined the flowerbeds surrounding Bentley's. She inhaled deeply. Just relax, she told herself. Just relax.

The sound of a vehicle around front caught her attention and she peered around the corner. Channel 7 News.

Early.

She raced back inside to hear Francine whistle.

"Ladies. Front and center."

A drill sergeant would have been a better career choice. Angeline gathered with the eight other employees.

"They're here. Is everything ready?"

"Yes, ma'am." Angeline glanced at the others. No one else spoke.

"Good. Remember, Latoya Cower is interviewing *me*. Head to your stations and try not to stare at the camera. If you're needed, I'll ask. Angeline, you meet them at the door and bring them here." Francine positioned herself near their most expensive gown.

"Yes, ma'am." Angeline stood at her desk, and while waiting for whatever took the news crew so long, sorted papers into paid and unpaid. She rubbed her brow which ached from lack of sleep and a building headache. She'd tossed and turned the night before, but this time her insomnia wasn't Bentley's fault. Elaine's words wouldn't leave her. *You have to let it go.*

But she couldn't get Jessie off her mind. The look of horror on Jessie's face when Angeline pulled Matt away at the fundraiser haunted her. Later, she'd stepped into the bathroom and discovered Jessie throwing up. Had that been her fault? And what could she do about it now?

"They're coming up the walk." Glenda's shrill voice rang out. "The news team *and* Olivia Bentley."

Angeline pasted on her best smile, opened the door, and admitted Latoya and Olivia to Bentley's. Show time.

Chapter Eleven

Homer scowled at the dark-green shed, the lions guarding its contents. He rubbed the head of the lion next to the building; its gritty exterior scratched his palm. They used to sit in front of Wayne and Elizabeth's trailer when Jessie was little. What good were they now?

He scrubbed his hand over his face. He should quit using this building as a safe place to spill out his pain. Twenty dollars a week could be put in savings instead of going to that boy for mowing. These lions would bring several good dollars at a yard sale and could help pay for Jessie's wedding.

Homer lifted the heavy padlock and inserted the key. He glanced at the second padlock next to it and wondered why he'd bothered to add a second lock. A swift yank pulled the rusty metal door open. He flipped on the light, illuminating the contents of the building, a picture of the past.

His past.

He peered at the space closest to him, a meticulously organized area. Large totes lined shelves on the walls, hand-written labels adorning each one. All sizes and all colors. On the floor stood a ten-speed bicycle, oiled and shiny. Beside it was a child's bike.

Homer reached into his pocket for a handkerchief. He swiped at his eyes before lifting the pink tote closest to him from the shelf and setting it on the floor. His breath caught in his throat.

Elizabeth's special dresses.

He lifted the lid and unfolded the top dress, a light purple floral print. One of his daughter's favorites. The light scent of perfume still clung to the garment … or maybe he imagined it. He inhaled, then replaced the dress, shut the lid, and lifted the box to the shelf.

Elizabeth's knick-knacks. Elizabeth's china. Each tote labeled and stacked. Memory after memory. A mouse scurried near the purple tote in the corner. His face crumpled as a sob escaped his lips.

Jessie's toys. Not just any toys. Inside the tub lay her softball glove. Her bat. Her bicycle helmet. He'd removed them from the house right after the accident.

He trudged toward the other side of the shed. A motorcycle had tumbled on its side, seat ripped. He fingered the dents he'd hammered into it. Men's clothing lay on the ground or had been thrown on top of an old tool bench, nests for mice and spiders.

No way would Wayne get his stuff without signing the divorce papers …

Everything Wayne left lay useless and trampled. Every dent he placed, every rip he made was his means to vent the overwhelming anger. Only problem, it had not helped.

Nothing did.

He turned back to the door. The orange tote filled with Elizabeth's pictures. Tears blurred his vision. Why his only daughter? He lifted the lid, then shut it. Some days it was too hard. Like today.

***

The sun beat down on the porch, sending waves of heat jumbling with a slight breeze. Jessie arched her back, trying to release the tension. She'd swapped the burden of worrying about Papaw for the burden of her absent father. Not a good trade.

Papaw and Mamaw sat together on the glider, waiting for the Channel 7 team to arrive. She perched on the swing beside Matt, holding on to his arm.

Mamaw glanced toward the road. A white van kicked up dust. "I bet that's the news people."

"I believe it is." Matt stood and jingled the keys in his pocket. "I'll go put Bear in the barn."

"Then come right back." Jessie swatted his arm. "You're not getting out of this."

Latoya Cower exited the van after it stopped beside the house, followed by a young man carrying camera equipment. She waved. Said, "Hello, Jessie," then grabbed a few items from the backseat and hurried across the yard.

Latoya smoothed her jacket as she mounted the steps. "Are you ready for this?"

Jessie drew a deep breath. This was part of moving forward with her life. "Yes, ma'am. I'd like you to meet my grandfather, Homer Smith, and my grandmother, Martha."

Mamaw beamed. "Ms. Cower, this means so much to us."

Papaw grunted and Jessie swallowed a spoonful of frustration at his stubbornness.

Matt rounded the corner and joined them on the porch.

"And you remember my fiancé Matt," Jessie said.

Latoya nodded as she extended her hand. "How are you?"

"I'm good," he answered, taking the woman's proffered hand in his own, then releasing just as quickly.

"We're proud of what y'all are doing but it's not like we didn't want to give Jessie her dream dress." Papaw shuffled his feet. "Times have been tough."

"And this is where Channel 7 News can help," Latoya said. "Along with Estelle Granger, The Dress Boutique, and Lulu's Fabrics. Did you happen to see our story last night?"

"About Bentley's?" Jessie said. "Of course. It was a wonderful piece. Olivia Bentley seemed very proud of her boutique."

"I noticed you asked a lot of questions about wedding dress designers," Mamaw pried. "What was that all about?"

"You'll see in tonight's story." She looked around. "Now, then. Let's get started."

***

Angeline glanced at the clock sitting on her mantel above the gas logs.

Five minutes until six. She could wait. Having to deal with Francine and Glenda every day had given her a master's degree in patience. She grabbed the remote and flipped on Channel 7 News.

After a lengthy stretch, she sank into the overstuffed chair with a double burger, fries, and chocolate milkshake on the TV tray beside her. Time to fuel up on comfort food. The story on Bentley's the night before had been a success. Francine even commented on how well everything looked. Tonight would be another wedding installment and Angeline didn't want to miss it in case Francine had any questions for her in the morning.

Angeline lost focus as the top news stories rolled across the screen. She pondered her latest phone conversation with Elaine. Angeline's behavior of late had been awful, and she'd admitted it. Elaine had given her hope that life could be different. Her cousin shared how different people handled grief. Anger and bitterness were not unusual reactions.

Angeline accepted an invitation to the Wednesday night service at Elaine's church. Maybe she could finally unravel all the tangles left inside her heart by her father's death. Did God remember the small child who had once prayed by her bed?

She looked up at the mention of Jessie Smith's name only to see Jessie's face fill the screen. The camera panned to show an old woman and the man who came to Bentley's. And Matt. She turned up the volume.

"And with the help of Estelle Granger, The Dress Boutique, and Lulu's Fabrics, Jessie is going to get her dream wedding gown." Latoya's smile faded and the camera panned closer. "But there's another piece to this story you should know. One that will make tonight's story all the more poignant. Homer Smith tried to gain help at Bentley's, but was turned away."

Olivia Bentley came into view on the television and Angeline's milkshake slipped from her hand and sloshed onto the tray. She grabbed several tissues from a nearby box and mopped at the spill, her eyes never leaving the screen.

Latoya continued. "I followed up on this story by going back to

Bentley's after hours."

Olivia Bentley, hair disheveled, stood outside of the store clutching a handkerchief. "I don't know what happened with Mr. Smith. But I promise you one thing. We will get to the bottom of why the poor—I mean *distinguished*—gentleman wasn't offered assistance. We serve the *whole* public here at Bentley's." Her distress magnified as the camera zoomed in.

Angeline placed her head in her hands. She couldn't believe this was happening. And she'd taken credit for sending Jessie's grandfather away. Her everything-in-its-place world was coming unraveled faster than she could make sense of it.

Why?

This couldn't bode well for Bentley's *or* her job.

***

A ringing phone jarred Jessie from her nap. She'd been reading when the activity and emotion of the day caught up with her. She fumbled for the phone on the bed. A local but unfamiliar number.

She cleared her throat. "Hello?"

"Jessie, this is Latoya Cower. I didn't mean to call so late, but I had to let you know."

She wiped sleep from her eyes. "Know what?"

"After the story aired tonight, the switchboard lit up. We've been bombarded with people who want to help."

"Help?" She pulled herself to a sitting position and flipped on the lamp. "With what?"

"With your dream wedding. Local businesses have offered to donate items: flowers, tuxedo rental, decorations, and even style your hair on the big day. Many people are asking where they can donate money. You have a *lot* of friends."

"I—I can't believe it," She gasped. All this? For her and Matt? "Why would people do this?"

"I think one caller summed it up best. She said, 'In the South, especially here in Riverview, we support our own. Jessie's been a bright light in this community as long as I can remember.' So, if you don't mind, we'll come by the school tomorrow to complete this story. We're also setting up a bank account to hold the money until the wedding. I need to let the viewers know what's going on."

"Of course." They conversed a few moments longer, then Jessie hung up and telephoned Matt. Her heart pounded as Latoya's news flooded through her.

"Matt?" She let out a giggle. "You're not going to believe who called me."

"Who?"

"Latoya Cower from Channel 7." Jessie relayed the information she'd been given.

"You're kidding." He whistled.

"No. Really. They want to help." Jessie pulled her chair toward her. She had to get up. "I've got to go tell Mamaw and Papaw."

"Okay. Call me in the morning."

"I love you." She hung up the phone. A lump grew in her throat and her eyes watered. She would have a beautiful wedding and it wouldn't cost her grandparents a thing. Maybe Papaw could relax now.

She moved into the chair and made her way to their bedroom. The door was open and she stopped in the doorway. "Mamaw."

"What is it, darling?" Her grandmother called out from the darkness. "Something wrong?"

"Jessie?" Papaw grunted. He flipped on the lamp beside him.

"We need to talk."

Mamaw rose and wrapped her robe around her, moving after Jessie into the kitchen. Papaw followed.

"I had to wake you. Latoya Cower called," Jessie said. "It's unreal." She replayed her earlier conversation.

"How wonderful." Mamaw clutched her hands. "Here we were troubled about the money, and God provided it through this town. I shouldn't have doubted Him."

"I can't believe it." Papaw pulled a tissue from its holder and rubbed his nose.

They sat up a while talking about the future and wedding plans until Jessie smothered a yawn. "Well, I've got to go back to bed, or I'll never get up in the morning. At least we're off for the Fourth of July."

She wheeled to her room and moved back into the bed. Staring at the ceiling, she prayed. *God, You are beyond good to me. I ask for help, and You give me a whole wedding. I didn't find my father, but You are a father to me.*

She snuggled on her pillow and wedding dreams swirled in her head. How could she thank all the people who were being so kind? Maybe through social media. Would Latoya let her post something on their Facebook page?

Facebook. Her father. In one short second her joy waned. Why didn't he want her? She clenched her fists. And why couldn't she let go of the impossible? He didn't want to be in her life. So be it. No more time to be double-minded. She had to focus on the ones who did love her.

Period.

***

A rumble of thunder echoed in Angeline's Lexus while she waited for the early morning rain to let up enough to run inside. She couldn't delay the inevitable—facing Francine. Olivia Bentley had been so upset. Probably still was.

Angeline opened the door enough to raise her blue paisley umbrella before darting out of the car and toward the store. On the porch, she shook the water from her umbrella before propping it by the door, then entered. If she could only shake out her nerves.

Glenda's leer greeted her. "Did you see it?"

"Of course." Angeline sidled to her desk, the quiet deafening. She grabbed a paper towel and wiped off her shoes.

Glenda followed her. "Francine said to come to her office as soon as you arrive. I can't imagine why."

Angeline paced toward the office to whatever fate awaited her. She knocked on the door, then entered. Glenda waited behind her, leaning against the doorframe like a vulture on the side of a busy highway. *Maybe it will only be a reprimand.*

Yeah, right.

"Angeline." Francine stood behind her desk, an empty moving box in front of her. "I guess you saw the news."

The sneer on Francine's face matched Glenda's. Not good. "Yes, ma'am."

Francine folded her arms. "Good. Then you won't be surprised when I tell you that Olivia Bentley told *me* to inform *you* that your services would no longer be required." She handed Angeline the box. "Glenda will be taking your place. Gather your things. Your last paycheck is in the middle drawer of your desk."

The room closed in on Angeline. She shut her eyes to absorb the news. No job and a townhouse with a mortgage. Was this payback from God for what she had done to Jessie?

"Don't worry, Angeline," Glenda said. "I'll take good care of your desk."

Angeline didn't answer. What could she say? Glenda couldn't do her job and they both knew it, but Francine and Olivia Bentley would find that out soon enough. Until then, Glenda would suffer as Angeline had under Francine. Good luck.

She gathered her belongings and pocketed the check before exiting with as much dignity as she could muster. She pressed her key and opened the trunk of the Lexus, then threw the box into the large space. She slid into the car and blinked back angry tears. Life wasn't fair.

Francine taught her how to run Bentley's and she had gone by the book. This only led to her being fired, with Francine protecting her own interests. Did anyone truly care about her except Elaine? Did God? Then why hadn't things gotten better, instead of worse?

She started the car and drove away, only slowing when she neared her neighborhood.

She shook the tears away. *Let's get real here. What now?*

Her mind wouldn't function. *Be like Scarlett, Ang, and think about it tomorrow.* She'd have lots of time in the next few days. The rain stopped as she pulled into her driveway and her phone rang. She glanced down. Elaine.

Not now.

She didn't answer, but unloaded the box then tramped toward her front door. As soon as she made it inside, she dropped the box onto a chair, plopped down on the sofa and lit a cigarette.

The phone rang twice more and she continued to ignore it. What did it matter?

Later in the afternoon, a knock on the door startled her. Somewhere between a game show and a soap opera, she'd fallen asleep. She blinked as the knocking continued, then reached for her pack of cigarettes and lit another before rising to answer.

She spied through the peephole. Elaine. What did she want? She opened the door and motioned for her cousin to come inside.

"Ang, what's going on?" Elaine stepped in, hands on her hips. "Why didn't you answer my calls?"

"I'd rather not talk about it." She slinked back to the sofa and Elaine found her way to the other end.

"I saw the news. Tell me what happened."

She shrugged. "I got fired. I was the one who turned that old man down." She stood and crossed to the French doors that led out to the patio and then on to the back yard. "Anyone could see he couldn't afford Bentley's." She turned back to face Elaine before taking another draw of her cigarette. "If Francine or anyone else would have been in my place, they would've done the same thing."

"I'm so sorry." Elaine swatted at the smoke that billowed with each spoken word.

"Sorry?" Angeline crushed out the cigarette in a nearby ashtray. "Well sorry won't pay for this townhouse, will it?"

***

Angeline drove to Riverview on Friday evening. Central City had been a bust. She'd approached all the dress shops in town. Several were closed because of the Fourth of July holiday, and the rest treated her with total indifference. They wouldn't even consider the resume she'd brought with her.

Did everyone watch the Channel 7 News? She coasted through downtown, and spied a newspaper box in front of the Riverview Diner and figured the want ads could help. A large slice of chocolate pie wouldn't hurt either.

Angeline bought a paper, entered the café, and found it had emptied considerably from the usual early supper crowd. Two old men leaned against the counter, probably catching up on the day's gossip and farm news. The sign near the door said to seat yourself, so she walked toward a corner table, only to see Matt and Jessie sitting there. She spun on her heels to leave.

"Angeline, wait," Jessie's voice halted her. "Please don't go."

She turned, newspaper tucked under her arm. "Why not?"

Matt glanced at Jessie, who nodded, then motioned to the chair across from them. "Join us." His expression turned to pity. "We heard you lost your job."

Angeline didn't move. Instead, she focused on the tacky wallpaper above Jessie and Matt's heads. "Bad news travels faster than good. So, you want to humiliate me by rubbing it in? Well, you're too late. Plenty of people have already beat you to it."

"Of course not." Jessie shook her head. "I wouldn't want my worst enemy fired from her job."

The words stung Angeline like a slap to the face. "*Your* worst enemy? Well, I guess that would be me." Angeline blew out a breath. "My life couldn't get much more horrible anyway."

"Please sit," Jessie encouraged her again. "I talked to Elaine last night."

Elaine? Angeline could see no hatred in Jessie's expression. She glanced at Matt and resigned herself to finally pull out the chair and perch on its edge. "How do you know my cousin?"

"We go to church together." Jessie took a sip of her soda. "I didn't know you were cousins until last night when she asked the young adult class to pray for you to find a job."

"And did you? Pray for me? After the way I treated you?" Angeline turned her attention to Matt. "Both of you?"

"I won't lie," Jessie answered for the two of them. "It wasn't easy. I talked to Elaine after class, and she mentioned you lost your father and didn't get along with your mother. I can relate."

Angeline squirmed in her chair. "How?"

"I haven't had the traditional family. I lost my mother, and my father rejected me. I don't even know where he is." She glanced toward the front door. "And Elaine told me your father was at the wreck when it happened. I never knew that."

Angeline leaned back. How could she not know? "He *thought* it was his fault you were crippled. He shouldn't have moved you. He died believing that lie. But it wasn't true, you know." Her father's memory was all she had left to cling to. Her voice lowered to a whisper. "I know it wasn't."

"No." Jessie's tone fell flat. "The doctor didn't think so. From what he told my grandparents at the time, the damage was done on impact."

Angeline rubbed her forehead. Jessie didn't blame her dad. So, could she still harbor blame toward Jessie? Or maybe she should let it go like Elaine said. "My dad couldn't move past it. I hated you because of the wreck." She was so tired. So, so tired of carrying this anger. This burden. This *hatred*. "But I—I guess it wasn't your fault."

"And it wasn't his either." Jessie straightened. "I have to focus forward, leave the past behind."

"I'm trying to do that too." Angeline lifted her chin. Maybe she *could* change.

"What's past is past," Jessie said. "Anyway, the reason I want to talk is to tell you about Estelle Granger."

"Isn't that the woman making your dress?"

"It is. Since Latoya mentioned her on the news, she's been flooded with requests for dresses and other clothes. She's going to have to hire a manager/bookkeeper to help her and two seamstresses. I told her I knew someone who would be a good manager."

"You suggested *me*?" Angeline leaned forward. Jessie had to be kidding. She waited for the joke to be sprung. "You would do that?"

Jessie nodded. "God has done so much for me and Matt and—"

"Do you want the job or not?" Matt held up his cell phone. "Estelle sent her phone number if you want to talk."

Angeline's stomach twisted. Go from Bentley's to working for—for someone just starting out? No. She couldn't. Then again, she really loved the townhouse. And her car. And eating … She sighed. "I'll take the number. Thanks."

"Here it is." Matt tapped on the face of his phone until it revealed his contacts. Movement behind her indicated that the waitress approached with their supper. "Why don't you stay and eat with us?"

"I can't." Angeline typed in the number, then placed her phone in her purse. "I've got a lot to do." Like swallow a ton of pride if she was going to take a job like this.

Angeline stood as the waitress set the plates on the table. Awkward. What else could she say? "I'll see you around, I guess."

She couldn't help but notice Matt reach for Jessie's hand across the table. They were probably going to say grace or something … she couldn't bear that right now. Just couldn't bear it. She turned with a nod, then hurried to her car, slid inside, and laid her head on the steering wheel. Okay. What just happened? She stopped for a paper and pie, but found Jessie, Matt, and a job. Shouldn't there be a happy dance? Or something? Maybe.

And maybe someday she'd look back and laugh about the direction her life had taken.

Maybe. But not today.

Chapter Twelve

Homer walked outside after breakfast and braced against the humidity that fogged his glasses. He trekked to the barn, wetting his boots with the remnants of the morning dew, then opened the door and loaded his wheelbarrow with wire cutters and an empty roll to wrap the old barbed wire on. Today the fence would come down, and the old trailer spot would be remade for Jessie and Matt. New memories on a fresh, clear day.

Bear waddled into the barn, nudging against Homer's leg. He reached down and scratched him behind the ears. "Bear, old boy, it's time to tear the fence down. You going to help me?"

Bear's overweight body wagged with his tail. He pushed himself to jump up, but failed. Homer drove the wheelbarrow out of the barn and through the open gate. Together, Homer and Bear trooped through the tall wiregrass to the corner.

Homer surveyed the land with a careful eye and stopped at a certain fencepost. "This should give the kids about two acres, Bear." The dog plopped down by the post. "Of course, one day, all of our land will be Jessie's, but this will be a nice plot to start with."

He snipped the wire and pulled staples from each post, dropping them into the wheelbarrow. Each rusty staple he tugged from the secure piece of wood seemed to release a little of the sorrow in his heart.

After allowing a small smile, he reached down to rub Bear again. "Jessie's gonna get her wedding. Maybe God still hears an old codger like me. Or at least He hears Jessie and Martha."

The sadness of not having Elizabeth during this special time still wrestled with the good that was happening. Today, though, the good was winning.

***

Angeline knocked on the door of the small vinyl-sided house which rested in an older neighborhood right outside of Central City. She drew a deep breath and straightened her navy linen jacket, which complemented her white linen pants. Had she overdone it with her choice of outfit? She rolled her eyes. Of course, but she had to treat this like it was a professional job interview. "Think *townhouse*," she whispered.

Estelle sounded pleasant over the phone but what did that mean? Francine seemed nice at first. And could this woman even run a business that could stay afloat against an establishment like Bentley's? Working there, with its mask of everything good, had warped her somehow. She had simply adored going to work, even with the negatives. There was just something about saying "I work at Bentley's." But thoughts of Elaine, the Smiths, even Glenda, jarred her back to reality, each in a different way. A shudder raced up her spine. She did *not* want to end up like Francine … or even her own mother.

The door opened and a middle-aged lady in a patriotic tee and wrinkled Capri pants peered out. "Angeline, is it? I'm Estelle. So glad you came." She beckoned Angeline inside.

"Hello." Obviously, Estelle wasn't worried about first impressions. Angeline stepped inside and glanced around at the cluttered living room. A sewing machine squatted in the corner, squares of fabric spilled off of chairs and end tables, and pieces of patterns lined the couch. What had she gotten herself into?

"Ignore the untidiness. We'll go in the kitchen." Estelle scooped up dirty dishes from the table and deposited them in the sink. "Sit down and I'll grab us a cup of coffee. Cream and sugar?"

Angeline pulled out a chair and slid onto the cushioned seat. "No, ma'am. Black's fine." Her eyes widened. How could she work with someone this disorganized?

Estelle set the cups on the table and poured the steamy liquid, first in Angeline's, then in her own. She returned the coffeepot before stirring generous amounts of sugar in her own cup. "I know you must be thinking it's time to run." She laughed and the sides of her mouth crinkled in a pleasing way. She continued to stir her coffee. "I'm in the process of leasing the empty shop on the courthouse square here in Central City. Do you know the one that used to house Sula's Tots to Teens?"

Angeline nodded. "Sula's used to be a chic little shop. Expensive."

"Exactly. *I* think it's why they went out of business. But that's neither here nor there. It will be a good size for our little dress shop. To start, I only want to design and sew clothes for the public, specializing in wedding dresses. And tuxedo rentals to bring in a bit more money. Maybe in the future, it could become a full-scale bridal boutique." Estelle lifted her cup and blew on the steaming liquid. "And I have even more dreams."

"Oh?" Angeline clutched her cup, noting the word "Peace" printed in different fonts around the blue mug. An interesting choice, but she couldn't help but wonder if starting over would help her find that peace she was looking for.

"The beginning will be a little difficult." Estelle sipped her drink, then set it down. "It's taken my savings to lease the store and pay the first few months' expenses. I've given a two-week notice at the dollar store where I've been working, so I'll have a small check left to help." She leaned over as if she were about to share the secrets of the world. "Now, listen. I won't be able to pay you much. Nothing like Bentley's to start with, but I believe we'll grow. My first cousins, Sophia and Lenora, have agreed to help me start this venture as my seamstresses."

Angeline chewed her lip. This would be a fresh start full of uncertainty. No doubt about that. But ... "How do I fit in? I take it that, aside from my paycheck, this place will be nothing like Bentley's."

"Oh, I hope not." Estelle leaned forward. "I envision a different atmosphere to start with. Not snobbish, but welcoming. Inviting to everyone. I want ladies comfortable while searching for a wedding gown, prom dress, or ready-made clothing, just like they were home. *Your* job will be to take my vision and make it a reality. And I want to either start or help a local charity to clothe the needy as my way of giving back to the community."

Angeline gulped. "Is that all?"

"I've heard you're good at organization. If you want the job and don't mind the struggle to get it off the ground, then you're my manager." Estelle stood, reached for the coffeepot and refilled her cup. "For me, it's time to step out and make my ideas a reality."

Angeline swallowed a sip of coffee. *Could* she take this untidy vision and make it work? Maybe. Not working for uptight Francine, but instead a creative woman who cared for the needs of others.

Since she'd met Matt and Jessie in the diner, decisions seemed to pause at her doorstep, waiting for a yes or no. Okay. Yes. It was time to let go of the anger and resentment and allow her father to rest in peace. She couldn't change her past, but she could step into a different future, one brimming over with possibilities.

She straightened and her lips parted into a smile. "I believe I can help you with this dream. Tell me more."

***

The last light of the evening sky illuminated the porch with a tinge of coral. Matt joined Jessie on the swing, his arm holding her steady. Thank goodness, some of the stress had lifted off her shoulders. He hadn't really known how to fix it. She still had mixed emotions over her father, but for now, she seemed better.

"Matt," she said softly, interrupting both the silence and his thoughts. "Tell me you love me again."

Matt placed a kiss on her lips, then squeezed her shoulder. "You know I love you."

"I wanted to hear it again." She snuggled against his chest. "Are you coming by Monday after work?"

He nodded. "I'm going to help your grandfather put up the new fence. He needs to get it done and get the cows out of the small corral." Matt glanced at the barn, knowing the time to had come to start helping out more. "We'll get that spot fenced and cleaned up and then we can look for a mobile home to move there."

"I can't wait." Jessie gripped his hand. "In a few months, I'll be Mrs. Matt Jansen."

"The name does have a nice ring to it."

Her phone sounded on the swing beside her. "Speaking of rings."

She picked up the phone and answered. "Hello? … Ms. Cower, how are you? … Good. … You *what*?"

Matt sat up. From the tone of her voice, he couldn't decide if this was good news or not.

Jessie's eyes teared. "They *are*? That's so generous. … Tell them we said thank you. … Good-bye." She ended the call.

He gripped her hand. "What is it?"

"Ms. Cower said there's a company that makes standing wheelchairs. Th—they offered to rent me one free for the wedding so I can stand in our pictures."

He brushed a tear from her cheek. His words wouldn't come. He'd heard of these chairs, but the price was way out of reach.

"Matt. I'll be able to look you in the eyes during the ceremony."

He cleared his throat. "I can't imagine anything better. When will they deliver it?"

"They'll bring it to the house early that morning and show us how it works." Her eyes widened. "What if I can't operate it? What if it won't work with the dress?"

"Whoa." Matt grasped both of her hands. "This is a good thing. They wouldn't wait to bring it that day if we couldn't handle it. I'll be right beside you, remember?"

"I'm sorry. It is a blessing. Mamaw will cry again."

"I think she'll cry a *lot* before this wedding is over. And worry." A few fretful thoughts strayed near the corners of his mind as well. Would everything go smoothly that day?

Only time would show. God proved He was with them time and time again. They could enter the next phase of their life without fear.

Jessie shivered, then giggled.

Matt raised his brow. "What is it?"

Jessie opened her arms wide. "Wedding. Here we come."

***

Saturday, October 13

Jessie huddled beneath the multicolored quilt. Her migraine had finally retreated to a hollow ache. How could she get married in three weeks when she too often could barely face getting out of bed?

She reached for her phone, nestled under her pillow, unplugged it from the charger, then pulled herself to a seated position among the pillows. She rubbed sleep-deprived eyes and shoved aside hopeless thoughts which tried to surface. Headaches didn't last forever. The wedding would soon be here.

Someone tapped on the door. "Jessie?"

"Come in." The feebleness in her voice irritated her. She cleared her throat.

"How are you feeling this morning?" Her grandmother hugged a pile of clean laundry. She set it on the dresser and pushed clothes into drawers despite the small amount of light coming through the door.

"You can turn the light on." Jessie stretched. "My headache's gone."

"Thank the good Lord." Mamaw turned the light dimmer halfway. "At least it's Saturday and you don't have to go to work."

"The headache's my fault. I've overstressed lately, all this planning and figuring. But I'll be fine before Monday."

"I tried to warn you." Mamaw walked over to the bed and planted a kiss on the top of her head. "I'm going to fix breakfast. You want oatmeal and hot tea?"

"You know me well."

Her grandmother left and Jessie counted herself blessed. Mamaw was one special lady.

Jessie rubbed her thumbs against her temple. Catering, invitations, the dress. But those details weren't what brought on the headache. She could thank yesterday's late afternoon Facebook message for that. She grasped her phone and scrolled to it.

Jessie, I'm sorry I didn't answer your friend request on Facebook a few months ago. I couldn't handle it at the time.

Wayne must have re-opened his account just to contact her. But for this? After all these years, she was only worth two sentences? Wasn't it enough that she had the normal bride jitters *and* was confined to a wheelchair? Now that she had heard from him, she wished she'd not heard from him at all. This message didn't get her any nearer to closure. Why had God even laid it on her heart to contact her father? Maybe it hadn't been God, but her own thoughts.

The aching deep in her heart pushed its way to the surface, catching in her throat. She couldn't stand the repeat of his rejection and swiped at unshed tears, fighting for control. Why get so upset? She'd known this could happen when she decided to contact her father.

But did it have to hurt so badly?

At the time, her desire to know outweighed the pain. Now, as the pain hindered her ability to think, she clenched her teeth. No. Don't give in to despair. You tried. Failed. Move on. She deleted the post—and her father—from her life. Once again.

***

The kitchen table lay hidden under stacks of paper, notebooks, and magazines. Jessie rubbed her temples.

Focus. Millie will be here soon. What was I supposed to have accomplished?

She took another sip of her soft drink. The caffeine should help. If only the wedding could magically happen.

But this was real life. Somehow, she had to pull it all together.

Her phone rang and she glanced at the screen.

Millie.

"Hello?"

"Hey. I'm getting ready to leave. Got the guest list ready?"

Jessie covered her face with her hand. "I—uh—kinda forgot."

"*Forgot?*" Millie's voice rose. "Forgot you were supposed to have a *completed* list by the time I get there, so we can get the invitations finished? They should've already been mailed."

And Jessie longed to be more independent? She couldn't remember anything lately. "I did start it. It's hidden under all this stuff. Mamaw's finishing her list of family members. I already have the names of all the friends and family Matt's inviting."

"What's going on? No. Don't tell me now. Work on the list. I'll be there in a few minutes. You can fill me in then."

"Okay."

Jessie hung up the phone and dug through the papers in front of her until she found the yellow notepad with names. *How do you eat an elephant? One bite at a time.* Millie's favorite expression. She could do this.

Mamaw entered the kitchen through the back door. "I've got the sheets hung on the line. Don't let me forget to bring them in before dark."

"I'll try, but you're asking the wrong person." Jessie continued to sort through the mess, making several smaller piles of information. "I can't keep much straight at the moment. Millie will be here soon. Look over this list and see if we forgot anyone."

Mamaw pulled up a chair. Her lips moved silently as she eyed the list. "I think we have everyone in my and your papaw's family here. If we leave someone out, I'll never hear the end of it. Take my cousin, Lilac Johnson. She wouldn't come if we offered a thousand dollars. No, I take it back. She would come for the money. And no other reason. But she'd tell everyone in three counties if we don't invite her." She handed Jessie the notepad.

Jessie scrawled another name and address. "I always felt sorry for her. Who names their child *Lilac*? Don't you think she was picked on by the other kids?"

"If you really knew her, you wouldn't ask." Mamaw rearranged the pile of addresses and two old address books to the side of the table. "Just add these last names to the main list."

A knock sounded from the other room.

"I'll get it," Papaw called out. "Come in." The screen door creaked. "They're in the kitchen."

"I'm here." Millie bounded into the room, plopping in the chair across from Jessie. Her blond hair now boasted a pink streak which somehow suited her. "Tony was miffed I was coming over, but I told him we had to get this wedding rolling."

Jessie's eyes widened. "I don't want to cause trouble between you and Tony."

"You're not." Millie waved her hand. "Tony hasn't forgotten our wedding two years ago. He's picking at me. He thinks the world of you and Matt. Now let me see that list."

Mamaw stood. "If y'all don't need me, I'm going to finish the chores."

Jessie handed Millie the notebook. "Thanks, Mamaw, for helping. And don't forget to bring in the sheets," she half-teased.

"Okay." She moved into the living room. "Come on, Homer. You can help me outside."

The door slammed. Millie's smile drooped. "Your grandparents are so sweet. I wish mine didn't live seven hundred miles away." She flipped open her iPad and scrolled down it. "Here it is. Jessie's wedding."

"I'm sorry I'm so scatterbrained." Jessie set down her cola. "Do you want something to drink?"

"No thanks. We just finished supper." She ran her finger down the iPad. "Now let me think. I have the guest list complete with addresses. We've ordered flowers. What about using Patsy's catering? Did your grandmother agree?"

"Finally." Jessie fumbled through another pile of papers, and pulled a pink sheet from the stack. She and Matt had to convince Mamaw that they had money for catering and she didn't need to cook. The new caterer in Central City offered her a fifty percent discount.

"So many people have given us good prices for the wedding. I still think some of them just want the positive advertisement from Channel 7."

"Could be." Jessie shrugged. "We're *supposed* to try and believe the best about people."

"I didn't say which ones." Millie loaded the addresses into her iPad. "I guess I'm a little suspicious. You can't always trust people nowadays. They hide things. Speaking of hiding, what's wrong with you? You've been majorly distracted the last couple of days. Give."

Jessie laid down her pencil. Time to confess. "I got a message on my Facebook page from my father."

"Your *father*?" Millie leaned on her elbows. "He finally replied? What'd he say?"

"That he was sorry he didn't answer my friend request. He couldn't *handle it*." Jessie air quoted the last two words, then reached for her can of soda, hand trembling.

Empty.

"Well." Millie huffed. "Look at all he's done for this family, running off and abandoning everything and everyone after the accident. Even before, if you count the divorce, which I do. And he says *he* can't handle it?"

Jessie recoiled. Even if her father was basically no good, she hated to hear it from others. "There's probably a reason." But she couldn't see one.

"Yeah, there is. He's still drinking." She shook her head. "I'm sorry. I know this is painful, but it infuriates me. I've seen you suffer. And you deserve to be happy."

"You're right." Jessie straightened. This time was for her and Matt … and the family. It would be joyous, no matter what. "The message upset me, but I'll work through it."

"Did you tell Matt?"

"He saw it when I did. Made him so mad. Anyway, he said it was Wayne's loss."

Millie reached over and hugged Jessie. "That's what I love about Matt. He's super intelligent."

After finishing the invitations, Millie departed and Jessie carefully placed the wedding material back into separate files. Everything once again in its place. Control was back, for now.

One thing still fretted her mind, but she wasn't ready to talk about it. Not even to Millie. What about the honeymoon?

Jessie had no control over *that* little detail. What would Matt think when it was just the two of them? Alone at the cabin?

But Matt loved her the way she was. He wanted no secrets. She chewed on her lip. Could she really open up to him, abandon herself with no fear of rejection? No more hiding behind a façade of perfectionism. God would have to help her learn to be dependent on Him and not on herself. That meant relinquishing control.

But how could she live without fear if she didn't have control?

The empty place in her heart left by her mother's death and her father's abandonment reemerged with a vengeance. She placed her head in her hands. *God help me work through all this emotion. You can fill this emptiness with Your love. I need You. I'm getting too discouraged to try.*

Chapter Thirteen

Angeline stood behind the antique white counter and tapped her foot to the upbeat music playing in the background. Contemporary Christian music wasn't too bad. Some of it she liked almost as well as country.

Almost.

She studied the small shop around her—the walls a subtle gray with white accents. The diamond tufted-back loveseat and rectangular coffee table in the corner spoke of modern comfort. They'd placed rolls of fabric to adorn the right wall at the front of the store. Mannequins— one dressed in a lime green pantsuit and the other in a stylish black dress—stood on her left. A third wore a trendy wedding gown. She couldn't help but smile. Estelle's dream had come to life and she had helped: The Central City Creative Clothier.

The small dressing room in the corner by the counter took up little space for tuxedo fittings. Large dressing rooms and a wall of mirrors were stationed in the sizeable back room along with the seamstress' area.

Less than three months since the July grand opening, and they were already on the map when it came to custom-fit clothing. The shop's calm, inviting atmosphere made her and their customers feel at home. The ambiance was warm … and so different than Bentley's.

The hum of sewing machines filtered through the closed door to the back room where Estelle and her seamstresses custom-designed and fitted clothing. Angeline glanced at the day's fittings on the computer screen in front of her.

"Angeline." Estelle came through the doorway, a multi-colored scarf fashioned around her neck. "Are you almost ready?"

"Yes, ma'am."

Jessie would be here shortly. Who would have ever thought she would be the one helping Jessie with her wedding dress? And that there could even be a friendship?

The bell jingled above the door. Angeline hurried to hold it open as Martha and Jessie entered.

"Come in, come in," Estelle called out.

"Hello, ladies." Martha hugged Estelle, then Angeline.

Angeline gave her a quick hug back, then moved behind the counter. Everyone who came into Estelle's shop hugged a little too much for her comfort.

Estelle then hugged Jessie who said, "We're getting down to the final stages of the dress. I'm so excited."

"Oh, and look at this idea Angeline had." Estelle reached behind the counter and picked up a swatch of orange material. "You can see it's the same color material as the bridesmaid's dresses but much sturdier. We're going to make covers for your wheelchair seat and back to match. They'll attach with a fabric hook and loop fastener."

"That'll look wonderful," Jessie said. "How did you think of it?"

"I saw it on Pinterest." Angeline picked up her phone and pulled up a picture, showing it to everyone. "I knew it would be easy to do."

"You are so creative," Martha said. "I'm glad you're working with Estelle."

"Thank you." Angeline swallowed the lump rising in her throat. How any of the Smiths could be nice to her after the way she acted was still beyond her. Instead of treating her like an enemy—like someone who had tried to ruin their granddaughter's wedding plans, not to mention her life—they instead treated her like family.

She frowned. Could she ever have a relationship with her mother like Jessie and Martha had? If miracles still happened.

Estelle motioned. "This way."

They followed Estelle past the sewing machines into the large fitting area. At some point, Angeline envisioned this space divided with walls. But that wasn't going to happen until the finances were more stable.

"Hey, we missed you in class Wednesday night." Jessie rolled near the mirrors, then locked the wheels of her chair. "We had a good discussion of young people in today's church."

Angeline focused on the large mirror in front of her. "I've been fighting this sinus thing. I—uh, went to bed early." She still wasn't at all sure about this Christianity stuff. She had so many questions and only a few answers.

"You need a humidifier. Stop it before it starts." Martha patted her arm. "I hope you make it to church Sunday. Oh, and Ben should be here shortly. Could you watch the door while I help Jessie with the gown? Wouldn't want him back here."

Ben? Who was Ben? Most likely one of the groomsmen. Angeline returned to the front.

She stood in the doorway and peeked back at Jessie as Martha and Estelle helped slip the dress on and then helped her back into the chair. Estelle adjusted the train of the gown directly to the chair, just like they'd discussed.

"It's almost like I'm not in this chair. The gown covers a lot."

"Try wheeling around the room and we'll see what we need to do," Estelle suggested.

Jessie wheeled forward with no problems until she turned to the left. Part of the gown lodged in the wheel. "Oh no." She reached down and tried to untangle it. "I didn't ruin it, did I?"

"No, dear." Estelle dislodged the fabric and put a pin where it caught. "I'll need to readjust the train right here and maybe raise the back hem a little more. Overall, I think the gown is perfect."

"You look beautiful," Angeline called out.

When the bell jingled again, Angeline stepped fully into the front room, shutting the door behind her. A young man ambled toward the counter, intense green eyes smiling from under tousled straw-colored hair.

"May I help you?" Angeline sized up his faded jeans and button up shirt, sleeves rolled.

Farmer.

"I'm Ben Stevens, cousin of the groom. Matt said I needed to be measured for the tux." He winked. "I'm one of the groomsmen, you know."

Flirt.

"One moment." She turned, pushing through the door to the back. "Ms. Granger. Ben Stevens is here to be measured for his tux."

"You'll have to get his measurements, dear." Estelle knelt beside Jessie, re-pinning the sides of the dress. "We're having trouble back here, and Jessie's going to have to try the dress on again."

Angeline closed her eyes and breathed out a sigh. Just part of the job. She'd measured men before. This guy, although young and kinda cute, was no different from the others.

As she made her way to the counter, she shot a glimpse at Ben who looked out the shop window. Broad shoulders. Muscular build. Hmm. Must work hard on the farm.

He turned and caught her staring. His grin widened, displaying a cute dimple. For a moment, she was transported back to elementary school, and to being in trouble for passing a note. This would never do. "I—I'll need to m—measure you." Her cheeks overheated. Good grief. She couldn't even talk straight.

She ducked behind the counter and dug out a tape measure from a box overflowing with sewing supplies. *Calm down. He's only a customer.*

But when she straightened, he'd moved closer. The scent of his cologne—all woodsy and spice—tickled her nose. "I, uh—"

He leaned against the counter. "Where should I stand?'

Not too close, for starters. Was he trying to embarrass her?

"Right here." She pointed to a spot by the mirror, picked up her clipboard, and drew another deep breath.

I'm a professional. I did this at Bentley's all the time. Even flirted with a few guys myself.

As she stole a glance in the mirror, she swallowed again. He wasn't as tall as Matt, but much more powerfully built, and the same charm swirled about him. "First your shoulders."

She stretched the tape across his shoulders, then jotted down the number. Calm down. Maybe some conversation. "So, are you kin to Matt's mom or dad?"

"Matt's dad and my mom are first cousins."

"I see. Now I need to measure your chest and waist. Can you inhale and hold it?" She moved closer and fumbled the tape. It hit the floor.

He swiped it up. "Need this?" He glanced at the tape then twirled it like a lasso.

The heat rose to her cheeks. "Yes. Hold still." She puffed out her words. Change that. He was nothing like Matt. "Please."

She wrapped the tape measure around his chest, his really broad chest. She swallowed, then stepped back. The laughter in his eyes totally disarmed her. She wrote the numbers down. Try again. "Are you from around here?"

"We live right outside of Central City, near New Hope Baptist Church. How about you?"

"In Riverview." She recorded his waist measurement next, not daring to look up. Then it hit her. The inseam. She bit her lip.

"What is it?" He must have noticed her indecision.

"I need the measurement of your inseam. If you could hold it, well—you know …"

Why had she taken this job again? Her face had to be the color of a fire engine. If only she could disappear.

"Sure, I can." He held the tape to the inside of the leg of his jeans and she grabbed the end and pulled it to the back of the heel of his snake skin cowboy boot. Don't look up.

"You got that?" He towered over her.

"Yes." She stood, then moved behind the counter. Sweat broke out on her forehead as Martha opened the door.

"Angeline, we need you—why, hello, Ben."

Angeline tucked the tape back in the basket. He hadn't taken his eyes off her.

Martha stepped over to Ben and hugged him. "I'm so glad to see you."

A reprieve. Angeline forced her shoulders to relax.

Martha turned. "If you're finished here, dear, Estelle needs you in the back."

And a welcome distraction. Now to escape. "I'm finished." She nodded to Ben. "Good-bye."

"One thing," Ben called to her as she started through the doorway. She caught her breath. "Yes?"

"When can I see you again?" He winked, throwing her emotions in a quandary.

Angeline Springer go out with someone as conceited as him? It didn't matter how good he looked. "When you come to pick up your tux." She flounced away, ignoring his laughter, without a glance back.

***

Matt filled his truck with gas at the Quik Stop, then started home. Less than three weeks to the wedding, and so much to do. Jessie's anxiety over the details had been compounded by the email from her father. He slammed his hand on the steering wheel and his foot to the gas, then eased up. No need to have a wreck. Especially not over Jessie's miserable father.

He slowed and turned down Blue Ridge Road to see Ben's car in his driveway. Matt glided up until he parked next to Ben's 1972 Dodge Charger, then hopped out. The junked vehicle they'd worked on for over a year was now a one-of-a-kind, sleek, black machine.

Ben leaned against the door, staring down at his phone.

"Hey, what's going on?" Matt asked.

Ben held up his hand. "I'm trying to find someone on Facebook. I met the cutest little thing today, but she didn't want to give me the time of day."

"What else is new? You probably ran her off." Matt pushed his cousin's shoulder. "What's her name? Maybe I know her."

Ben kept scrolling. "Angeline. I didn't catch her last name, but she works at the shop where we're getting our tuxes and she's from Riverview."

"You can stop looking." Matt shook his head recognizing trouble when he smelled it. "It's Angeline Springer."

Ben tapped his chin. "Angeline Springer. Wait. She was a cheerleader—?"

"At Riverview." Matt finished his sentence.

"Oh, I remember her." Ben frowned. "Didn't she go after you once? Kinda loose, wasn't she?"

"Yep," Matt said with instant regret. "But I believe she's changed. Jessie and I helped her get a job with Estelle. She's come to church a few times."

"Do you think she'll be there on Sunday?" Ben rubbed his chin. "Because I think I'll be visiting. Right after I send her a friend request on Facebook."

"You're more than welcome to church." Matt opened his truck door. "I've got to get to Jessie's." He chuckled. "See you Sunday."

Matt put it in reverse. Angeline and Ben? That would almost be too bizarre. And with their personalities? Destructive.

As he left his driveway, he glanced back at his cousin. He never had real feelings for Angeline and Jessie had forgiven him. A new relationship might be a good thing for both of them—Ben and Angeline.

If Ben didn't blow it.

Minutes later, Matt turned down Jessie's drive. Her grandfather stood outside the barn, so he pulled nearby and got out. "Hey, Mr. Smith."

"Hey, Matt." The old man maneuvered the water hose over the cow trough. "Jessie's not back from town yet."

Matt dug the toe of his boot into the muddied ground. "That's okay. I kinda wanted to talk to you."

"What 'cha need?" Homer cut off the water, then wrapped the hose around the yard hydrant.

"You know the doublewide Jessie and I found? Well, we finished the paperwork and are waiting for final approval on the loan. They can deliver it the week before the wedding."

Homer brushed his hands on his overalls. "You're cutting it mighty close."

They walked to the porch.

"I know." Matt plopped on the porch swing while Homer took his usual place on the old metal glider. He rubbed his chin. "It worries me."

"Is the trailer the only thing fretting you?"

Matt glanced up. "You noticed?"

"You're as antsy as a nervous goat. You worried about taking care of Jessie? She's a wonderful girl and independent as all get out." Homer pulled off his cap and brushed his hand through thick gray hair. "But she can concern you."

"I want to do my best for her."

"And you will, son. Me and Martha will be around if you need us. Your parents too. Jessie's strong and you two will make it."

"You're right, Mr. Smith." Matt leaned back as Martha's car pulled into the driveway. "Last minute jitters, I guess."

"Yep." Homer pulled his cap back on his head and grunted. "And the way I figure it, they won't get better 'til you're married."

Chapter Fourteen

The late afternoon sun splashed through the window above the sink, casting merry shadows across the kitchen. Jessie arched her back. She'd sat too long in the chair. Matt pushed the pile of documents to the center of the table, and drank from his Mountain Dew. "I think that's the last of the paperwork. I hope so anyway."

"Me, too." Jessie rubbed her brow. "I'm so ready." She reached out and grasped Matt's hand. Who would have thought getting married and buying a home required so much paperwork?

"Your head's not hurting, is it?" Matt stood and moved behind Jessie to rub her shoulders gently. "You promised me you'd try not to stress. About anything."

"I'm getting married in a couple of weeks. What's to stress about?" Her laughter carried a hollow sound. Who was she kidding? "My head's fine, but keep it up. There, at the base of my neck." She reached back to the tense spot. He gently kneaded the tight muscle. She sighed. "Much better."

"You said the caterer is lined up. Isn't that the most important thing?"

"Spoken like a true male." Jessie rolled her eyes. Hadn't he looked at all the paperwork, same as her? "You don't have a clue. What about the invitations? Or flowers? Estelle finishing the dress?"

"I guess that's important, too." Matt continued to massage between her shoulders.

Papaw trudged into the kitchen and stopped to pour a glass of water. He coughed, sloshing water on the counter.

"Your cough isn't sounding so good." Jessie shook her head. He didn't take care of himself. "You'd better go to the doctor, Papaw. I can't have you sick at the wedding."

"You sound like Martha." He cleared his throat, fighting with the child-proof cap on a cough syrup bottle. "I'll be fine. Going to take a dose of this cough syrup 'for I go to bed."

Matt leaned over and kissed Jessie's cheek. "I've got to go. I'll call you after a while." He kissed her again. "Now, stop worrying."

"All right. No more worry." Jessie glanced at Papaw as Matt headed toward the back door. "I mean, what could happen?"

The door banged behind Matt.

"Papaw, are you sure you're all right?"

Homer placed the bottle on the window sill. "Of course. This stuff tastes terrible, but the pharmacist says it'll clear me up."

"I hope so." Her grandfather ambled toward the bedroom. She blew out a breath. What would she do if something happened to him?

***

A chilly wind blasted Angeline as she hurried to her Lexus. Ah, the luxury of starting the motor from inside her home and having it warm when she climbed in. She sat her purse beside her and gripped the steering wheel.

"Take a deep breath. You can do this." She spoke out loud. "People go to church every Sunday."

She tugged at her skirt. Was it long enough? This new lifestyle had been more difficult to adjust to, at least the church part. What did these people expect of her? So far everyone had been nice. They actually seemed okay with the bad girl turns to good scenario.

Did they see her that way or was it just her imagination?

She drove the short route to Riverview Community Church, then dashed inside to prevent the late fall wind from destroying her hair. She shook hands with the lady in the foyer handing out bulletins and caught a glimpse of herself in the door reflection. *Hair looks perfect. Skirt not too short.* Now to grab a seat in the back row.

Angeline drew a sharp breath. The back row was occupied by Jessie,

Matt, and *Ben*? Where was Elaine? She glanced over the half-full church but couldn't find her.

Jessie waved from the other end where she sat. "Angeline. Over here."

She couldn't avoid Ben now. Angeline passed behind the last pew and Jessie's wheelchair which stood in the corner. Jessie scooted down so she could slide in beside her.

"I'm so glad you came." Jessie hugged her. "And Ben's visiting. He said you two talked the other day at the shop."

"We did." Angeline extracted herself from Jessie's embrace.

"Hey, there." Ben leaned forward and flashed a smile. "We meet again."

"Hey." Her pulse quickened, but she wouldn't let *him* know. She nodded then turned back to Jessie. Maybe Ben would take the hint she was ignoring him. "Jessie, when are you coming for another fitting?"

"Ms. Granger is actually coming to the house Wednesday to bring the dress. Maybe you can come with her."

"I don't know. I'll probably need to watch the shop." She reduced her voice to a whisper as the pastor called for the opening prayer. Time to concentrate. "I'll talk to you after church."

She dared cast a glance at Ben. He winked, then grinned. She shifted in her seat. How annoying. He must have been waiting for her to look.

After the prayer, the worship band moved right into their opening song, and Angeline found herself swaying with the music. The melody soothed her, and she wished it wouldn't stop. If only she didn't have to deal with the people.

Another prayer at the end of worship and then the pastor poured out his message, which was fairly interesting. So, why did she have so much trouble concentrating? She blinked and forced herself to pay attention to what the pastor said about a man owing a great debt and having it forgiven, yet refusing to forgive a small debt didn't make sense. Why wouldn't he? She pulled a pen from her purse and jotted down the Scripture reference on her bulletin so she could look it up later.

The pastor stepped away from the pulpit, eyes sweeping the congregation, then stopping. Her brow furrowed. Was he staring at her? "Is there someone in your life you haven't forgiven?" he asked. His words jolted her. But why? Hadn't she made amends with Matt and Jessie?

But what about her mother? Not that her mother's attitude was *her* fault. She wasn't the social maven who didn't have time for her own daughter.

Angeline picked at her fingernails during the altar call and her skin crawled as the pastor closed the service. Finally.

"Hey, you two want to grab a burger with me and Ben?" Matt slid out of the pew and brought Jessie her chair. "Or has your grandmother cooked?"

Jessie shook her head. "No. We have wedding decorating plans to discuss. Millie is meeting us here shortly."

"No problem." Matt nodded toward Ben. "We'll go pick up your grandfather and eat at the diner."

Martha called from the front of the church. "I'll be in the fellowship hall if you need me."

"Okay, Mamaw," Jessie said.

"You want to go with us men, Angeline?" Ben leaned against the pew, drumming on its back. Her heart fluttered to the beat.

"I better stay and help Jessie." No doubt about it. She needed to keep her distance from Ben. She'd been hurt by guys who attended church as often as ones who didn't.

As the crowd thinned she rested against the wall of the church. Ben had left without her and without an argument. Probably better that way. She had a feeling she wasn't ready for someone like him in her life.

A pert blonde in a fashionable pantsuit of turquoise be-bopped down the aisle toward them. Must be the wedding planner, Millie. Any time she'd come into the shop, Angeline had been out running errands.

"Sorry I'm late, guys. Our church service had a special baby dedication." She glanced at Angeline, tilting her head. "I'm Millie Lambert."

"Angeline Springer."

Millie's smile faded; the temperature in the room plummeted.

Millie turned her back on Angeline. "Now, Jessie, this is the way I envision we decorate."

Angeline flinched. Is this how Jessie's grandfather had felt standing in Bentley's? She deserved it, but did it have to hurt so badly? "I'll be back in a moment." She faded toward the bathroom, then exited the building, and hurried to her car to grab the bag in the trunk.

Why did she think her life could be different? Some things never changed.

***

Jessie wheeled around toward the back of the church. Maybe they could place bouquets of flowers at each side of the doorway and one near the prayer rail. Deep orange tulle bows attached to the pews would brighten up the dark wood. An arch of greenery would contrast her dress and the bridesmaids' dresses. She looked around for Millie. "Should you go check on Angeline?" she asked. "Maybe she's sick. She was headed toward the bathroom."

"Serves her right." Millie sniffed. "After the way she upset you at the fundraiser for Devin back in the summer? Here we were trying to raise awareness for pediatric Crohn's disease and she's trying to steal Matt from you."

Jessie's fingertips flew to her lips. "Shh. She'll hear you. We've been over this. Angeline apologized, and we set it straight. Now she's even attending church some. That's a good thing."

"But don't you worry she still might try to come between you and Matt?" Millie walked to the back and peered through the sanctuary door. "She's digging in the trunk of her car. She'll be back."

"I don't know. She seemed awful fidgety during the service. And to be honest, I don't worry about her stealing Matt. I only worry at some point *he'll* reconsider what he's doing. I mean, how crazy is it to marry someone you'll have to take care of?"

"Jessie Smith." Millie crossed her arms. "I don't know how much more Matt can show he loves you. Would you marry him if you could walk and he couldn't?"

Jessie sighed. "If I loved him, it wouldn't matter."

"It sounds to me like you doubt Matt's love for you."

"Does it?" Jessie couldn't imagine a man treating her better than Matt. "I won't say anything else negative. I promise."

"That's better." Millie puckered her brow, turning her head toward the door leading to the fellowship hall. "Hey, I hear your grandmother calling me. I'll be back in a minute."

Jessie hadn't heard anything. She wheeled back to the altar area. All was still. She ran her hand along the wooden prayer rail, then gripped it and bowed her head. *God, speak to me. I love Matt so much. I worry too much, and can't seem to change. Right now, before I go any further with this marriage, I place Matt in Your hands. If we're making a mistake, show us. I want to do the right thing. And God, help Angeline find You. She seems so unhappy at times. Amen.*

"Jessie, we need you." The call from the back of the building echoed through the tall structure.

"Coming." She pushed her way through the narrow hallway. God would show her what she needed to do, but she had to be patient. She would try to let go of worry, her heart open to His answer.

Jessie entered the kitchen, her breath quickening. Balloons, crepe paper, and a room full of women, including Estelle Granger, awaited her.

"Surprise!" Millie shouted.

Jessie's hand flew to her mouth. Another bridal shower.

Mamaw moved to her side. "You are surprised, aren't you, dear? I promised Millie I wouldn't tell."

Jessie's gaze took in the large cake on the table and pile of presents beside it. "But the family gave me a bridal shower already."

"We know," Millie said. "But Margaret wanted to do this. She asked what gifts you two hadn't received, so we could all bring something."

Jessie turned to Margaret, Pastor Allen's wife. "This is so sweet of you … and everyone."

Angeline brushed past Jessie and set a gift on the table before taking a seat in the back of the room by Estelle.

"Move over here." Millie pointed to an empty space beside the presents. "We'll open gifts first then eat."

Margaret picked up a notebook and pen from a nearby counter and pulled a chair beside Jessie. "I'll write down what you receive and who it's from. And of course, put the bows in a bag for your bouquet at the wedding rehearsal. Remember, each bow or ribbon you break means another baby." She raised her brows. "You better be careful."

Jessie couldn't help but smile. "I will."

The first gift bag contained a toaster, followed by a set of coffee mugs, and three blue towels. Millie handed the gifts to Mamaw, who displayed them on another table for all to see. She unwrapped more towels, a set of plates, and several kitchen gadgets. Angeline's present was next.

"Dish towels with sunflowers," Jessie said. "Thank you, Angeline. I love sunflowers."

As several ladies turned to look at her, Angeline reddened.

"Here's a gift." Millie handed her a small box wrapped in zebra-striped paper and hot pink ribbon. "From me, of course. Can you tell?"

Jessie carefully undid the tape and handed Margaret the bow. She opened the white box and pushed back the tissue paper. Lingerie. Jessie's eyes widened as she stared at the flimsy garment.

"Hold it up," Millie said, then giggled. "We're all women here."

Jessie raised the leopard print baby doll by the straps with trembling hands. Sheer and trimmed with neon pink. How embarrassing. Warmth flushed her cheeks.

Her face surely matched the color of this trim. With a pasted-on smile, she examined the tiny gown.

How could she handle the wedding, much less the honeymoon?

Chapter Fifteen

Jessie woke to the sound of a hacking cough echoing throughout the quiet of the house in early morning. Papaw wasn't getting better, but he had promised Jessie and Mamaw that he'd go to the doctor today.

Knowing she wouldn't be able to go back to sleep, she decided to check her email.

Fifteen messages. She deleted the spam and advertisements, then opened one from Millie. It held a completed look at all the wedding plans. Thanks goodness Millie had a knack for organization. It lessened the stress growing in Jessie.

She flipped from email to Facebook, immediately noting that she had one Facebook message. Her heart quickened until she saw that it was just Matt's sister saying hi. She took in a deep breath, exhaled, then another. *He cannot handle connecting with you, Jessie,* she reminded herself. *Don't expect anything and you won't get hurt.*

Or, she wouldn't be hurt any more than she had been already.

For a fleeting moment she thought to check for any activity from Wayne. She'd managed not to up until now. How could she? He didn't ask for any reply from her. Not one word asking how she was or what she'd been doing all these years. He could've at least asked.

Jessie's hand hovered over the mouse pad, trembling to look, but she shook her head almost as if she needed her own good sense to combat her desire to know the man who had fathered and then abandoned her.

Why bother? His account was probably deleted again. But how could she know? Would he have really answered if he didn't care at all?

Invite him to the wedding.

Now, where had that thought come from? God? Maybe ... or maybe just a longing to have her father in her life, like the fathers and

135

daughters she saw here and there—in town, at the school, at church. Why couldn't she have that kind of bond with Wayne?

Papaw's cough resounded again. Jessie shut her computer and pulled her wheelchair over so she could start getting ready for work. She needed to convince him to take better care of himself. She'd lost one father. She didn't intend to lose another.

***

Angeline parked near the food court of the Central City Mall. Time for a shopping spree. Her new job didn't afford her one, but if nothing else, she could hit the sales racks. She locked her car and hurried in through the wide side doors. Maybe shopping would be a salve on the fresh wounds inflicted by Millie's coldness.

Would she ever live down her past?

The Central City Mall housed several cute boutiques, a few department stores, and a well-stocked food court. She strolled down the wide-open interior. This was what she needed. A 75-percent-off sign drew her into the sporting goods store. Maybe they would have some Crimson Tide summer wear marked down.

She browsed one rack and moved to another when a familiar voice drew her attention.

"I think I'll need an eleven."

Ben.

One peek around the rack of sweatshirts and she spotted the shock of blond hair and broad shoulders. Her heart rate increased tenfold. Shouldn't he be out on a tractor or something instead of in the mall on Monday, upsetting her morning?

He laced up one trendy sneaker, then stood to try it out, turning her way before she could duck.

He waved. "Hey, Angeline," he said as though he'd fully expected to see her there.

No. She'd been caught staring again. She turned her head as if she didn't hear, but he limped across the room toward her, one sneaker still in hand.

"Are you avoiding me?" His brow furrowed. "Did I do something to upset you?"

"Of course not." Her mind raced for an answer, but there wasn't one. "What are you doing here?" She nodded at the shoe still in his hand. "Besides buying shoes?"

"Well, my next class doesn't start until twelve, so ..."

"Next class?"

"Chemistry. I'm in my second year at Central City Community College."

Heat rose in her neck, threatening her cheeks. "Oh? What are you majoring in?"

"Chemical engineering. I loved chemistry and math in high school, so I thought I'd combine the two and make them into a career." A salesman drifted by, eyeing the shoe in Ben's hand. "Oh, I'll take these." He pulled the other shoe off his foot, and handed both to the clerk, then turned back.

Angeline glanced at his stocking feet, then back up to his face to find him charming her with a goofy grin. She needed to say something. Anything. "Well. Glad someone likes math. I was never any good at it."

How bright did that sound? She pushed her bangs to the side, angry at herself. How could she be so inarticulate around this one single man?

"How about I buy you a coffee at the café across the hall?" He glanced around until he spotted the sales clerk. "As soon as I buy these shoes, I mean."

She nodded. "Okay." She took a step back. "I'll go get us a table."

He grinned again. "I won't argue." As he moved to retrieve his shoes, Angeline's stomach fluttered. Why was she letting her guard down? He was probably like the other guys.

Not that she'd ever know, she reasoned, unless she talked to him more.

She crossed over to the coffee shop and took a seat at a small table by the door. Ben joined her a few moments later, plopping in the chair across from her. The waitress greeted them; he ordered a strong cup of coffee, no sugar or cream. She ordered a hot chocolate with cream on the side.

"Cream on the side?" Ben asked her. "That's a new one for me."

"I like extra cream with my chocolate." She smiled in an effort to change the subject from her to him. "So, tell me about college."

"I've never told many people—anyone who thinks they really know me would be surprised but—" Ben stopped when their server returned to the table with their drinks. He looked up, smiled, and thanked her.

The server—in her fifties if she was a day—smiled back. Yep. Ben was a charmer.

Angeline added the extra cream to her chocolate. "You were saying?"

Ben cradled the hot beverage in his hand. "Um—yeah. I actually *like* school." He laughed lightly.

"Why would that be such a surprise?"

"You know ... being a *macho* football player—or at least by perception—you kind of hide information like that from the rest of the guys. But college is different because you're no longer trying to be the most popular man on campus. Now you're hunting a career."

"And you think you've found one?"

"I believe I have. Chemical engineering. Numbers and chemistry both fascinate me." He took a long swallow of his coffee. "Of course, I'm still taking basics."

"I wouldn't have thought you were a math geek." Angeline sipped her chocolate. Good looks *and* smart? Wonderful. "I guess you're *perfect*, like Matt and Jessie."

Ben's brow furrowed and she mentally kicked herself. She had to stop this. "Hardly," he said, then stared into the mall, clearing his throat. "I've definitely sowed some wild oats. Not something I like to talk about."

Her interest peaked. "I thought you church people had it all together."

He laughed. "Not *me*." He shook his head. "Enough of your interrogation. Tell me how you got interested in everything wedding."

Angeline settled in a little, feeling the warmth of the chocolate and the coffee. "Simple. I love design, managing, and beautiful things. After high school, Mother helped me land the job at Bentley's." She fiddled with her cup. "Working with Estelle is so much better though. And I'm considering doing some dress designing on my own. She's teaching me to sew."

"Now there's something." Ben leaned back. "I'd never think of you as a seamstress. Will wonders never cease?"

A giggle escaped her as the remaining tension fell from her shoulders. Maybe she'd met a man she could trust. And honest and open about the good and bad in life.

A friend.

Or maybe more …

***

Matt pushed open their barn door. Pungent smells of hay, manure, and livestock assailed him. A feeble *moo* sounded from one corner. The small black calf peered through the slats of the stall at him, tongue licking at the wood.

He shut the door. "I'm coming, boy."

Matt opened the door to the stall and held the large bottle of milk to the calf's mouth. The animal latched on and nursed.

"I know you miss your mama, but I'll have to do."

Farming had always been a full-time job for his family. Like his dad, he worked a full-time job *and* farmed. Now with the wedding fast approaching, how could he keep everything going and still have time for Jessie? Cut his sleep from a few hours to an even fewer?

"Hey, Matt? You in there?" Ben called from outside.

"Yeah. Come on in." He pulled the now empty bottle from the calf's mouth and scooped new feed into his trough as the calf tried to nuzzle his leg. "Go on, fellow."

He shut the stall, then picked up the hose to fill the calf's water bucket.

"Is this the little guy who lost its mother?" Ben reached through the slats to scratch the calf's nose, but instead pulled back a handful of slobber. He grimaced as he brought his hand up. "Yuck."

"That's him. When Mr. Smith called to see if we wanted to try and raise him, I said sure. I mean for seventy-five dollars, it was worth a try." He wound up the hose and replaced the feed scoop in the tub, popping the lid on tight. No need to feed any mice.

Ben wiped his hand across a bale of hay nearby. "I ran into Angeline at the mall," he announced. "She had coffee with me. She *likes* me. I can tell."

"You're kidding? From what you said the other day, she didn't like you too much at the tux fitting." He cuffed him on the shoulder. "What changed?"

"We talked for so long I was almost late for class. She's cautious, but nothing I can't handle." Ben followed Matt out of the barn. "My charm and good looks will win her over."

"Yeah, right." Matt leaned over the nearby fence post. The afternoon sun slipped behind the grove of trees so he shielded his eyes to count the cows in the field. Everyone accounted for. He turned to Ben. "When will you see her again?"

Ben pulled a weed woven into the barbed wire. "I don't know. I asked, but she wouldn't commit. Who can figure out a woman, huh?"

"I get you. I mean, Jessie texted me to tell me she was going to invite her father to the wedding." Matt shook his head. "And I told you how he didn't want anything to do with her."

"What did you tell her?"

"Do what you need to do." He shrugged.

"Do you think he'll come?"

"Nope. And all I can do is support her and be there when he doesn't answer."

"What if he does?"

Matt rubbed his chin. "I don't know. It'll depend on Jessie. But between you, me, and those cows out there, I hope he doesn't show up, especially if it's only going to make things worse." His phone vibrated from the holster on his hip. He pulled it out, then stared at the text.

His heart sank. Another problem.

"I've gotta go." He headed toward the house.

Ben called after him. "What's up?"

"They've put Jessie's grandfather in the hospital. Sent him straight from the doctor's. Jessie needs me to take her there."

Once inside, Matt hurried to shower and change into clean clothes. Ready, he scooped his keys from his bedside table, then squeezed his eyes shut. Another long night lay ahead of him.

Chapter Sixteen

Jessie pushed her chair closer to Papaw's hospital bed. Mamaw had moved to the far corner to take a phone call. The infusion pump in the small dimly lit room beeped with a steady whine. Occluded.

"Papaw," she said, "You've bent your IV line again. You have to sit still. Here." She reached to the line wrapped on the bed rail and straightened it, then sat back and looked around. The pale blue walls with the floral border tried to cheer her, but to Jessie, a hospital was still a hospital. The dry air filled with the odor of disinfectant and some kind of weird vanilla air freshener hung way too familiar.

Papaw pulled himself straighter in the bed. "Don't know why I need to be here. It's bronchitis. A little cough, is all."

"Dr. Robertson said you were a step away from pneumonia. Sit up." Mamaw laid her phone on the table, then fluffed his pillow. "And you're dehydrated. A day or two here will keep you from getting worse."

"If it wasn't for you, woman, I wouldn't stay here, getting poked and prodded." He glanced at Jessie. "But I wouldn't want to be sick at your wedding."

Jessie patted his hand and released a breath. When Mamaw told her they'd admitted him, she'd said all the right things but her heart seemed to stop and the air had grown thin. Her groan of a prayer was nowhere near faith-filled but had been heard.

Upon arriving at the hospital, the doctor assured them it was more precaution than anything. Papaw would be okay.

Matt sat in the chair in the corner, watching the local news flashing on the television overhead. He pointed at the screen. "Hey, did you see this?"

Jessie glanced at the television. "What?"

"The long-term weather forecast is giving a possibility of severe weather the week of our wedding."

"Oh, no." Mamaw clutched her hands. "But these weather people often miss the down-the-road forecasts, bless their hearts."

"Everything's going to be fine." Jessie refused to consider another problem. There was enough going on already. She stifled a yawn and glanced at the clock. Nine on the dot. Visiting hours were over. "Are you staying, Mamaw?"

Papaw shifted in the bed. "No, she isn't."

Mamaw crossed her arms. "Of course, I am. I'm not driving my car this late and I'm not leaving it here without me. No arguments. I'll sleep in this reclining chair and be comfortable. Now you two, go on home. You've both got to work in the morning."

"Okay." Jessie leaned toward Papaw and kissed his cheek. "Get better."

Mamaw came over and hugged them both, whispering in Jessie's ear, "He needs me more than he'll admit."

Jessie chuckled, then followed Matt into the hall. They stopped at the elevator and Matt pushed the button. "He didn't seem too sick—" The words stuck in her throat.

"Your papaw will be all right." Matt pushed the elevator button. "He's a fighter."

"I know. But I still worry about him." Jessie's lip trembled. "What would I do if something happened?"

"Don't even think those thoughts. You're starting to sound like your grandmother."

Matt stepped into the elevator as it opened to hold the door for Jessie.

"You're right," Jessie said, wheeling in. "Dr. Robertson said he'll be fine. The wedding will be fine and the marriage will be fine."

"Fine?" Matt bent over and caressed Jessie's lips with a long kiss while the elevator descended. He pulled away as the door opened. "Our marriage will be much better than fine."

"It will." Jessie rolled alongside Matt through the parking lot to his

144

truck. Once there, he picked her up and set her on the seat. She didn't release her hold until they'd exchanged another kiss. She longed to be with him, day and night. But a nagging fear clung to her, wrapping tendrils of dread around her heart. Would he still want her when it was just them and everything was unveiled?

***

The dark of her room welcomed Jessie as the noise of Matt's truck faded away. Before leaving, he'd fed and watered the cows and chickens, then made sure she locked the doors behind him. She flipped on the small lamp by her bed.

She needed to unwind before she could sleep.

She moved to her desk and flipped open her laptop. Her Pinterest page popped up and she spent several minutes glancing through the newest wedding pins. Her heart flooded with gratitude with the thought of so many people contributing to their wedding. She switched to Facebook.

Invite him.

That thought again. But how? She typed in his name. She scanned the ones that showed up and clicked on one with no profile picture.

It was him; her father. Time to send the message she'd been thinking of since yesterday. Her fingers hovered over the keyboard a moment before she wrote:

I respect your wishes to remain out of my life. The reason doesn't matter. However, I wanted to let you know that I'm getting married. His name is Matt Jansen. He's from a family that moved here when I was in the fifth grade. Our wedding will be Saturday, November 3rd at 3:00 PM at Riverview Community Church.

She took a breath, then continued. *If you want to come …*

Her finger twitched before she finally pushed send. She stared at the screen for a long moment, then turned away, wondering why she even bothered. He probably wouldn't reply. But no one could ever say *she* didn't try.

Her eyes misted. Less than two weeks to the wedding. Her papaw in the hospital.

And the new doublewide wouldn't arrive until the Wednesday before the wedding.

So close to time.

Every night now, when her mind tried to settle, the same thought invaded and kept her from sleeping. What would Matt think on their wedding night? He'd seen her in a bathing suit and never uttered a negative comment on her appearance. But nothing changed the fact that she was handicapped. That her legs lay lifeless, like dead branches from her body. Maybe even young brides with working legs worried about that first time. Would they be enough?

But she was *less* than whole.

Would she be able to be the woman Matt wanted? Needed?

"Maybe I should talk to someone." Her trembling voice resounded in the room, magnifying her aloneness. But who?

Not Mamaw. Millie. She was married, and surely had some jitters before her wedding. Maybe it would help to get all her fears in the open. Anything hidden can't be healed. The topic of emotional healing during Wednesday night church last week lay buried in her thoughts. She should have listened more closely.

A flash came in the corner of her screen. Someone had messaged her. She glanced at the top of her page and clicked on the icon.

Wayne.

She held her breath. What would it say? Part of her didn't want to know. What if it were hurtful, too much for her to bear? Her loneliness intensified as never before. *Please God, help me. Please.*

She clicked on the message and it popped up on the screen in front of her. *Dear Jessie.*

Tears dropped from her eyes. She reached for a tissue and whisked them away before continuing.

I was surprised to hear you are marrying. I guess I forgot how grown you must be. My counselor has encouraged me to reconnect with my family. Even though it's easier not to. But maybe it's time. If you really want me. Wayne.

Counselor? What kind of counselor? Like a therapist? Someone to help him wrestle out his feelings and emotions? Had memories of her and her mother finally gotten to him enough that he decided to do something about it. Or …

Maybe he'd changed, pulled his life together. She gripped the sides of her wheelchair. *If you really want me.* Did she? Wayne was a total stranger to her. One thing was for sure; she'd better break it to the family before she decided. Well, Mamaw and Matt anyway. No use upsetting Papaw.

A whirl of emotions lifted and dropped her at the same time. What had she been thinking to invite him?

She grabbed up her phone and dialed Matt's number.

"Hello?" His voice, though thick with sleep, gave her strength.

"Hey, Matt …" Her dry throat choked her.

"What's wrong? Is it your papaw?"

"No. I—I received a message from Wayne." She relayed what it said.

Matt paused. "Counselor? What kind of counselor?"

"He didn't say." She released a breath. "Maybe he is seeing someone to help him with his feelings about abandoning me. Or maybe …" A new thought struck her. "Maybe he went to a rehabilitation center for alcoholics or something. But now he said he would come if I really wanted him to. I'm freaking out. What will Mamaw and Papaw think?"

"Take another breath, Jessie."

She inhaled deeply, then let the air out slowly. "I think that deep down I didn't expect him to say yes."

"Hmm." He cleared his throat. "I guess if it were me, I'd want to meet him a few days before the wedding. Then you could get the awkward phase out of the way and it wouldn't be such a shock."

"That's a good idea." She shut her laptop. "I wouldn't be wound up like I'll probably be the day of our wedding."

"And why would you be *wound* up on the best day of your life? You *are* marrying the greatest guy around."

Her mind eased as she giggled. "And the most humble. And I

couldn't be happier, Matt Jansen."

"Me, too. See you tomorrow."

"Bye." She hung up, leaned over and switched off her light, wondering if she would be able to sleep. Her phone rang and she glanced at the screen. Mamaw.

"Hey. Is Papaw okay?"

"He's fine. I just wanted to make sure you made it home."

"I did. Matt fed the animals and made sure I locked the door when he left." She gripped the phone tighter. Now may not be the best time to share the news, but it was easier than in person. "And I—uh— Mamaw, I invited someone else to the wedding."

"Did you mail out one of the leftover invitations? I thought we counted everyone."

"No, ma'am. I sent out a Facebook message. To …" Jessie's voice trailed. She didn't want to hurt Mamaw, but it was too late to turn back. "To Wayne. I invited my father."

Silence. Jessie chewed her lip. *Please don't be crying.*

"Okay." Mamaw's voice was strained. "May I ask why?"

"I—uh—felt like I needed to. Just to be there, nothing else. And I'm going to tell him to come by a few days before so we can get, you know, reacquainted. Anyway, he might not come to the wedding itself. Or at all."

Mamaw sighed. "I just hope you don't get hurt over this."

"I had to try, Mamaw. I didn't want to go into this new part of my life without saying that I made an attempt to connect with him."

"We'll stand with you on this. You just get some rest. Goodnight."

"Goodnight." Jessie set down her phone. Her grandparents would be with her. They always had. And she would do as Matt suggested and meet Wayne ahead of time. If he *really* showed up … well, then she'd deal with Wayne Riggs.

***

Homer reached down and pushed the button to raise the bed. What was Martha talking about? Matt better not be getting cold feet. He shifted into a sitting position as Martha laid down her phone. "What's all this about Jessie getting hurt?"

"Now, Homer," she said. "I want you to promise me you won't get upset."

He stifled the cough that was building. "About what?"

She placed her hands on her hips and gave him *that* look of hers. "Jessie has gone and invited Wayne to the wedding."

"*What?*" The cough broke loose and he reached for his handkerchief, trying to stifle the noise. When he calmed down, Martha handed him the small plastic cup of water and he took several sips before speaking. "Why would she invite that sorry no-good excuse for a man? And I'm not even going to say *father*, because he isn't one."

"I don't know, Homer. She just felt like she needed to."

He gripped the cup. A wave of pain slipped over him. "Why? Does she want Wayne to walk her down the aisle?"

"Oh, no." Martha wrestled the cup from his hand. "She doesn't expect him to attend. And she's going to ask him to drop by a few days early."

The pain lifted. Not to replace him. Just to be there. Knowing Wayne, he probably wouldn't show anyway. "Well, I can tolerate him for a short time. For Jessie."

Martha nodded. "We can do this for her."

He closed his eyes. "I'd better rest." He'd need all his strength to hold back if Wayne dared show up. Especially if he dared to hurt his Jessie again.

Chapter Seventeen

Homer pushed back in his recliner and picked up the newspaper from the table beside him. He glanced around the familiar living room and almost smiled. Good to be home again. Two days in the hospital almost brought him to the point of planning an escape.

"Are you comfortable, Homer?" Martha bustled into the room, setting a cup of coffee, steam curling over it, on the coaster. "I asked Matt to come feed the animals again tonight so you won't have to worry about them."

Homer crossed his arms over his chest, stifling a cough. "I can feed my own animals. You need to quit fussing."

"Now, you just got home. Dr. Robertson said to take it easy for the rest of the day. Humor me." Martha lowered her voice. "At least, do it for Jessie. She's been so nervous lately. I'm afraid she's going to have another one of those headaches. It's all this stress with Wayne."

"I'm glad you told me if it's worrying her this bad." Homer coughed, then sipped his coffee. If it twern't one thing, it was another. "But she don't need to worry about me. If she *wants* him to come so bad, I can be civil." And he would.

***

Jessie lay stretched out on her bed, hearing every word her grandparents said as they sifted through the thin walls of the old house. She frowned as she pulled up Facebook on her phone. Were her jitters that noticeable? Apparently. Wasn't she covering them up with busyness and smiles?

Apparently *not*.

She'd waited long enough; the time had come to send a reply to

Wayne. Her fingers nervously pecked the keys.

I apologize for not replying sooner. Things around here have been hectic. I would love you to … No. Love was too strong a word. She backspaced and started again.

I would like you to attend the wedding, but would prefer that you come a few days early so we can get reacquainted. Jessie.

That was fair. It was *her* wedding and she didn't want to renew her acquaintance with her father on the day of the ceremony. Also, if he changed his mind, it wouldn't spoil the wedding. Matt's idea was perfect.

Jessie glanced at her wall calendar for the hundredth time that month. In a week, their home would arrive. Then the wedding on Saturday. She didn't want the ceremony itself to be complicated. She pulled up the wedding program on her phone that she and Millie had created and read through it again. Matt's dad would be his best man. His cousin, Ben, and Stu Wiley—his friend from work—would act as groomsmen.

Millie, of course, would be her matron of honor. Matt's younger sister, Sarah, and Jessie's third cousin, Amy, would be her bridesmaids. Papaw would give her away. Mamaw's great nieces would be flower girls, and help with the train on her dress while Papaw's great-nephew would bear the ring. Of course, Pastor Allen would marry them.

She then pulled up her Pinterest board and glanced at the chocolate-colored suits for the men and the deep orange bridesmaids' dresses. Millie would contrast in brown, which would look lovely with her light hair. Everything would be beautiful, more than she could ever have imagined.

Jessie glanced at the clock. Five o'clock. Matt should be here any minute to feed the animals.

Time to set all this aside and concentrate on my husband-to-be.

She pushed herself to a seated position, moved to the edge of the bed, and swung herself into the wheelchair. After running her hand over the comforter to smooth it, she pushed into the living room.

Papaw cleared his throat and reached for his coffee.

"How you feeling, Papaw?"

"Don't you start fussing." His mouth twitched at the corner. "It's bad enough that Martha here treats me like an old man."

"Only because you are an old man." Mamaw swiped at him with a dishrag. "Now act right while I go put on a pan of biscuits. I'll make enough for you to have some in the morning with your favorite chocolate gravy."

"Chocolate gravy? How about having it tonight?" He lifted his eyebrows. She rolled her eyes and scurried from the room.

"Now, Papaw," Jessie said. "Besides, you know I've already baked brownies for tonight. And we have ice cream."

"I guess brownies will tide me over until morning." He smiled. "They sure smell good." He folded the newspaper and placed it beside him, then reached for the television remote and flipped on the evening news.

The weatherman's voice shot from the speakers. "We're keeping an eye on next week's weather. Things could be shaping up for an unstable week."

Jessie inhaled sharply as Matt pushed through the screen door. "Weatherman talking about the weather? Or the wedding?"

"Oh, you're very funny." Jessie kissed the cheek he offered. "Sit."

"Let me go feed the animals first." Then looking at Papaw, he said, "How are you, Mr. Smith?"

Papaw didn't answer, only waved at him, letting Matt know he was consumed with the weather forecast. When a commercial came on, he looked up. "I told Martha, she shouldn't have bothered you. I could do my own feeding."

"I don't mind." Matt opened the creaking door. "I'll be back in a minute." He smiled at Jessie. "I smell chicken stew."

"And brownies," she said.

Matt grinned before he turned and walked out the door.

Jessie glanced out the window at the darkening sky. Would she have to deal with bad weather beside all the other distractions in her life? Two types of storms in her life had not ever been in any of her wedding plans.

Please God. Hold off the bad weather.

***

Main Street had grown dark and the street lamps glowed dimly around the courthouse square. Angeline left the newspaper office where she'd placed a quarter page ad announcing holiday specials at the Central City Creative Clothier. They were finally starting to turn a profit, so now was the time to advertise.

Estelle commended her on the way she managed the shop. How awesome was it to have free rein to make improvements? Francine had never listened to her.

Odd how something so devastating at the time turned out so well. Her phone beeped while she unlocked her car. An incoming text.

She plopped into her car, throwing her purse on the seat beside her. She scrolled down to the message.

Ben.

He'd asked for her number while at the coffee shop in the mall and against her better judgment, she'd given it to him. Was he going to be one of *those* guys who bugged a girl constantly? She glanced at his words.

Hi. Hope you had a good day at work. See you Friday at the fitting.

Short and to the point. No begging her to go out or anything. Maybe he would prove to be different.

"Okay, Ben Stevens. Let's put you to the test." She plugged her phone into the car charger. She wouldn't reply today. Would he still be interested come Friday? "Let's see if you're only after one thing," she said, as she reached for her seatbelt and pulled it around her. "Or if you're different from the rest.

She started her car, then pulled onto North Avenue. Just a quick stop at Big Market, then home. It seemed every time she'd meet a new guy, he wasn't what she thought he would be. Couldn't anyone be honest and open?

And what about church? Millie's disgruntled look colored every thought of fitting in. True, Millie attended a different church, but there were probably people at Jessie's church who thought the same way about her. *Tainted.* She gripped the steering wheel tighter and blinked away the tears forming in her eyes.

Jessie's church. Could it ever be *her* church?

Her high school classmates perceived her as easy and the people at Bentley's as uncaring. Jessie and her family seemed to think of her differently. But had her own self-perception changed? And could there be any hope for someone caught between who she was and who she wanted to be?

***

Homer shivered, the coolness seeping through his open flannel coat. His breath whitened in the early morning air as he fumbled to fasten the too-small buttons, then pulled the knitted hat tightly around his ears. Didn't matter how chilly it was; chores had to be done.

He poured corn into the chicken's bucket feeder and cleaned out the stalls. He tried to whistle an old song from his youth but his lips were too cold. Come to think of it, he couldn't remember the last time he whistled. His heart was glad over seeing Jessie about to marry and the money no longer a problem. He could provide.

The barn door groaned and Matt stepped through the doorway. "Hey, Mr. Smith."

He nodded. "Matt. Cold enough for ya?" Homer closed the lid on the feed. "Thought you'd be at work by now."

"It's colder than I like it. We're supposed to be fitted for our tuxes so I traded shifts with Lee. He normally works evenings." Matt set up an overturned bucket. "Thought I'd come by here first and see if you needed any help."

"No, son. I'm to finish these few chores, and then stay inside. Orders from Jessie and Martha." Homer shook his head. "It's too hard fighting both of 'em."

"I understand." Matt pushed his hands in his pockets and chuckled. "I wondered about doing a little bush hogging down at our home spot—a onceover so it will be ready for the mobile home Wednesday. I've got some piping to upgrade, and the electricity to hook up."

"Go right ahead."

Matt leaned against the barn door and looked out over the gray of the sky. "I hope it stays dry. Still a lot to do before next Saturday."

"Sure is."

"*Homer.*" Martha's shout pulled them outside. She waved from the porch. "You and Matt come here."

Matt shut the barn door and followed Homer to the house. "She sounds upset," he said.

"Martha is Martha." Homer walked up the back steps, and into the kitchen where she stood, phone in hand.

"Jessie called from the school. There's all kinds of trouble. The caterer has cancelled."

Trying to keep his emotions intact, Homer grabbed a mug and poured him some coffee. Not more worries.

"Cancelled?" Matt asked. "But we've already paid half the money."

"They're returning it. They told Jessie they're on the verge of bankruptcy. They haven't been there six months." Martha's hands went to her hips. "I believe there's more to it than this. How could they do this a week before the wedding?"

"What did Jessie say?" Matt wiped his brow.

"She's talking to Millie and then she'll call you when she gets her break. I know she wants you to go by the caterer and pick up the money while you're in Central City." Martha's voice trembled. "What then? I don't know."

Homer had to calm Martha down. "It'll be all right. Things always happen before weddings. That Millie's a smart girl. She'll figure out something."

"I'm sure she will," Matt said. "I'll go ahead and bush hog and then get cleaned up for the fitting. I'll make sure she calls y'all when we decide something."

"Bless you, Matt." Martha said. "Let us know what you do."

He put his hand on the back door. "I will."

Homer carried his cup of coffee to the recliner and plopped down. It seemed like yesterday when he'd knelt on this very floor and begged God to help him, but couldn't hear a reply.

God, You answered Jessie and Martha's prayers about the wedding. I'm stubborn, I know, but could You help them find a caterer?

Homer shook his head. Ten years ago, he'd raised a fist to heaven and declared there couldn't be a God. Not after what they'd been through. Lately, he'd seen a glimpse of hope.

Was it God only being good to Jessie? Or was God maybe giving him a glimpse of hope, too?

***

Jessie sat in the break room near the office while Millie scrolled her finger down her phone. How could so much go wrong trying to plan a wedding?

"I feel so bad about this." Millie frowned. "I recommended this caterer and with the discount they offered, I thought it would be ideal. Now their website's gone."

"You couldn't have known." Jessie flipped through the folder from the Central City bridal fair. Thankfully, it was still in her desk. "I see two caterers we could call in Central City and the diner here in Riverview will cater food, but not a wedding cake. I guess if we have to, we could call the supercenter."

"Let's try the caterers first." Millie dialed the number of the first and explained their situation. "Oh," she said a minute later. "Well, thank you, anyway."

Jessie cringed. They were in trouble. "No?"

"They're already booked for Saturday. You'd think there wouldn't be too many November weddings. Let me try the other number." She ran her finger down the list, then dialed. "Yes, this is Millie Lambert and I need a caterer on November third for a wedding at Riverview

Community Church," she said, obviously leaving a voice mail. "My number is 515-0986. Please call me as soon as possible."

Millie turned to Jessie. "Answering machine. Maybe they're setting up a wedding somewhere."

"Try the diner." Jessie sipped her diet soda. "Maybe we'll have two choices."

Millie dialed. "Yes, this is Millie Lambert and I'm looking for someone to cater a friend's wedding next Saturday, the third." There was a long pause. "Oh, I see. Thank you anyway."

"What?" Jessie rubbed her fingertips over her temples. "Another dead end?"

"They're doing the Hanley family reunion over at the recreation center. She has her whole staff involved." Millie looked at the clock on the wall. "I've got to get back to my class. Let's wait on calling the supercenter until I hear from the other caterer."

"Sounds good." Jessie wheeled back toward the office and texted Matt when she arrived. *Waiting on a call from a Central City caterer. Will let u know as soon as I know something. Call Mamaw for me please. Love you.*

She pushed send and busied herself with paperwork. Millie would find someone to cater for them. She had to. Only one prayer came to mind: *God, we need help.*

The rest of the morning crawled by with no reply. At lunch, Jessie ate in her office and checked her emails. She sorted them into files, then opened Facebook.

There had been no reply from Wayne since her last communication. Maybe today. She pulled up her messages. Scrolling halfway down, she found him.

Jessie. Have decided to come. Will arrive Tuesday and stay at a hotel in Central City. I know you're busy, so let me know when you want me to come to the farm. Wayne.

Seconds ticked by before she could close her mouth. He was coming. He was *really* coming. After ten years, she would finally speak to her father. She waited for a positive emotion—even a flicker of one—to hit her. Shouldn't she be happy? She'd thought she would, but what resurrected inside her was cold, unadulterated anger. He'd better have some answers—some *wonderful* reason why he hadn't come to see his only child.

She'd send Matt a text about his arrival but wait and tell Mamaw and Papaw when she returned home that evening. Hopefully, Papaw would still be okay.

But would *she*?

Chapter Eighteen

Matt swiped his hand through the air. He squinted at Ben in the driver's seat of the Charger. "You think you're wearing enough cologne? You haven't been this gaga over a girl, in oh, say two or three weeks."

"Hey, now. Angeline's not any girl. Sure, she has a hard edge, but there's something there." He coasted to the red light. "I'm planning on marrying this one."

Matt stared at him "Are you crazy? You only met her a few weeks ago."

"So? When a man knows, he knows. Didn't you know with Jessie?"

Matt shook his head in disbelief. "We met when we were children so … not right away."

The car moved forward with the traffic past the bank. A dog loped across the road, dodging cars. "Hurry, fella," Matt said. A sign displaying a cake flashed to the left. "That it?"

"Yeah. It should only take a minute. I hope they don't give me any problems." Matt breathed out as he exited the truck. Maybe they should have married at the court house. It would have certainly been easier.

He hurried inside. The front windows were already emptied of any display. Patsy Lester, who he and Jessie had ordered the wedding food from, crept out of the back room.

"Oh, Mr. Jansen." Her face reddened.

He grimaced. The lady had tears in her eyes. "Yes, ma'am. I came for the deposit."

"I'm so sorry." Her face crumpled. "I—I thought we could pull through, but ..." She reached into the cash register, pulled out a ticket and counted out the money, then handed it to him.

"Thank you, ma'am."

The woman grasped a handkerchief and Matt retreated. He crossed the sidewalk and jumped back in the car.

"How'd it go?" Ben started to back out. "Did you give her a piece of your mind for leaving you and Jessie in a bind like this?"

"Nah. She was about to cry. I can't handle crying women. But I got the money. Drive on to Central City and let's get this fitting out of the way." Surely Jessie and Millie could figure this catering thing out. It was beyond him.

The Central City Creative Clothier was planted on the left side of the square in the middle of town. Ben pulled into the front spot. "I want to make sure she sees *the* Charger."

"Yeah, maybe she'll marry you for your car."

"Ha. Ha. Are you insinuating she wouldn't marry me for my good looks and charming personality?"

"You said it, cuz. Not me."

Matt exited the car and pushed through the door, Ben lumbering behind. Near the shop window, a mannequin outfitted in a white tuxedo stood next to one in a pink prom gown. *Sure glad Jessie didn't want me in white.*

Angeline stood to the side of the counter, entering something into the computer. Her navy skirt hugged her curves, and her red crocheted blouse accentuated her tan complexion. Could she have dressed up for Ben? Maybe *she* liked *him*, too.

"Hello," she said, her faced turned to Matt. "The tuxes have arrived. I'll tell Estelle you're here."

Ben leaned against the counter. "No hello for me?"

"My hello was for both of you." She didn't meet his gaze as she exited to the back.

Ben scratched his head. "What's going on here? She talked like crazy at the mall."

"She's playing timid." Matt lowered his voice. "Remember, I'm the ex-crush."

"Don't remind me," Ben whispered back. "I'll have to try harder. You get fitted first and then go out and call Jessie. Give me a chance."

"Will do."

Ms. Granger entered the room with suits in hand, Angeline following. "Matt. Ben. So glad to see you again. The wedding's almost here. Are you ready?"

Same question everywhere he went. "We're getting there. Oh, Stu said he'd be here after two when he gets off work."

"Good, good." She hung the two tuxes on a metal rack by the door, then put on the glasses that hung on the chain around her neck. "Who's first?"

"That would be me." Matt accepted the suit she offered and moved toward the small dressing room in the corner. Now Ben and Angeline could be alone and maybe Ben wouldn't strike out.

"I'll be back in a minute." Estelle's voice faded as she crossed the room headed toward the back.

Matt stepped inside the small room and hung the suit on the hook.

"You look nice today." Ben's voice filtered into the dressing room. Matt shook his head. What a lame opening line. He wouldn't get anywhere unless he improved.

"Thank you." Her voice sounded stronger than before. "Is that your car out there?"

"Yeah. Matt and I worked a long time restoring my baby." Lack of pride in his *baby* had never been an issue with Ben. "She was a junker when I got her."

"How do you know it's a she?"

Matt grinned at Angeline's question as he fought with the tux jacket.

"She's temperamental and hard to get to know."

Matt groaned as he stepped from the dressing room.

Don't blow it, Ben.

Angeline crossed her arms. "Are you implying something?"

Ben paused. "I don't think so."

Time to intervene. "Angeline, I'm kinda in a hurry. The caterer cancelled and I've got to call Jessie back."

A look of shock and concern crossed her face. "This close to the wedding? That's terrible."

Estelle entered the room. "The jacket fits nice, Matt. Turn around." She checked from all angles. "The pants might be a little long. I'll place a temporary hem and I think you're good to go. Stand still." She reached for a pin cushion, squatted beside him, and began placing pins.

"Why did the caterer cancel?" Angeline asked.

"They didn't?" Estelle's voice raised an octave. "The one near the bank?"

Matt shrugged. "Yes, ma'am. They're going bankrupt."

"Well, I for one am not surprised." Estelle stood. "I wondered how they could rent such a nice place and do so much improvement without spending a fortune. Have you found someone else to cater?"

"I'm waiting to hear from Jessie now. When you're done here I'll get changed and go outside and call while Ben tries his tux on."

With Estelle done, Matt changed, then stepped outside. Muggy air slapped him. Way too warm after a chilly start to the day. Typical south. He'd be glad when it cooled and the threat of storms passed.

He leaned against the building. Not too many people out today. A young woman pushing a stroller with twin boys hurried by, followed by a girl chatting on a phone. He pulled his phone out from the holster at his hip and rang Jessie.

"Matt, I was about to call." Her words came in a flurry. "Millie heard from the caterer and they can work it out. They're going to put a rush order in for supplies and will be at the church early to set everything up. The price is a little higher, though."

He winced at the tremor in her voice. "It doesn't matter. This is for you and it will be worth it."

He glanced up as Ben emerged from the shop, frowning.

"It is," Jessie said. "And it will be perfect, no matter what. Can you go to one-twelve Darby Road? That's where Kinsley's Katering's located. I've ordered everything the same as before, but will you bring me a sample menu anyway? They said they would take the deposit—"

Her voice choked. "You did get the deposit, didn't you?"

"I did. It was no trouble. Ben and I will head right over there. I'll see you this evening." He said good-bye, then pushed his phone back in his holster and opened the car door. Ben said nothing as he cranked the motor.

Must not be good. "Well?"

"It went nowhere. While I was trying on the tux, she disappeared. I had a nice talk with Ms. Granger, though."

"What did *she* say?"

Ben shrugged. "She told me to not push Angeline too hard. Said she's had a lot of hurt in her life, and if I truly liked her, I'd be careful. Am I that transparent?"

"You're plumb goofy." Matt grinned. "But it's okay. I've always been that way around Jessie. When you're in love, you can't help yourself."

"I agree with you there. Maybe I'll see her Sunday. She can't hide from me at church."

***

Angeline had retreated to the bathroom when Ben stepped into the fitting room. Now she stayed out of sight in the back, waiting for him to leave. What was wrong with her? Here was an attractive guy, who acted decent, and she was running like a rabbit at the opening of hunting season.

Before he arrived with Matt, she rehearsed lots of things they could talk about, but the minute he stepped into the shop and she got a whiff of his spicy scent and those green eyes, it all left her. He probably thought she was temperamental. Well, she couldn't stay hidden forever.

The bell to the front entrance jangled and Estelle hurried through the door.

"You okay? Anything I can do?"

Angeline slumped into a nearby chair. "I froze up. I don't know what happened."

"Well, it's evident you like this young man." Estelle smiled at her.

"He comes from a good family, being Irene's boy and all. I'm sure you'll be able to talk to him next time. Just try to relax."

Estelle patted her shoulder and carried the tuxes to the back. *Next* time? A hundred things had changed in her life over the past few months. Was any relationship worth going through more?

Angeline wandered to one of the sewing machines to practice on the simple pattern Estelle had given her. She threaded the white thread through the eye of the needle then fed the cloth through the machine, creating a tight stitch. She clipped the threads and held it up, frowning as she traced her finger over the pucker.

"Let me see." Estelle leaned over and studied the material. "You have the tension too tight. Now loosen it and try again."

"Sewing is harder than I thought." Angeline pinned another piece together.

"If you want to design wedding dresses someday, you have to have a deeper understanding on how they come together. Sewing is a necessary skill."

Angeline began again, this time with a smile. "I'm glad I have you to teach me."

As Estelle walked toward the front, Angeline sighed. So different than Bentley's. And Ben? When she thought of that tousled blond hair and his goofy ways, she couldn't help but smile once more. Maybe he would be worth it.

***

Jessie stared out the truck window. Their home spot. Matt opened the passenger's door and helped her into the readied wheelchair. The freshly cut grass still carried its fragrance; the biting tang forced her to rub her nose. Nearby trees danced in the stiff breeze, leaves spilling to the ground at each twist and turn.

Familiar, yet soon to be different. The small elm tree to her left had a few bright yellow leaves clinging to life mixed with dead ones.

The story of her life.

Their beautiful new home was on its way a day early and she'd wanted to be here with Matt when it arrived. The electricity would be hooked up tomorrow. At least the weather was warmer and Papaw had stopped coughing. He and Ben had arrived earlier and now stood talking by the fence. Mamaw stayed back at the house to cook enough lunch to feed everyone.

Her father could be in Central City by now. Jessie rubbed the back of her neck and determined to message him shortly.

Matt grasped her hand. "Are you okay? I'm talking to you, but you're not hearing me."

She looked up at his concerned face. "I'm sorry ... what did you say?"

"I said, wasn't it great that your grandfather traded his last calf to buy a porch for us from the Hendersons?"

Jessie brushed all other thoughts from her mind. Worrying would not help. "Papaw is the greatest. You know he's already scrounged up enough lumber to build a ramp." She waved toward the men. "Hey, Ben."

"Hey, there." Ben ambled toward them. "Are we ready to tie the knot?"

"More than ready," Jessie said. "The stress is enough to make me want to run away."

Matt turned sharply. "I hope you're kidding."

She winked. Better not give Matt anything else to stress about. "What do you think?" She looked down, then back up with a grin. "How far do you think I could roll anyway?"

"There it is." Ben pointed toward the end of the dirt road as half the doublewide home, pulled by a large truck and trailed by the other half, created a mountain of dust. Still another truck with concrete blocks and tie-down straps followed.

She hugged herself as it drew closer. The clay vinyl siding matched perfectly with the brownish-gray shingles. Her own place.

"I'm glad the rain held off," Matt said. "Going to make this a piece of cake."

Ben moved over by her. "You talked to Angeline lately?"

"No. I've been so busy." Truth was, she'd noticed Angeline's absence at church. Had Ben scared her off? The house stopped before the driveway. "Matt, I think I better move over by the gate so I'll be out of the way."

"Okay." He pushed her through the rutted yard to a safe distance. "After we get married, I'm going to cut up the yard with the tiller and sow more grass. I'll get these clumps out of here."

Within the next hour, both sides of the home were placed in position, set, and the tedious work of blocking it up and tying it down began. It would take all day. Then it would still have to be underpinned so it would be ready when they returned from the Smoky Mountains.

Jessie drew in a deep breath. The honeymoon. She still hadn't spoken to Millie about her worries of the wedding night and what would follow. Maybe Friday morning they could talk.

A brown Honda Civic passed the woods to Jessie's left and pulled off to the shoulder of the road near the place she sat. A man exited the car, followed by a young girl, maybe six or seven years old. Jessie's hand went to her mouth.

Wayne.

Her childhood backyard returned to her. "Come on, Jessie. Focus. If you can't hit these simple pitches, you'll never be able to play softball."

Her father pitched the ball to her again and she bit her lip, swinging hard. Too hard.

"You've got to keep your eye on the ball, not your swing. Try again."

She tossed back the ball, then perched the bat on her shoulder, swiping the bangs from her eyes. She *would* hit the ball.

The pitch hung low. She lined up and swung. The ball thudded against the bat, sputtering along the ground to her left.

"Jessie. Wayne. Supper's ready." Mama stood at the door of their home, waving.

She ran to her father and they walked in together. "How'd I do?"

"Better." He patted her shoulder. "Better."

Jessie squeezed tears from her eyes, clearing the brief memory away.

Yes, his hair had grayed and his face now boasted a beard. His thinness mimicked a drought-stricken individual, but the face hadn't changed. Not really. A lump rose in her throat as her father crossed the grass, the girl trailing behind. She had a small build, her blond hair hanging in waves past her shoulders.

Matt returned to her and placed a hand on Jessie's shoulder. "Your father?"

"Yeah. It's him." Her voice lowered to a whisper.

She glanced over at Papaw, who stood still as a windless day.

"Jessie?" Wayne stopped several feet away from the couple. "I tried to message you, but you didn't answer. I thought I'd drive by and see the old trailer spot, but then I saw y'all out here and … well …"

He kicked at the ground with his foot. The little girl fidgeted but remained quiet.

"Hello, Wayne." She couldn't bring herself to call him "Dad," the one thing he hadn't been to her. "We've been setting up our new home." She looked up. "This is Matt."

"Matt." Wayne kept his distance but nodded at his future son-in law. "It's nice," he said, glancing over at the doublewide. "They about got it ready?"

"What about me?" The girl tugged at Wayne's shirt. He nodded an approval. The child smiled and, permission granted, walked over to Jessie. "I'm Shay."

Jessie's stomach tumbled. Who was this child? "What a pretty name."

A flush crept across Wayne's face. "Jessie, Shay is my daughter. Your half-sister."

She had a *sister*? She pressed her lips together. Shay's hair was blond but the nose and chin were the same. She looked more like their father.

Jessie wanted to throw up. Scream. Something. Instead, she could only stare at the child.

"Mr. Smith." Wayne's voice pulled her from her trance. By now, Papaw had joined them, his weathered hand resting near the base of her neck.

"Wayne."

"Been a long time."

"Yes, it has."

An awkward pause ensued before Wayne took a step back. "Jessie, I was wondering when we could talk. Maybe tomorrow?"

Talk? How could she talk when she couldn't even put two thoughts together?

Papaw intervened. "How about me and Martha bring her to the Riverview Diner? I expect you remember where it is. Your little girl could sit with us while you two talk."

"I can do that," he answered, keeping his eyes on Jessie. "How about noon?"

"Okay." Jessie finally breathed.

"Good. I'll see you there." His chin jutted upward. "Come on, sweetheart. Let's go …"

"But …" the child said.

"It's okay," he said. "We'll see her again tomorrow."

"Bye, Jessie," she said.

Jessie couldn't help but smile. After all, none of this was her fault. The accident. Her mother's death. Her abandoned childhood. "See you tomorrow," she said as Wayne turned and walked away.

Again.

Shay turned back when she reached the car. "Bye, Jessie," she said, waving frantically. "I'll see you tomorrow."

"Bye-bye, Shay." Her voice broke when she said the name. She had a sister. Whether or not she could work things out with her father, she wasn't an only child any more. Still, no tears would come though. Why had he stayed with this child and not with her?

Matt knelt beside Jessie, massaging her hand. "You okay?"

She stared after the car pulling away. "I don't know. My father is back and I have a sister." And what about Papaw? She looked up, hoping to read his expression, but he'd walked away, crossing the field toward the house. "I need to see about Papaw."

"Sure," he said.

As they drove to the house, Jessie stared down the road in the direction Wayne and Shay had taken. Tomorrow. She would know more then.

Yes, tomorrow.

***

Martha added sweet tea to Matt's glass for the fifth time, though he'd not gotten close to emptying it. Homer could not focus on the meal before him, though Matt and Ben munched their ham sandwiches with no problem.

But neither one of them had ever lost a child. Raised a grandchild. And come face to face with the man he'd wanted to kill ten years ago. Funny ... some of the anger melted away with how sickly Wayne looked. And the little girl. So much like Jessie.

"Papaw, you need to eat something," Jessie said.

"I'll eat after a while." The lump in his throat returned. He picked up his cup and swallowed some of the now lukewarm coffee.

"Tell me again. What was the little girl like?" Martha turned toward Homer. "I'm her ... uh ... half-grandmother, aren't I?"

"I'm not sure how that works." How could they handle this major change in the structure of the family? Jessie had hardly said two words, since they'd come back in the house. Wayne was upsetting his Jessie again. He rubbed his aching temple.

He'd told Martha he could be civil but right now he wanted to hit someone. Hard.

"I think I'm going to sit on the porch." Jessie pushed from the table. "I'll finish eating later."

Matt jumped up and followed her out the door. "I'll join you."

"That was wonderful, Mrs. Smith." Ben bunched the napkin on his plate and stood. "I'm going back to see what all we still have to do."

"Why don't you go too, Homer? Give Matt a little time with Jessie." Martha started gathering dishes. "So much happening."

Might as well. Maybe he could work out these emotions on the new ramp. He followed Ben out the door.

"I'll be there in a minute." He waved Ben on and trudged to the barn. He loaded a couple of hammers, a tin of nails, and his handsaw onto the wheelbarrow. Did he need anything else? A flash of green caught his eye. The tarp had slid off the paint cans. He adjusted it back. The time to visit the shed to unleash his anguish had ended. The wedding only days away, life was real and he couldn't hide anymore.

***

Jessie reached the swing, then dropped her head into her hands. She squeezed her eyes shut. "I don't know if I can do this."

The shuffle of paws announced Bear's approach. He rubbed his nose against her hands and licked her. She raised up. "I'm okay, boy."

"Come on." Matt helped her into the swing, then held her close while Bear deposited himself on the welcome mat. "Listen … you don't have to go tomorrow. I'll go to the diner and tell him it's not the right time." Jessie shook her head against the suggestion. "Jessie, you have to do what's best for you."

She laid her head on his shoulder, clutching his arm tight. "I don't know what's best for *me* anymore. Since I decided to start this and prayed to God to let it happen, I should let it play out. But I didn't want to begin our married life with all this upset."

Matt pushed the swing with his foot. "I know."

"He abandoned me." Jessie clenched her hands. "And then fathered another daughter who calls him *Daddy*. Well, what about *me*? What about all the things *I* missed and can never have back?"

"He's the one who missed out, not having you around." Matt's voice soothed her frayed nerves. "All I know is there are a lot of people who love you and have cared all these years. Me. Your grandparents. Your friends at school and church. Even the townspeople who've helped us with this wedding."

"I know you're right. But—what I don't understand is why couldn't *he* care?"

"He's an idiot. You can't change that, Jessie, and some people will never change. Go ahead and prepare yourself for that … just in case."

Jessie lifted her chin. Matt was right; she couldn't alter Wayne or give way to the conflicting thoughts filling her mind. This was *her* wedding week. "Whether any of this works or not, I still have much to be thankful for. I need to see him tomorrow no matter if he comes to the wedding or not. For closure. Will you meet us there?"

"Of course." Matt kissed her cheek.

She relaxed her hands from the fists she'd made. Let it go.

She gazed up at Matt's face. He smiled and kissed her again. Her arms encircled his neck as their lips met once more.

After a few moments, Jessie slipped into a more peaceful state of mind. Their home was set up. She would see the inside tomorrow when they finished the ramp. All the nice gifts from the bridal showers the church and family had given them would be moved from Mamaw and Papaw's spare bedroom to her new home. Life would be good, with or without her father.

No matter what happened tomorrow.

Chapter Nineteen

Light gray clouds dotted the horizon, drawing Homer's attention from the old John Deere tractor. Storm clouds? He chugged down the driveway toward Jessie and Matt's trailer.

The Weather Channel had not decided how far south the bad weather would come. Small tornadoes were fairly common in November, but it had been twenty years since a damaging storm had hit. That cyclone had been a bad one, though. One a body wouldn't forget.

He turned onto the dirt road and traveled the short distance to Matt and Jessie's. Their neighbor would bring the porch at eight. He glanced at his pocket watch as he braked near the trailer. Almost that time now. They could attach the porch and then the ramp. With Ben and Matt, they should be done in time.

To make it to the diner.

"Wayne." Homer muttered under his breath. Why did Jessie have to go and look up that sorry excuse for a human on her computer?

He slapped his hand on the steering wheel. Stop. Now was the time to face all this like a man, the one Jessie needed him to be.

He glanced up to see a flatbed trailer loaded with the porch approaching the house. Matt and Ben followed behind in Matt's truck. Beyond them, the clouds thinned a little, the sun trying to break through. Maybe the rain would pass.

They would use the bucket on his tractor to move the porch to the back. Jessie wanted it there so she could sit outside and enjoy the view of the woods and the fields. It wasn't a big porch, just enough for the young couple. In the future, they could build a nicer one on the front; maybe even put a roof on it. He'd make sure it was fixed right.

Within an hour, they'd positioned the porch and were ready to attach it, and then the ramp. By evening, Jessie should have a way into her new home. He pulled the watch from his overall pocket again. Plenty of time.

How would he deal with Wayne at noon? And entertain his other child? He stifled a sigh. Just hold on a few more days, Homer. The wedding will be over and life will be normal.

He readjusted his cap. Who was he kidding? This was the new normal and he'd better get used to it.

***

Jessie glanced at the television as a children's costume commercial came on. Could it already be Halloween? The holiday hadn't entered her mind when they picked out the date for the wedding. A day of tricks and treats.

The day one hid behind masks.

Maybe she needed one. Seemed a perfect irony for meeting her father at the diner. She wouldn't let it ruin her morning though.

As she pushed into the kitchen, the mixed aroma of hot apple muffins and coffee made her smile. Could there be anything better on an autumn morning? If only the cooler weather had come and stayed. Summer still had a foothold on the season, one it wouldn't relinquish.

Where was Papaw? Had he eaten? He worked too hard. She opened her mouth to tell Mamaw, who sat at the table, still in her gown and robe, then closed it. Stop worrying. They had to get the programs finished. Jesse had printed them on the computer using a pattern from the hobby store. Mamaw folded one, placing the foiled autumn leaf neatly on the front.

"Hey, darling. Want something to eat?" Mamaw laid the program on the table.

"I will in a minute. Let's get these done first." She grasped the next one from the stack. The ushers would hand them to the guests as they arrived. She had written a special thank you on the back, and they'd already mailed thank you cards to each person who'd help make their wedding day special through the donations. They would decorate the church tomorrow, and Saturday would be the special day she'd remember forever.

"Jessie. Do these leaves look all right?" Mamaw held up another program. "I wish Millie were here to do this."

"They look fine. Millie took a vacation day tomorrow so she can decorate. I couldn't ask her to take two. Anyway, she's going to Central City for us after school to pick up the extra decorations and tablecloths for the reception."

"I know. It's only I want everything to be lovely. And I'm nervous about this lunch today. For you, that is." Mamaw picked up the scrap paper and carried it to the garbage can.

Jessie folded the last one. "I'm starting to wish I'd never contacted him. But then I never would have known about a sister." Her eyes threatened tears, but she pushed them back. No time for emotions now.

Her stomach growled. She pushed over to the counter and retrieved the warm muffin from the plate, crunching into the crusty top. The cinnamon mingled with the brown sugar pacified her taste buds. Bliss in a bite.

Mamaw jumped up and poured Jessie some coffee. "Now, listen. About today—and about the—well, of course, we'll love the girl. And don't you worry about her at the diner. I made a nice bag of Halloween candy for her." She pointed to items resting on the counter. "I'd already bought these coloring books with three crayons to give out to trick-or-treaters tonight, so I'll bring one for her. You can take as long as you need."

Need? Jessie bit her lip. Couldn't anyone understand she didn't know how long she needed or what she should say? She should act like a Christian and do and say all the right things. Few *right* things were on her mind at this moment.

Mamaw began to pack the rest of the muffins into a gallon bag. "Are you sure you'll be all right, darling? You don't have to do this, you know."

"Matt told me the same thing last night." Jessie twisted her engagement ring. She would do this for herself and her sister. "No, I started, and I'm going to see it through. No matter how it turns out, I'm still loved and accepted by so many people and God loves me. So regardless, I'll go."

Maybe if she said it enough, she would start to believe it.

Someone banged on the back door. Ben opened the creaky screen and looked in. "Hello, Mrs. Smith, Jessie. Homer said you were making us a thermos of coffee." He sniffed the air. "And snacks."

"Oh, my. I meant to bring it out to you, but I've been busy helping Jessie." Mamaw put two thermoses of coffee in a small tote and added some Styrofoam cups. She picked up the baked goods and handed everything to Ben. "Now remember to share," she said in a half-tease.

Ben grinned. "I promise. Oh, and Jessie, I talked to Angeline last night. We were on the phone for hours." He waggled his brow. "She can't resist me."

"Uh-huh." Jessie rolled her eyes. "You keep believing that."

"Now you sound like Matt. I heard she's invited to the rehearsal dinner so maybe I'll get to see her there. Well, I gotta go."

Jessie shook her head. Same old Ben. Now if only her problems were so simple. As she left the kitchen for her bedroom, her mind strayed to the diner. Today would either make or break her relationship with her father.

***

The Riverview Diner bustled with lunch regulars, local workers on their break, and harried waitresses. The aroma of fried chicken met her as Jessie parted the crowd, finding their normal table in the corner unoccupied. She glanced around. Good. Her father hadn't arrived yet.

"Grab your regular seat, honey." Consuela, a longtime server, smiled. Her black hair was smoothed back in a ponytail, which accented her deep mahogany eyes. "I be back in a moment."

Jessie pushed to the table and sat with her back to the crowd. If she gave vent to her feelings and people stared, so be it. She wouldn't see them. Mamaw and Papaw pulled up a chair on each side of her. Maybe meeting at such a busy time wasn't a good idea.

She reached to the middle of the table, straightened the salt and pepper shakers and smoothed a wrinkle in the bright red tablecloth. She pulled two napkins from the holder and placed them in front of her.

Consuela returned with her order pad. "You want the special? Sweet tea?"

"We don't want to order yet, except for the drinks," Mamaw said. "We're expecting a few friends. And could you save us the table over there by the window please?"

"It kinda far from here, no?" Consuela furrowed her brow.

"It's okay," Papaw grunted.

"Three teas," Jessie managed to say.

"Make it four." Matt slid into the fourth chair.

"Now Matt is good customer." Consuela patted his shoulder and hustled away to fill the order.

"It's ten 'til twelve." Jessie glanced at her phone, then at Matt. "They should be here any minute now."

He reached over and took her hand. The simple gesture almost brought her to tears but she bit her lip and blinked them away.

Within a minute, Consuela dropped off their drinks. Each time the bell dinged with the opening of the door, Jessie tensed. More customers going in or out.

The bell jingled and a little voice rang out. "There she is."

She stiffened as Shay bounced over. "Hi, Jessie."

Jessie focused past Shay and on to Wayne. Time slowed. Papaw, Mamaw, and Matt stood.

"Shay, this is my mamaw, Miss Martha. And you remember my papaw and Matt."

"Hi." Shay raised a hand, then shifted from foot to foot as if she'd grown unsure about the situation at hand. What had Wayne told her?

Mamaw nodded. "Hello, Wayne. Shay, Mister Homer and Matt

and I are going to move over there." Mamaw's kind smile seemed to erase the unease from Shay's face. "Won't you sit with us? I brought you some Halloween treats. See, Consuela saved the table."

Matt bent to kiss Jessie's cheek. "I'm here for you," he whispered toward her ear. He straightened, nodded toward Wayne, then followed Papaw across the restaurant.

Wayne pulled out the chair opposite Jessie. "Thanks for meeting with me." He adjusted his John Deere cap as though he needed to.

Jessie reached for another napkin, but returned her hand to clutch the glass of tea instead. "Well, I'm the one who reached out to you."

He nodded. "You—uh—you doing okay?"

She clenched her teeth. *Okay?* Ten years and that's the best he could come up with? As he'd said, she had been the one to call for this meeting. The least she could do is be honest. "I don't know if *okay* is the right word. Do you?"

He frowned, refusing to meet her eyes, instead focusing on picking at his thumbnail. He finally took a deep breath. Blew it out. "I wanted to explain. For a long time, I have."

Jessie opened her mouth to speak, but then Consuela approached the table again. "Something to drink?" she asked Wayne.

He ordered a sweet tea then watched as she walked away.

"Okay," Jessie said, bringing his attention back to her.

"To start with, Jessie, I've been sober fifteen months now." His eyes held onto hers. "And I have some of my parental rights back with Shay."

"Oh ... you're *not* married?"

"No. Divorced. Erica—my wife—my *ex*-wife—couldn't take the drinking any more than your mother could." He shrugged. "Not that I blame them now, but back then, somehow I kept thinking someone would accept me and my problem without question."

Consuela returned to the table again, set a glass of sweet tea in front of Wayne, said, "Let me know if you need anything else," and then walked away.

Wayne wrapped callused, sun-darkened fingers around the glass, then took a long swallow, leaving Jessie with her thoughts.

Fifteen months. For an alcoholic, that was close to a lifetime. So ... that was good, right? A second divorce—not so great. But— "Wait. If you're not married, who is the Joy Riggs I saw on Facebook?" Jessie tapped her fingers against the table and bit her lip again. "Another daughter?" No, wait a minute. No. The woman in the picture was too old to be—which meant— "Another *wife?*"

Wayne set the glass on the table and looked at her, nearly dumbfounded. "Gosh, no. No, no. Joy's a sister I didn't know I had." His voice dropped, though it now sounded strong and sure of itself. "I found out two years ago that my father and one of his girlfriends had her. And—wait till you hear this part—I mean, you think your life is messy—my mother *knew*, but never told me."

Her heart twisted. "Well, then I guess I have a half-sister *and* an aunt I've never known about." Jessie took a long sip from her glass, hand trembling. She was ready to cut to the chase. "Why didn't you come back after I got out of the hospital? Do you know the pain you caused me?"

His shoulders drooped. "Can I tell you something? This may not make a hill of beans worth of difference ... but it might—it could ..." His voice trailed, but in expectation.

Jessie drew a breath. He waited for her to give him the go-ahead. "What? What could?"

Wayne wiped his hand across his face. His brow furrowed as if what he was about to say pained him beyond what Jessie had ever thought him capable. He looked down at the table where he'd laced his fingers together, then up again, directly into her eyes. "My mother—your grandmother—"

"Who I also never knew," Jessie cut in, reminding him that in his absence, she'd not only missed his love, but that of a paternal grandmother.

"Yeah, well ... her name was Mary, okay? Mary Bourke. *Her* father—my grandfather—was one mean man." His eyes crinkled at the edges. "And when I say *mean*, I'm not saying a little. He drank hard and swore harder … even at his kids." Wayne blew out a sigh. "Mom used to tell me about how her mother was so scared of him—Mom was the oldest of the three kids—that she'd knuckle under to whatever he said or did … even to his own kids." Wayne shook his head, looked back down to his thumbs, and then up again. "My mother *hated* her mother."

"Hate is a strong word."

Wayne blinked. "Is it?"

Jessie felt heat in her cheeks. "Go on."

Wayne's neck hunched further into his shoulders. "My mother was sixteen when she met Scott Riggs."

"Your father."

"Yeah. He was twenty-four—nearly ten years older and as Mom said, 'Oh, so charming'—and the next thing she knew she was pregnant with me. Mom told me more than once that if she'd had her way of things, I'd never made it to the world, but back then …"

The reality of her father's words hit Jessie straight in the heart. Had her paternal grandmother ended her unplanned pregnancy, Wayne would have never been … and neither would she. "She *told* you that?"

Wayne chuckled. "Oh, yeah. That and so much more. See, Jessie, my mom and dad were forced—and I do mean *forced*—to get married, but that didn't mean they liked it. Dad traveled with his job more than he stayed home, leaving me and Mom and enough whiskey bottles to fill the entire county. That's how my mom dealt with her life." Wayne glanced over to where Papaw and Mamaw sat with Shay and Matt, then to her again. "I don't know how it would have turned out if your mother and I stayed together or if there'd never been an accident, but I'll tell you this much. You've been raised knowing love and with three squares in your belly every single day. You've been raised warm in the winter and cool in the summer." He jabbed himself in the chest and for a moment Jessie thought she saw tears well up in his eyes. "Me? I ate stale Cheerios without milk and called it supper while my mother lay passed out on the couch. At times, I went to bed hungry, even. There were times …" His voice trailed again. "Nah. Let's not go there."

Jessie sat silent, trying to imagine the little boy her father had been. Hungry. Or cold. Or afraid. But the picture was replaced by the memory of her mother's grave and of herself as a child, learning to get in and out of the wheelchair unassisted. So *she* wouldn't be a burden on her grandparents. "Are you telling me that's why you left?"

"Leaving is what my old man did." Wayne shrugged. "Mom's drinking got to the point that he'd rather leave her to rot and me to fend for myself. And that's exactly what he did."

"But you were his child." The words sounded more like a question than a statement.

"I was his *offspring*. He blamed me for being tied down at twenty-four to a broken sixteen-year-old with a chip on her shoulder—and never stopped until the day she died."

"She died?"

"Yeah. Back in 2013. Breast cancer." Something between a chuckle and a groan came from deep inside Wayne's chest. "Five years earlier, she found out about Joy—and that my father had been living a double life. So she divorced him—"

"They'd stayed married all that time?"

"Believe it or not. Married on paper, mind you. I haven't seen my father since I was about sixteen and hadn't said much to her until she called to say she was dying." He shrugged, then raised his hand. "As if I wanted to know."

"What did you do?"

He swallowed. "Do you know a song—it comes from back in the 70s—called 'Cat's in the Cradle'?"

Jessie shook her head.

"A great song. It's by Harry Chapin, who you also probably never heard of."

Jessie shook her head.

"You should look him up. Anyway, the song talks about how we become our parents ... or our kids become us ... or something like that."

Jessie pressed her lips together. No. She was *not* her father. She was her mother and Mamaw and Papaw, but she was not Wayne Riggs.

"Anyway, by then I was drinking harder than ever. I kept in touch with her but this wasn't a Hallmark movie or anything."

"And your father?" My *grandfather* ...

"He married Joy's mother as soon as he and my mother were divorced, which was five years or so before she died. After Mom died, I went looking for him, I—I don't even know why. Like they would care that she died. Well, that's when I found out about Joy. And decided it was time to get help. Time to stop blaming everything on my mother's drinking and my father's absence. Time to stop playing 'Cat's in the Cradle'." He sighed again. "To answer your original question, Jessie, when the accident happened, I couldn't get a grip on Elizabeth's death and your injury. I wanted to pretend it didn't happen. When I wasn't working, I was in the bar, or out with the guys trying to forget. Then I met Erica and it became easier and easier to pretend it never happened." He swatted at a tear. "None of it."

She flinched. He made the bad decisions, not her. She had a right to be angry. "At school, the kids would ask me why my dad didn't bring me to school, or attend the Christmas program, or eat lunch with me on parents' day. After the accident ... you—you just disappeared. Right when I needed you." She took a breath. Released it. "Why couldn't you care?" Jessie's voice had risen until the people at the next table stared. She lowered it again. "I'm so tired of being hurt," she said around the knot in her throat.

"I'm sorry. I'm not trying to make *any* excuses here. I only want you to know—to have—a little of the background. My—my counselor at the mission told me—"

"*Your* counselor? I needed a counselor to fight the hatred trying to fester in my heart. If not for my church and God, I couldn't have handled it." Jessie wiped unabashed tears, which slid down her cheeks. The mention of God calmed her and she sought for the right words. "But—but I *have* to forgive you. Pastor Allen said it's not a feeling; it's a choice. In some ways, that's why I needed to find you." She jabbed at her chest with her index finger. "I didn't want to enter my marriage carrying that much anger."

Wayne cleared his throat. "The mission where I meet with the counselor preaches a lot about God. They gave me a Bible, and I'm reading it some." He glanced across the room again. "I want to change for Shay."

"But not for me."

"That's not fair, Jessie," he shot back, his eyes filled with a short-lived flame. "I didn't try to contact you because—"

"I thought one of the rules of sobriety is to make amends with anyone you've hurt," she challenged. Jessie didn't know much about being clean and sober, but she'd heard it discussed once on a television show.

"I—I thought you'd never want to see me, and, sweetheart, I sure didn't blame you if you didn't."

"Well, I did."

She stared at him for a good thirty seconds, waiting. Studying. Alcohol had abused him as hard as he had abused it, but fragments of the handsome man he'd once been lingered. And he had been. And she remembered *that* man. The one her mother had fallen in love with. The man in the back yard, tossing a ball to her. Tickling her before bedtime. Humming as he worked outside …

Wayne closed his eyes as deep lines formed across his forehead. "I'm *sorry*. If I could go back and change it—but, Jessie … I can't. Much as I might want to exchange myself for your mama. Her be here and me be gone. As much as I'd like to change what happened to you in the accident. I—I *can't*."

The words sounded sincere, but Jessie wasn't ready—not yet. Not fully. She said nothing, only looked down at her lap, aware of the wheelchair she'd been trapped by for so long.

Finally, Wayne slid his chair away from the table. "Well … that's all I came to say."

Shay jumped up and ran to them. Jessie gave her a small smile. Such a sweet child and the only reason this day was bearable. She took a shaky breath. "Shay. I want you to come sometimes and visit our farm if your mom doesn't mind." She pulled a scrap of paper and a pen from her purse and scribbled it down. "Here's my phone number."

"I'd like that." Shay took the paper and smiled. Her eyes sought her father's face. "Can I?"

"Like Jessie said, you'll have to ask your mother."

Shay looked at Jessie again and smiled. "I'll ask her."

Wayne cleared his throat. "I think it would be better if we didn't come to the wedding. I wouldn't want to ruin your big day." He straightened his cap. "But I'm glad I got to see you. To let you know that I'm sorry." He paused. "And I am, Jessie."

Jessie searched her heart for a long moment, trying to find a part of her that wanted her father at the wedding. The dream of her family being one again crumbled with the accident. The fairy-tale ending with her parents beside her as she walked down the aisle, or a wonderful time of restoration and magic, *wasn't* going to happen.

This was real life. She couldn't make herself feel different, and she was *not* going to put on a mask and fake it. God calmed her soul, but there was still a lot of healing to be done. No, if they were to have a relationship, it would take time. And it would take both of them.

She forced another smile. "I'm glad you let me meet Shay."

"I'm trying to get on the right track." He stepped back. "Maybe I can."

He grasped Shay's hand and turned toward the door.

"Bye." Shay waved as they walked away. "I'll talk to my mother."

Jessie turned her chair and sent an easy smile her way. "You do that."

Matt hurried back to the table and pulled his chair close to Jessie, wrapping his arm around her shoulder. She slumped against him, and gripped his arm so tight she was sure it hurt him. "Please. Take me home."

Her energy had left. How would she ever make it through the days ahead?

She said little on the way home and once they arrived, went straight to her room. She moved onto her bed, then pounded her pillow into shape.

God, why didn't life turn out like I wanted? Why does everything have to be so hard? I'm tired of trying while life beats me down. Heal my brokenness.

She closed her eyes and spoke into the room's quiet. "And heal Wayne. He needs you."

Later that evening, Jessie turned off the light and worked herself into the bed and under the covers. Their shelter offered little comfort against the day's events that replayed in her mind. She still had no answers. Somehow, she would survive this just as she had all the years spent in the chair, times of teasing at school, the stares of others. She would keep her eyes on Jesus, the one who guided her when she couldn't see.

Shay's bright smile flashed by. A sister. It was her last memory before fading off to sleep.

Chapter Twenty

Jessie opened her eyes slowly. Bright sunshine peeked through the blinds in her room. Her ceiling fan made lazy circles with a slight tick as the pull chain tapped against the globe. She adored sleeping under the breeze they made. She would have to get Matt to put a ceiling fan in their bedroom

Their bedroom. Tomorrow would be the wedding, then the honeymoon. Her mouth grew dry. She *had* to talk to Millie.

She mentally went over her to-do list for the day. Decorate the church at ten, a mani-pedi at two, and rehearsal at four. The day hadn't even started yet and already weariness crept over her. She rubbed her temples. *It's the stress from Wednesday.* She had to put it behind her and move on.

Time for a hot shower and hair-washing. That always helped. Within the hour, she finished and dressed in jeans and a fuzzy pink sweater. She stole a look in the mirror, her reflection reminding her of Shay. The sister she'd never known about, just like her father had never known about his sister.

Her father … she'd almost forgotten about Wayne. Well, for a few minutes, anyway.

Mamaw entered her room, carrying a load of laundry she laid on the dresser. "You look real nice. Are you all ready?"

"I think so. I wanted to have everything close to done, because I won't have much time before the rehearsal dinner. And you know how Pam loves to take pictures." Jessie cleared her throat. "I love Matt's mother, but I wish she wasn't such a shutterbug."

"It'll be fine. I'm just glad Matt's family decided to have the rehearsal dinner at The Riverview Senior Center."

"Me too. It's so close to the church," Jessie said. A frown creased her heart. "Are you sure you're not doing too much? I worry about you and Papaw."

Mamaw stopped in the doorway. "Now don't fret about us. We'll have plenty of time to rest after the wedding. Your papaw is ready to be finished with all this, but … I'll admit he is also concerned about the weather." She looked toward one of the windows. "It's just too warm for November and they're thinking the cold front is supposed to come in tomorrow. I'm afraid it'll be a stormy wedding day."

Jessie released a sigh. *Unsettled weather? Then it'll fit right in.*

***

Angeline punched the order into the computer. Five turquoise bridesmaid dresses for a February wedding. She glanced at the clock. Nine-thirty already. She and Estelle were going to be late to decorate the church. Couldn't be helped.

She still had to place the wedding gown order for Savannah Leland's cousin, Felicia, onto the delivery truck. Felicia was already on her way to Tampa for her beach wedding.

How in the world someone could leave their gown for a few final touches to be overnighted was beyond her ability to understand.

She called into the back room. "Estelle, is Felicia's dress almost ready?"

"Just finished." Estelle hurried through the door. "It's folded and bagged on the small table. I've got to run to Lulu's Fabric. I'll be back in a minute."

The bell on the door jangled, startling Angeline. She glanced up to see Ben sauntering over to the counter.

"Hey …" he drawled. "You ready for this wedding?"

"Not quite." The store's phone rang for what seemed like the tenth time that morning. "We're behind on everything." The phone rang again. "Hold on." She drew a deep breath and answered. "Central City Creative Clothier. How can I help you?"

Ben leaned against the counter. She tried to focus on the call, but his beautiful green eyes fascinated her. Between his musky cologne and well-fitting shirt, concentration proved nearly impossible. She blinked and diverted her attention to the countertop.

"For an anniversary dinner next month? Hold on and let me pull up the schedule." She scanned the calendar on the computer. They should have time, though the fitting might have to be on a Tuesday.

Ben drummed his fingers near where she tried to work. She looked up through her lashes. A slight smile graced his face and, from her close view, the few freckles on his nose made him that much cuter.

"Oh, yes, ma'am. I'm still here." She blushed and Ben's grin widened. Caught again. "I think we can do that … Can you come in Tuesday at two? … Yes, we're closed on Mondays … All right. I'll need some information please."

The bell jangled again, catching her attention. The delivery truck. Of course. When it rained … "I'm sorry. How do you spell your last name?"

"I'm here to pick up a delivery." The woman glanced at her clipboard, then back at her vehicle, which blocked in several cars. "And I need to hurry so I can move the truck."

Angeline glanced at the large pre-postage box at her feet … she hadn't managed to put the wedding dress in it and seal it up. "Hold on, ma'am," she said to the caller on the phone. She covered the mouthpiece of the landline with her hand. "Ben, could you grab that white garment bag for me from the table in the back? Please?"

He bowed slightly. "At your service."

Angeline returned to her call, trying to ignore the delivery lady. "Okay. The street address please." She typed it in, then reached for the box, laying it on the counter. "And that's Central City? … Yes … Now a phone number."

A horn blasted outside, catching everyone's attention. Ben stepped back into the room, handing Angeline the large white bag. She juggled the phone between her ear and shoulder while carefully arranging the bagged dress in the box, then sealed it, and added tape for extra protection. She handed it to the delivery lady who grabbed the box and hurried out the door.

"Yes, ma'am," she said, returning her full attention to the call. "We'll see you on Tuesday." Angeline hung up the phone and shook her head. "Whew."

"I didn't know you stayed so busy here," Ben said. "You're coming to the rehearsal dinner, aren't you?"

"No, I'm going to Lenora's in the mall for a manicure around eight. Look at these nails." She held out her fingers. "They need some serious attention."

"How about I meet you there later?" Ben said. "Right after the dinner we're taking Matt to Slider's to watch the high school championship game. I'll leave early."

Her heart pitter pattered. *Don't blow this. Just play it cool.* "You can if you want. But I have too much to do tomorrow to stay out late. I'll be helping Estelle at the church before the wedding."

"All right. See you there." He winked, then turned to push through the door, holding it open for an approaching Estelle.

Angeline watched him cross the road and climb into the Charger.

Estelle raised her eyebrows. "He's a nice-looking young man, isn't he?"

Angeline cleared her throat. *Nice-looking* was putting it mildly. "He is."

"Did you get the dress shipped?"

"Yes, ma'am."

"Okay. I know it's Friday but I told Sophia and Lenora to take the day off so we could help decorate the church. When we get back, we'll take the dress and train over to Jessie's house."

"Sounds good." Angeline shut down the computer, then followed Estelle out the door, her mind still on Ben. Finally, a guy she could trust. Maybe one day her mother would get a son-in-law and that grandbaby she always harped on about.

***

Millie trotted past Jessie and added another basket of orange chrysanthemums to the right of the simple arch, which had been placed in front of the prayer altar. She and Matt would soon repeat their vows to each other there. A lifetime of promises she intended to keep.

Angeline and Estelle were beautifying the fellowship hall for the reception, alongside Amy and Sarah, leaving Millie and Jessie to add the final touches in the main sanctuary.

The blend of live autumn leaves and the mums from the florist contrasted with the light green seating in the auditorium. Jessie glanced back at the entryway. Two old pieces of picket fence stood on each side of the door, wrapped in ivy and leaves with more mums in pots beside them. Orange tulle decorated the end of each row of seats and brown ribbon adorned the baskets at the arch. A dream wedding.

"Oh, Millie, it's more than I could've imagined."

Millie circled the room, taking it all in. "Yes, I think it's perfect." She glanced at the list in her hand. "The florist will bring the bouquet, boutonnieres, and corsages for the parents and grandparents first thing in the morning. I told her to put them in the extra refrigerator in the back storage room so no one will mess with them. Not like I think anyone will. It's all in order."

She slid into a seat by Jessie, kicked off her clogs, and rubbed her right foot. "Whew. I've got to sit a minute. Now tell me what's troubling you. You've been way too quiet. Is it your father?"

Jessie picked at her fingernails. Their meeting still played in a continual loop in her head. But something was more pressing. "No. I have to let that go. I can't deal with it now." She shrugged. "After Matt and I return—um—from the honeymoon ..." She felt the rush of heat in her cheeks. "Then, I'll think about it."

"So, then what is it?"

Jessie took a deep breath. Let it go slowly. "All right. Here goes. I'm a little nervous about tomorrow night."

"*Oh.*" Millie nodded. "And I'm guessing you don't mean the wedding reception."

"Hardly." Jessie pressed her elbows against her sides. "I love Matt so much. I don't want to disappoint him. What if he—well, he—I might not—well you know—" Her voice trailed. A bead of sweat formed above her lip. Had someone turned up the heat?

"I fought the same thoughts when Tony and I got married. I mean, Tony had a less than stellar past and I wondered if I would measure up to the girls he had been with before."

"I didn't know." Jessie gulped. Matt said there had been no one else. But after the whole Angeline thing, had he been honest with her?

"Well, it's something he's not proud of. Especially since he became a Christian." Millie patted Jessie's hand. "That's between us."

"But you're normal and I'm not." Jessie glanced at her useless legs. "It couldn't be as hard for you."

"None of us are normal, sweetie." Millie leaned forward. "Everyone has hang-ups and differences, but Matt loves you. He's going to be thrilled to be with you, and if you love him with all your heart, you'll meet his needs." She cocked a brow. "That's what you're bothered about, huh?"

"Yeah." Jessie felt new heat rise in her cheeks, all the way from her belly. Someone had *definitely* messed with the thermostat in the church.

"You and Matt will work through this like you have every other challenge you've faced. I mean, look what a nice home you have. I'm so glad I came by last night to see it. When you get back from your honeymoon, I'll help decorate if you want."

Jessie relaxed. "That'll be great. If we have time before Saturday, we'll add a few pieces of the furniture we've found that's put in storage. But if not, that's fine. Anyway, I can't wait to see the Smokies. I know it's gorgeous and Matt rented a cabin for us that overlooks a lake. I'd like to see Cades Cove and Gatlinburg."

"I don't know how much time you'll get to sightsee." Millie chuckled and slipped her shoes back on. "I don't remember us leaving the room too often."

Jessie gulped. There it was again …

Behind them, the church doors opened and Matt and Ben stepped inside. Matt walked halfway up the aisle and let out a whistle. "Wow. Looks like a different place."

"Isn't it wonderful?" Jessie said.

He surveyed the room. "Real nice. I believe we could get married here."

A grin broke on Ben's face. "How about the rehearsal dinner first?" His hands came to rest on his hips. "Hey, we stopped at Matt's, and the men are out back smoking a ham for tonight. And you wouldn't *believe* the rest of the food. Corn on the cob, chocolate cake, creamed potatoes."

"I know how good Matt's family cooks," Jessie said. "I've eaten there on Thanksgiving."

Angeline peeked around the doorway just beyond the prayer altar. "Hey, Jessie. We need you all to come see what you think. We're close to being finished."

Millie stood. "On our way."

Angeline led them down the hall and into the large fellowship room. Floral arrangements of sunflowers and cattails adorned the tables for a country-themed reception. The groom's table had burlap and wheat for decoration and another fall arrangement with a picket fence adorned a focal point along the back wall.

"Y'all did such a good job," Jessie said. "I hardly recognize this room."

Matt crossed the room. "What's this piece of fence for?"

"Decoration. We'll take some of our pictures there. And when they bring the food with our sunflower wedding cake, the fruit and vegetable table and the chocolate strawberries on your cake, everything will be a country dream."

The bride's table stood in the center and would draw all attention tomorrow. Jessie imagined the four-tiered fondant cake decorated with live sunflowers and brown ribbon. She clasped her hands to her chest. Wonderful.

When Angeline laughed, Jessie turned to see Ben standing close to her, pointing to something out the window. Probably his all-important ride. Could Angeline and Ben actually become a couple?

And was Ben a *good* influence? Angeline hadn't been at church lately. She'd shown interest at first. But did she know God?

She clasped Matt's hand. "Everything is as finished as it can be here. And it's nearly time for my nail appointment."

"Your wish is my command." The corny line rolled from his lips. "See y'all this afternoon."

"We'll lock up. Don't worry." Millie shooed them toward the door. "Matt, drive careful."

Jessie couldn't contain her smile. Everything was almost in place for their day, the happily ever after she'd wondered about coming true since the accident. Nothing could stop it now.

***

Angeline glanced at her watch. They needed to hurry. Closely followed by Estelle, she crossed the church parking lot and climbed into the car. Estelle opened the passenger door and slid inside, then fastened her seat belt. "We need to go back to Central City and pick up Jessie's dress."

"I was thinking the same thing." Angeline pulled a pack of chewing gum from her purse and offered Estelle a piece before putting the car into drive. "Things are pretty well wrapped up here."

She turned on the highway toward Central City wondering if she should have accepted a date with Ben after the rehearsal. Well, it wasn't a *date*. She'd only agreed to wait for him at the mall. She turned to Estelle. "I need some advice."

"Sure, hon."

"Do you ever have a choice to make with a lot of options, and don't know which one is right?"

Estelle smiled. "Often."

"How do you know what to do?" Angeline tapped her hand on the steering wheel. "To start with, first thing this morning my mother called. I haven't heard from her in months. She says she's lonely and wants me to come by Sunday. Until today her social life met her needs. And Ben. I've been burnt so often by trusting guys. I mean, once upon a time I tried to live right, but guys ignored me. Then when I changed, well, it didn't turn out too good either. All this gives me a headache."

"If I were you," Estelle said. "First I'd ask God for wisdom. Then I'd listen to my heart and see if I had peace about what to do."

"But I don't know if God hears me." Angeline sighed. "I asked Him to not let my dad die after he had the heart attack, but he died anyway."

Estelle laid a hand on Angeline's shoulder. "I don't understand why things happen sometimes. But I know God does listen to someone sincerely seeking Him. He doesn't turn anyone away. Even when we don't understand His ways, we can trust He has our best in mind."

"I feel judged at church," Angeline blurted.

"Then *people* have a problem and not you." Estelle shook her head. "No one should judge anyone or their motives in a condemning way. That's between them and God. Now, about your mother. Do you want to see her?"

"I don't know. Part of me wishes we could have a relationship, but the other part is tired of being hurt. The same thing goes with Ben." Angeline passed through the last green light before they reached the shop.

"I think it's time to step out and take a chance again," Estelle said. "This time you have friends to back you, real friends, like me and the Smiths if it doesn't work out. And in time, I believe you will receive acceptance and love in your life."

Angeline gripped the steering wheel. Acceptance and love. Could it happen to someone with her past?

Chapter Twenty-One

Angeline grabbed the door to the Creative Clothier, the wind working just as hard to tug it from her hand. "I wish this weather would make up its mind. Cold one day, hot the next. Now this wind."

"That's just the South." Estelle laughed. "Check the messages while I get the dress."

Angeline looked at the old-fashioned answering machine on the desk, but the counter said zero. "No messages."

"Angeline." Estelle's voice was sharp. "Come here."

Angeline scurried through the door to the sewing area. Estelle stood by the small table, clutching a tea stained gown, a white garment bag at her feet. "This is Felicia's dress. Where is Jessie's?"

"What?" Angeline gripped the chair beside her, her breath gone. Her mind replayed the morning, the phone, the delivery truck, the gown in the white bag.

She groaned. She *couldn't* have.

Ben couldn't have.

"No."

"I told you Felicia's was on the small table. Jessie's was on the cutting table." Estelle released the gown to its fullness. "Yes, they're similar, but this one has a different lace around the neckline and no ribbon. How could you ship it?" She sank into a chair. "We've got to get it back."

Angeline ran back to the computer, scanned the list of numbers and dialed. "Hello. I had a delivery picked up at the Creative Clothier, a rush order. I need it back ... You already shipped it? ... But I— ... Yes, I understand."

The phone slipped from her hand, onto the counter. Jessie's dress was on its way to Florida. She shuddered. They would *blame* her. Say

199

she did it on purpose.

Estelle moved beside her, gown still in hand. "Could they—?"

"No." Angeline shook her head. "It's too late. And it's all my fault." Tears slid from her eyes. She'd ruined Jessie's wedding, just like she'd vowed to do the day Homer Smith walked into Bentley's.

But back then she'd hated Jessie. Now her only hatred was toward herself. She buried her face in her hands. "Stupid. Stupid."

"That won't help." Estelle slipped her arm around Angeline. "First, I have to get this dress to Felicia and then we have to tell Jessie. Then we'll think of something. I still have the train anyway."

"You—you go ship the dress. I'll go to Jessie's house. I can't tell her on the phone." Angeline grabbed her purse. She had to go, even though Jessie would never forgive her.

And she'd never forgive herself.

Never.

***

Homer sat on the porch, fanning himself with the magazine he'd just pulled from the mailbox. Still too hot. From down the road a piece a gray car raced over the dirt, stirring up a cloud of dust. The vehicle flew up their driveway. He stood. Had something happened? Not another car wreck. He couldn't swallow.

The girl who used to work for Bentley's climbed out of the car. What was her name?

"Mr. Smith." She hurried toward the house, face all a-panic, but stopped short of the porch. "Is Jessie here?"

"We're expecting her and Matt back at any time. Is something wrong?"

Martha opened the screen door and joined them. "What is it?"

To his dismay, tears that pooled in the girl's eyes made a hasty descent. "I—I'm Angeline, remember? I work with Estelle at the Creative Clothier." She went on to explain the terrible mistake she'd made in regard to Jessie's wedding gown. "Now I don't know what to do."

Martha stepped from the porch and stood beside the shaken girl, hand clutched to her heart. "You—you *lost* Jessie's dress?"

"Not exactly. It's just not *here*." Angeline brushed her cheeks with the back of her hand. "I can't believe I made such a mistake. I'm so stupid. Go ahead. Hate me. I deserve it."

Homer closed his eyes. No dress. Was God playing some kind of cruel joke? Or was this girl just acting? She had been awful mean at Bentley's.

Lord, is there anything I can do?

He opened his eyes and stared at the dark green glider beside him. Then he trudged down the steps, passing Martha and Angeline and walked toward his truck. Before he opened the door, he turned back. "When Matt and Jessie get here, send them to the green shed on Uncle Seth's land."

Martha threw up her hands. "Homer, have you lost your mind?"

He shrugged, half-heartedly. "Just send them."

He started the truck then drove from the house. He tuned out everything, barely aware of the road. Soon the green shed appeared. He parked and got out of his truck.

The shed door protested as always when he turned the key. Jessie would be here soon. He entered, found the pink tote, and set it up on the rickety card table nearby.

Soon enough, the noise of a car outside told him they were here.

"Papaw?"

A sudden coldness attacked the core of his being. He turned to the doorway, gripping the shed post near him. He couldn't hide what he'd done anymore.

***

Jessie pushed through the doorway, Matt behind her. She covered her mouth with her hand then lowered it. Her dreams had shattered once again, when Angeline told them what happened. Matt accused her, but Jessie stopped him. It wouldn't help. Instead she said all the right things and left Mamaw to comfort Angeline.

But why did Papaw want her *here*? What was he concealing in this old shed?

"The lions outside used to stand by your trailer. Do you remember?" Papaw still gripped the post, face sagging into more wrinkles. He pulled a handkerchief from his pocket. "When you and your mama lived there, she liked these lions at the nursery and I got them for her."

A flash of a memory came. "Maybe I do. They seem familiar. But what is all this? Papaw, I'm tired of your secrecy. You're the one who paid Jeff to mow this yard, aren't you? What are you hiding?"

"Nothing. I mean, I did let the boy mow the yard." He wiped his brow with the handkerchief still in his trembling hand. "And I've been meaning to tell you about this place. I—I couldn't bring myself to."

"Tell me now." Jessie pulled herself straight in her chair and pushed toward the nearest plastic container. "What are all these totes and the wrecked motorcycle?"

Papaw glanced around. "Your mother's things. *And* Wayne's."

She gasped. This junk belonged to her parents? She sought to push through the cobwebs of her childhood memories, but failed. Nothing was familiar here. Only the lions outside.

Jessie rolled up to Papaw. "You told me all Mama's things were destroyed by the bad storm while I was still in the hospital. Why did you lie?"

"I didn't lie. Not exactly. The outbuilding was wrecked. But I was able to save the totes, so I brought them here to Uncle's old shed. And the motorcycle was in my way in the barn."

"And Mamaw didn't tell me either." Jessie hugged herself and rubbed her arms. Lies. Everyone lied. Wayne. Papaw. Mamaw. Even Matt. How many more secrets could there be?

Homer wiped his hand over his forehead. "Martha didn't know, since she stayed with you all the time. She never knew. I was going to tell you both when I was ready."

"When you were *ready*?" Jessie's voice echoed in the small space.

"Why would you do this to me? I deserved to know. It's my mother's stuff."

Homer walked away from her and stood beside the broken motorcycle. "I know. But you have to believe me. I did it to protect you."

Jessie stifled a scream. "How could a *lie* protect me? By withholding the memories of my parents? I'm not a child anymore. I'm a grown woman about to be married."

The pain tousled in Jessie's stomach. If only she could vomit. Her parents' effects, locked away in a building, less than five miles from where she lived, and he'd never told her.

"I—I only wanted what was best for you. I was stubborn, I guess. I couldn't forgive myself for not keeping you safe. If I'd been more careful, the car wreck might not have happened. I couldn't stand to look at these things."

Jessie folded her arms over her stomach. "Papaw, how crazy. Mama was grown. You couldn't have stopped the wreck. And we could have worked through this together."

If she'd only been given the chance.

"And I couldn't forgive your father either." Homer walked across the room. "I mean, after the accident he came to the hospital. When he heard the doctors say you were paralyzed, he just up and left." Homer slammed his fist against the metal wall. "The coward. Left it all on me and Martha. How *could* I forgive him?"

"So, this shed is like a shrine to Mama and revenge aimed at my father?" What had he been thinking? "You blamed God and tried to fix this yourself, and it's nothing but a great big mess."

She turned to Matt. "I've got to get out of here. Help me."

He crossed to where she was and grasped the wheelchair handles. She closed her eyes and covered her face with her hands then moved them when someone grasped the arms of her chair.

Papaw.

"Jessie. Listen to me." His face had reddened, and his hands shook. His voice, however, was strong and sure. "You've never been married, child. You've haven't yet known the joy of holding your own baby in your arms, a feeling more special than life itself. My *only* child. Only one God blessed me and your mamaw with. And to have the life of that child when she's still just a young woman ripped away from you in a moment. You've never stood beside your only child's casket, and gently pushed the hair from her face as you said good-bye for the last time."

It was more than she could bear. "Oh, Papaw."

Tears trickled down his cheeks. "I need you to forgive me."

She could … if God could. But would God hear the cry of the man who'd turned his back on Him? *I already have.* The words flowed through her heart, a whisper of hope. Her shoulders lightened and a weight lifted.

She reached for the hand of the man who'd done so much for her. "I forgive you. How could I not? You and Mamaw have done everything for me. You've given up so much." She squeezed his hand. "But you still should have told me."

"I should have. I'm sorry." He walked over to the pink tote, lifting the lid. "Here, maybe you could use this."

Jessie inhaled as he pulled a champagne gown from its container, careful to keep it from the ground. "Is that my mother's?"

"It is." He handed it to her. "Maybe Ms. Granger can do something with it. Your mama weren't no bigger than you when she married."

She hugged the gown to her, closing her eyes and breathing deeply. Hand lotion. A floral perfume. A memory unfolded like a late winter buttercup captured by a slow-motion camera.

"Mama." Jessie stood, looking in the closet in her parent's bedroom. "Is this your wedding gown? Please try it on. I want to see you in it."

She turned from the folded pile of laundry on the bed and shook her head. "I don't have time."

Jessie shifted from foot to foot. "Please. Pretty please."

"All right." Mama smiled and the corners of her eyes crinkled in a way that Jessie loved. "Close your eyes and I'll surprise you."

Jessie placed her hands over her eyes, being careful not to peek. It was such a beautiful gown.

"Okay." Only a few moments had elapsed. "You can look."

"Oh, Mama." Jessie's eyes widened seeing her mother dressed like a princess. "You are so pretty."

Mama's face lit up. "Thank you, darling." She pulled her long chestnut hair to one side so it cascaded over the strapless vision of champagne lace.

"Come look." Jessie pulled her into the bathroom and pointed at the mirror. "See how pretty?"

Mama didn't say a word. Her smile faded, replaced by a single tear.

Something inside Jessie broke. She'd made Mama cry. "I'm sorry. I'm so sorry."

"For what?" She brushed the tear aside. "I'm okay. Really."

But she wasn't. Jessie could never hurt her like that again. She needed to do everything right.

"Jessie." Matt's voice scattered the memory. "You okay?"

She opened her eyes. "I—I could see Mama. She was so real, like I could reach out and take her hand again."

Somehow her perfectionist tendencies now made sense. Had she taken her mother's happiness on as her responsibility? She glanced around. Maybe more memories would awaken through her mother's belongings and she could work her way through them.

"Uh, Jessie." Matt glanced toward the door. "I know this is all overwhelming, but—"

Jessie drew in a breath. "We have a wedding tomorrow." She held the dress tighter. "We have to see what Estelle can do with Mama's dress."

They followed Papaw back to the house, and a sense of security settled over her. She had a family now and finally a connection to a family back then. The past and present joined hands and walked in unison.

This was what it was like to belong.

Chapter Twenty-Two

Angeline glanced at her phone for at least the tenth time. Three-thirty. The clock on the wall of the Creative Clothier read the same. "Jessie, you and Matt better be on your way to rehearsal."

"Yes, dear. Go ahead." Estelle laid another pattern piece on the table. "Mr. Lindon at the dry cleaner should be calling any minute." She straightened, placing her hands on her hips. "It was so sweet of him to put cleaning the dress ahead of everything. And I have this pattern to go by. You saw how well the gown fits already."

"You're right." Jessie's voice trembled. "I'm ready."

After they were gone, Angeline slapped the counter. She hadn't missed the tremor in Jessie's hand or the hollow smile she wore. Sure, Jessie told her she understood, but could anyone?

Really?

She had ruined Jessie and Matt's wedding day before the day even came.

Nothing could change that. Her mother's gown was presentable, but nothing next to the extravagant one Estelle created. At least the train's color would coordinate with this one. The only saving grace of this whole day.

"Angeline. Come here." Estelle motioned. "Sit."

Angeline plopped onto the hard chair. "Yes, ma'am."

Estelle pulled another chair close. "Listen. We're going to get this done. The measurements are close. Just a tuck here, a small hem—"

"I *wrecked* their wedding." Angeline shook her head. "Everyone can be nice about it, but this is—is like the stupidest thing anyone's ever done. I shipped her dress away to *Florida*."

"It was an accident, a mistake." Estelle crossed her arms. "Or are you above making mistakes?"

"Well, no—"

"Then don't read more into it. I'm looking at it as a blessing in disguise. Now Jessie will marry Matt in her mother's gown, something old *and* precious beyond words. If Mr. Smith would have been honest before this, Jessie probably would have married in that dress anyway. He'd never gone to Bentley's, you'd still be working there, and I wouldn't have realized my dream. So, yes, I loved the dress I made her, but this will be even more special."

Angeline bit her lip. She would still be at Bentley's, cold and cowed under Francine's leadership. Her life had taken a turn for the better over the summer. Still ... "But all the people who helped provide for the dress. What will they think when she marries in another?"

"I've thought of that already. We'll pay Lulu's and the others for their donations, and Jessie's dress will be our showcase gown when we get it back. She won't mind posing in a picture I'm sure."

"And I'll pay them out of my check." Angeline breathed easier.

The phone rang. "Now that's probably Mr. Lindon. Go pick up the dress and let's get started."

Angeline took the call, then hurried across the square to the dry cleaners. She would do all she could to help Jessie and Matt with the wedding. In some small way, maybe it would make amends.

It would take all afternoon to finish the dress. There'd be no time to get her nails done now. She'd have to cancel the appointment.

Oh ... Ben.

She passed the post office and stopped walking, pulled out her phone, and typed a text explaining what had happened, then hit SEND.

A moment later, her phone chimed.

Can I come by the shop later?

Angeline allowed a small smile and keyed in an answer. *If you want to.*

She dropped the phone into her purse. It wasn't the same as a date, but no matter. Nothing was more important than finishing the dress and atoning for her mistake.

She deserved to suffer.

***

Jessie crossed her arms to still her unsteadiness. Millie scurried sock-footed to the front of the church, adjusting a sagging bow on one of the seats along the way. Estelle would fix the dress. After rehearsal, she'd try it on. Everything would work out. So, then why wouldn't her mind accept it?

Millie rapped on the podium with a rolled-up newspaper. "Attention, people. We need to go through this one more time."

A few groans echoed through the room. They'd run through the entire ceremony twice already.

"I don't think I can wait any longer." Jessie rolled up alongside Millie. "I want to check on the dress. Anyway, the natives are getting restless." She glanced at Ben, Matt, and Stu who laughed near the foyer door. "And hungry, I'm sure."

"Okay." Millie moved the podium over a few inches. "Jessie says we're good. Now on to the senior center for a delicious supper." The room quickly emptied.

"Make sure and save me some ham," Matt called out to Ben. "I told Mom to start without us. We'll be there as soon as we can."

Millie turned in the direction of the fellowship hall. "I'll be back in a minute. I want to take one last look. I'm *so* glad you're using silk flowers for all the arrangements. Now we don't have to rush here early in the morning and set up." Millie skipped to the back, still shoeless.

Jessie watched her retreating figure. "I don't know what I'd have done without her."

"Uh-huh." Matt stole a kiss. "How are you holding up?"

"I'll be better when the dress is ready." She surveyed the room. "Everything has turned out good. Looks nice. But—"

Matt clasped her hand, massaging out the tightness. "But what?"

She gazed into his eyes. He loved her, and really cared. Nothing else mattered. "No. I'm not going there. I was going to say I wish the dress wasn't on its way to Florida. I wish my father and I could have worked something out. And I wish I wasn't in this chair, and my mother was alive. You see? It never ends." Jessie clasped her hands together and sighed. "I can't go back and live in regret anymore. I'm going to be grateful for the people who are in my life. No more could have or should have. It is what it is."

Matt leaned over and kissed her again and they were lost in the moment until a throat cleared.

Millie stood nearby, arms crossed, tapping her foot. Jessie stole one more kiss, then smiled. "Is everything set in the back?"

"It is." Millie slipped on her shoes. "Now, go try on the dress and hurry back to the dinner. We have a wedding to attend tomorrow." Millie snatched up her oversized purse and headed toward the door.

She and Matt followed. She paused at the doorway for one more look at her autumn wedding. Tomorrow at this time, she'd be on her way to the mountains. And she would be Mrs. Matt Jansen.

***

The noise escalated to a notch below unbearable at Slider's, the championship game tied at halftime. Matt pushed the plate of wings toward Stu. "Here, I can't eat these. I want to live to see my wedding."

They'd met Estelle and Angeline at the shop and Jessie tried on the dress with its temporary stitching, as Estelle called it. Of course, Jessie wouldn't let him see her in the dress, but it must have been okay by her reaction. The rehearsal dinner was great, and she'd finally relaxed.

Mr. and Mrs. Smith were taking her home, so he'd joined the guys to watch the ballgame, a bachelor party of sorts.

The last night he'd spend as a single man.

Since he and Jessie had gotten serious in their relationship, his time with the guys had decreased drastically. Ben couldn't believe this didn't bother him, but Matt was ready to marry, raise a family, and start a new chapter in his life.

Stu laughed. "Ben here is the one who ordered blazing, not me.

Who's he talking to over there?"

Ben leaned against the bar, pointing at the television screen to his right as an oversized, rowdy man placed a hand on his shoulder.

Mike Peters from Central City High, back in the day. Matt shook his head. Someone out of Ben's past he could do without. Mike pulled many of the football team into his *party* mentality, and as a result, they had a losing record their senior year. Ben needed to watch his back.

Maybe Matt needed to watch it for him.

"Come on. One more drink." Mike's voice boomed above the noise of the overhead televisions and crowd of excited fans

Ben shrugged his shoulders and took the tall glass from the buzzed man. He swallowed it down and wiped his mouth on his sleeve.

Matt grimaced. Not good. If Ben didn't slow down, he wouldn't be able to walk out of the place.

Mike grabbed a glass from the bartender and handed it to Ben. Time to do something. Matt walked over.

"Hey, if it ain't the teetotaler from high school." Mike pushed against Matt. "Heard you were getting married."

"Yeah, Mike, I am." Matt grasped Ben's arm. "Come on, man."

"Hey, who are you? His daddy? Let him have some fun." Mike swung an awkward punch at Matt, but he sidestepped it. Instead, it landed on a woman's shoulder.

The woman clutched her arm. "Hey, watch it." The man beside her pushed Mike against the bar. Matt dodged another man who also tried to settle Mike down.

Stu turned from the television and headed across the room toward them. He grabbed Ben's other arm and together Stu and Matt maneuvered him toward the door as a burly worker pushed his way toward Mike.

"I think Mike's in trouble." Ben slurred and almost tripped, stumbling out the door.

Matt propelled him toward the car. "Man, what did you drink in there? And how many? You don't want to hang out with a character like Mike." They reached the Charger and leaned Ben against the door.

"Drink? I lost count. Probably whiskey. A jack-n-coke maybe?" He shook off Matt's arm, and struggled to unlock his car with the key. "I—I'm okay. I can drive. I've got to meet Angeline at the shop."

Stu turned to Matt. "You go on home. I'll drive him there and then home. Don't worry. We'll be at the wedding tomorrow."

Stu wrestled the key from Ben. "Hey, you promised I could drive this decked-out ride. Get in and let me see what she'll do." He waited until Ben strapped himself into the passenger's side, then slid into the driver's seat, raced the motor, and pulled out of the mall parking lot onto the main highway.

Matt unlocked his car, looking up when the Charger revved as it sped toward downtown. Better call Jessie so she could warn Angeline.

***

Angeline walked into the front area of the shop. The dress had been easier to alter than she could've dreamed. Finally. She could breathe again. After Estelle sewed in the permanent stitches, she'd drop it off at Jessie's.

Her phone vibrated in her purse on the counter. She pulled it from the handbag, scowling at her fingernails. "Hello."

"Angeline, this is your mother."

Angeline bit her lip. Should have looked to see who it was. "Hello, Mother."

"You haven't called me back."

The whine in her mother's voice unnerved her. "I know. I've been busy."

Maybe lightning wouldn't strike her down for her lies.

"I know you have. I just wondered if you were still going to eat lunch with me Sunday. I know you go to church now. Elaine told me. So I was thinking we could meet about one o'clock?"

Angeline rubbed her forehead. Forgive as you want to be forgiven and move on. That meant her mother, too. "Okay. Do I need to bring anything?"

"No." Her mother sounded stronger. "Just yourself."

"I'll be there." She glanced out the window. Ben's car pulled in front of the shop. "Oh, I've got to go, Mother. Bye."

Her heart fluttered as he stepped from the passenger side. The pale blue in Ben's shirt stood out against his tanned skin and without his ever-present ball cap—well—he looked even better, although ... *wobbly*? Stu jumped out and ran ahead, opening the door.

Ben ambled to the door and pushed past him. "Hey, Angeline."

She stepped from behind the counter. "Hi, Ben. Stu."

"Hey, Ang. You look great." Ben reached over and pulled her close, hugging too tightly.

The smell of whiskey sickened her. She pushed him away. "*What* is your problem?"

"We went to Slider's." Stu shrugged. "And Ben—"

"*My* problem?" Ben moved closer again. "I feel good, baby. We watched the game. You know, took Matt out for his last night before the prison term starts." Ben hooted like a proverbial schoolboy at a football game for several moments.

Angeline's face overheated and she looked over her shoulder toward the back, hopeful Estelle couldn't hear him above the machine.

She backed away, hands on her hips. Drunk. Another guy like all the rest. Let *peace* decide? Well, now she had. "Stu, you better take him home to dry out."

Ben grabbed her arm. "No, I don't want to leave, Ang."

She brought her foot down on his instep. His yelp soothed her feelings. He released her and she pushed him toward the door.

"Ow. Man, my foot." Ben grabbed Stu's arm as he stumbled outside. A police officer checking the mostly empty town square moved in their direction. Would serve him right if he got arrested.

"It's okay, officer." Stu's voice carried as the door closed. "I'm taking him home—"

Angeline leaned against the door. Angry tears streamed down her face. Here was yet another guy who couldn't get his act together. God must be having a good laugh over this one.

She would go to the wedding tomorrow and be civil, and afterward, she'd cut ties with them all. No more church or God or broken promises. It was all a joke.

Estelle sang out from the back. "I'm finished."

"Good." Angeline pushed away from the door and headed toward the back. "Do you need me? If not, I'm heading home."

"You go right on. I'll see you tomorrow."

"Okay." At least she didn't have to explain.

Angeline drove through Central City and stopped at the last red light. Her stomach growled as she spied Callie's Chicken Shack. Angeline pulled into the drive-thru, ordered chicken nuggets, fries, and a sweet tea. A few moments later, she pulled back onto the highway, nibbling the fries.

Her phone rang. She glanced down. Jessie. *I sure don't need to talk to her.*

But the phone rang every three minutes until Angeline finally answered. "Hello?"

"Hey. Are you okay? Matt called and said Ben had been drinking and I should warn you. I called earlier but couldn't get you."

"We were working on the gown, so I probably didn't hear the phone." Angeline lied. "But your warning is too late. Ben hadn't just been drinking. He was smashed. And he's an idiot." She swallowed a sob. "I don't know why I ever trusted him or you or your church or your God. My life's never going to change."

Jessie didn't reply.

Angeline glimpsed the screen. "Are you still there?"

"I'm here. I just don't know what to say. Other than that I'm sorry."

Angeline sighed, regret filling her even as air left her. "It's not your fault. You've been perfect through all this."

"That's the problem. I'm *not* perfect. Maybe quiet so people don't notice, but I've been angry and hurt too. It drives me crazy at times because … my mom isn't here, and … I can't *make* my dad act like I thought he should and him showing up recently only feels like about a decade too late."

Angeline slowed, then pulled into the driveway of her townhouse. "Well, Jessie, you seem to handle it better than me."

"There's only one reason, then," said Jessie. "A change came in my life five years ago when I finally gave up."

Angeline stopped the car and shut off the motor. "What do you mean, gave up?"

"Knowing all the answers. I wanted God to tell me why things happened the way they did. I wanted to understand everything. Put it in a box." Jessie's voice broke. "When I was fifteen, I finally surrendered my need to know. I asked God to be in control because, let's face it, my being in control wasn't getting me anywhere."

Angeline bit her lip. "I'm not doing too well either."

"He can—"

"Look," Angeline said quickly. She couldn't bear a sermon right then. "I have to go. Pray for me." She clicked the phone off and leaned her head against the back of the seat.

"God? *Can* I trust you?"

But her question hung in the air.

Chapter Twenty-Three

Someone knocked at the door. Homer climbed out of the recliner and looked through the screen. Ms. Granger. She carried a large dress bag and two other bags. Elizabeth's gown. He held the door open. "Come in."

Martha and Jessie came out of the kitchen. After a time of greeting, Estelle unzipped the bag, held up the dress, and pointed out the adjustments.

Martha dabbed at her eyes. Homer could only stare, his mind drifting to another wedding, many years ago.

"How do I look, Papa?" Elizabeth whirled around, laughing out loud.

"You're a dream, baby girl. A real dream." His voice cracked then, as she stood in front of him.

He shook his head. That was then. He retreated to his recliner and turned on the weather channel. He couldn't go back.

"Homer, she's going to try it on. We'll be back in a minute."

He nodded as they filed into Jessie's bedroom, then focused on the weather. Still a good chance of storms, some severe. They couldn't be sure whether the storms would hit in early or late afternoon. He hoped late. Real late. The weatherman continued to talk about weather in other parts of the country, but the focus was clearly on the south.

"It fits." Estelle came back through the doorway. "She doesn't want you to see her in it until tomorrow." She blew out a puff of air. "It'll be a busy day."

"Yes, ma'am." He stood and escorted her to the door. "Thanks again. You've helped so much."

"I'm so glad I could," Estelle said. "It's been worth every minute, though I could've used less drama."

Couldn't we all? Homer followed her onto the porch, then waited as she pulled from the driveway down the gravel road. More had happened today than he could process.

He looked at the sky. Stars sparkled in between the cloud cover. The secret was out and they didn't hate him. It sure lifted a load off his mind. Maybe he should think about what Martha said about coming back to church.

Maybe.

***

The dress hung in her closet and the house lay dark and quiet. Jessie rearranged her pillow. *Thank you, God, for the miracles I've seen today. Papaw, the gown, and finally peace. And please God, help Angeline find You. I don't know what else to do or say to her.*

The security light by the barn squeezed its glow through the slits in Jessie's blinds. She shivered and pulled her comforter to her chin. Her last night as a single woman. Soon she and Matt would become one and a new chapter in her life would begin.

This would be a complete cycle from the days after the wreck. After she had awakened back then, she wanted to die. Instead she dealt with the months of therapy. Her shoulders rounded. Her dependence on so many people, especially her grandparents, was what she hated most. She should be taking care of them, not the other way around.

She shook her head. It was time to let everything go—the façade of always being full of joy and bravery through the struggles and trials. True, God gave her courage to battle through the issues, but not as often as she pretended. Instead of trusting people and discussing her shortcomings, she hid them in perfectionism. Since she'd been friends with Angeline, she'd noticed the lack of trust and Angeline's defensiveness. She often acted that way too. Deep down, the fear of being abandoned again never left.

Jessie bit her lip. It wasn't her mother's fault she died in that wreck. Death and abandonment were twin agonies, ones that still hurt. Jessie had covered it up by trying to remain in control. Deep hurt can never be covered though, and the mess oozed through at the most inconvenient times. Now was the time to stop trying and start trusting.

Jessie shifted in the bed, squeezing her pillow tight. Could she still be a Christian while she struggled with these thoughts, feelings, emotions? Why did she keep doing this to herself?

Shame.

Guilt.

Disappointment. Despair. Anguish. Anger. Hate. Disillusionment.

All these emotions screamed inside of her after the wreck, but she'd stuffed them down until they rebelled.

It was now time to free them and accept what her God had to offer.

Freedom.

Acceptance.

Honor. Joy. Grace. Love. Peace. Contentment.

She closed her eyes. *Father God. I'm finished. For too long, I've refused to let go of my past. It's been my control, my will, instead of Yours. I've bottled things inside when I should have handed them to You. You're the only one big enough to hold them, to deal with them. I give it all to You this day. Forgive me.*

Could He really forgive her? Again?

I have. The words whispered to her, caressing her with a love that healed. She lay there several moments, soaking in a peace she'd not felt since ... maybe never.

She flung out her arms, then giggled. Freedom. She had brought the bad to God and He'd covered her with mercy. She had purpose beside the wheelchair and could move forward. Everything might not always be good, but God was. He held her tight as peace replaced anguish.

Jessie pushed the covers from her crippled legs and touched them. A revelation exploded in her heart. Her lack of independence was not her problem. What held her back from trusting God and others was the emotional and mental devastation stemming from the death of her mother and abandonment by her father.

God, I give You my father. Heal him and if possible reestablish our relationship. And I give You my mother. I know You already hold her in Your arms. And please love on Shay.

Jessie's soft whisper filled the room like a melody. "I am free. I am free. I am free, for You are God and You love me."

The pressure lifted even more, and she snuggled back beneath the covers until sweet sleep secured her.

***

Jessie sat on the back porch, hot tea in hand. The cow's low mooing echoed across the field. It was early yet, right at the brink of sunrise. Coral rays of morning slipped over the horizon, mingling with thin clouds. She stared across open pastures, spying Matt's house in the distance.

Today she would marry. Her grandparents were wonderful, but it was time to be out on her own.

A cabinet door banged inside. Mamaw starting breakfast. A stiff breeze dislodged the few leaves left on the oak beside her. The clouds were bunched and speeding by. Storm rising.

She guided her chair into the kitchen where Papaw nursed a cup of coffee at the table.

"Do you two want bacon or sausage with your eggs?" Mamaw placed a skillet on the stove's burner as she reached for a whisk. "They're scrambled eggs."

Papaw pushed back from the table. "Either's fine. I'm going to turn to the weather and see what's happening. It's supposed to rain today."

"And on your day, Jessie." Mamaw clucked. "I'm glad everything's finished at the church. I hope the caterer arrives early enough to get everything inside before the rain hits."

Jessie nodded. "They'll be there at nine so it'll be okay."

Papaw grunted as he stepped into the living room and turned on the television, Jessie behind him.

The weatherman's voice blared into the silence of the room. "It's hard to predict this very unstable weather pattern. The TORCON value for this storm system is a five. Now for those of you who haven't heard of this rating system, five is a medium possibility of a tornado forming. Stay tuned to this station or your weather station apps to keep up with this approaching system."

A commercial broke in, and Papaw turned off the television. "Fifty-fifty chance. I don't have one of those apps to watch the weather at the church, but I bet Ben does."

Jessie held up her phone. "I do and so does Matt."

"You're going to be too busy. I'll get Ben to keep up with it all. Don't *you* worry about it."

"Jessie, do you need any help getting ready?" Mamaw peeked into the living room. "I'm almost finished with breakfast."

"I'm fine, Mamaw. I've had my shower earlier. Millie's going to do my makeup at the church. We need to be there by twelve."

"When are they coming with the chair?"

"At nine." Jessie moved over to look out the window. Matt's truck had turned into their driveway. A lone butterfly tumbled inside of her.

"That's good." Mamaw turned back to the kitchen. "You two come eat when you're ready."

"Okay," Jessie said. "Matt's here."

"I thought you weren't going to see him until the wedding." Mamaw called from the kitchen. "The groom isn't supposed—"

"As soon as he helps me with the chair, I'm sending him on." She pushed to the door. "I'm not counting the day as starting until then."

Matt jogged across the yard and up the steps.

He stepped inside and removed his jacket, tossing it on the arm of the couch. "It's misting rain. Maybe it will quit soon." He bent to kiss her. New butterflies joined in.

"Breakfast is getting cold." Mamaw called from the kitchen. "Y'all come on."

They'd barely finished eating when the wheelchair arrived. It looked similar to the one she currently owned, but white for the wedding.

"You control it from here." The young man who delivered the chair pointed to the push handles. "Just pull beside the chair and you can transfer." He explained the directions and then waited as Jessie scooted into the new chair.

She grasped the handles. In a moment, she'd be standing, eye to eye with her family. Not looking up at them. She licked her dry lips. "Now what?"

"We lock it at your knees and above your waist." He pulled the padded knee supports and locked them into place with a click. The chest support pressed against her ribs as she rested her arms on it. "Now you can't fall, so don't worry about that. Just start pressing the push handles and it will raise you manually."

She gripped the curved metal and applied pressure. Nothing happened. She pushed harder and it moved a little. She released the breath she'd been holding. "I'll have to build more muscle."

"Do you want me to help?" Matt moved forward.

"No. I want to do this. But Mamaw, can you get the full-length mirror please? I want to see myself when I'm standing."

Mamaw left the room and Jessie continued using the pumping motion. Her blood circulated as she rose, causing a moment of lightheadedness but she didn't care. Three more pushes and she stood upright.

Matt stepped in front of her. His mouth widened into a grin. "Wow."

"Come closer." She stretched her arms around his neck and hugged him, then he kissed her. "This is so amazing," she said with a giggle. She glanced at Papaw who scrubbed his hand over his face. Her eyes immediately flushed with tears, but she blinked them away.

Today was her wedding day and she was standing.

Mamaw emerged with the mirror. "Oh, Jessie."

She handed Papaw the mirror and hugged Jessie, then stepped back.

Jessie beheld her image. She was upright with Matt beside her. The white bars would blend in somewhat with her wedding gown, and, after the wedding, she would have real standing photos.

"Thank you so much." She turned to the man who brought the

wheelchair. "You'll never know what this means to me."

"I'm glad we were able to help. One more thing—you reverse the process to lower it." He looked around the room. "I'll be back in the morning to pick it up. Did anyone have a question before I leave?"

"No." Matt reached out and shook his hand. "Thanks again, man."

"Here's my number in case you need me." He handed Matt a card, then turned toward the door. "I'll see you in the morning."

Jessie continued to gaze into the mirror, mesmerized by her standing self.

"One day, I'll get you one of these," Matt said. "I promise."

"I know you will." She lowered herself and practiced moving the chair around the room. The rain beat down harder for a moment, then let up. It didn't matter. It would still be a perfect day.

***

Angeline pulled the Lexus into the parking area beside the catering van. Ben's car wasn't here. Good. He was absolutely the last person she wanted to see, and if she hadn't promised Estelle she'd help, she would have ditched this day.

The rain had let up for a moment so she stepped from her car and smoothed her Ceylon blue dress. Where was Estelle's car? Millie rushed across the parking lot toward her, probably to tell her to leave. She cringed. Well, that was fine with her.

"Angeline." Millie stopped. "I'm glad to see you. I—uh—need to apologize."

"I'm sorry—*what?*"

Millie toyed with her bracelets "Yeah. The other day when I saw you, all I could think of was you hurting Jessie. You know she's my best friend." She shrugged. "Well, she said I acted snobby. I was wrong. Can you forgive me?"

Angeline stared. "Ye—yes, of course." She almost laughed. "I'm not used to people apologizing to me, though."

"You're not? I get to apologize a lot I'm afraid. My mouth runs way out ahead of my brain. Oh, and you're wearing a gorgeous dress. I love the color."

"Thank you. Estelle's not here yet, so … do you need any help?" She turned around at the rumble of a motor. The black Charger pulled into the church's parking lot.

Great.

"Yes. You could give me your opinion on the reception area." Millie trotted toward the fellowship hall door.

Angeline had to be careful in her three-inch wedge heels not to turn an ankle, but she hurried to get inside before Ben parked and got out of the car. There was nothing he could say or she wanted to hear that would make a difference. He pulled up to the fellowship door and hopped out.

"Hey, Angeline, wait up."

Millie giggled. "Well, come in when you're done visiting." She pushed through the door.

Angeline gritted her teeth. There would be no visiting. She turned toward Ben, arms crossed. "I have nothing to say to you."

"I'm sorry, Angeline. Stu said I acted like a real jerk." He rubbed his hand over his eyes. "I'm afraid I don't remember last night too well."

"It's my fault for trusting you. You acted all trustworthy and sweet. Well, you're like all the other guys. Jerks." The fine mist of rain had resumed so she turned to go inside. "I've got to help Millie."

"I don't know what else I can say besides I'm sorry. I mess up a lot, but I keep trying to get my act together." He opened the door for her. "I didn't mean to hurt you."

For a moment, he almost gained her sympathy. His eyes were bloodshot and he squinted, despite the clouds hiding the sun. Probably had a headache to match. Good. Most guys would defend themselves or make excuses. She would give him points for honesty. But he had blown any chance with her.

"I accept your apology. But I need to go." She crossed the hallway into the reception area to where Millie stood. "Now what did you need help with?"

She crossed Ben from her mind. She wouldn't make that mistake again.

Chapter Twenty-Four

A bracing wind whipped Jessie's hair as Papaw helped her from the car parked near the back door of the church. Matt was already there, so she'd texted him to retreat to the groomsmen's room. They wouldn't see each other again until she started down the aisle. Pictures would be taken *after* the ceremony. The old-timey tradition of the groom not seeing the bride was one she wanted to honor.

Papaw opened the church door. "The weather's getting worse, I think. I'm going to ask Matt what he thinks."

"Good idea." Mamaw carried her own dress and Papaw's suit, and fought a gust as it tried to rip them from her hands. "What a wind. I'm glad Deidre's going to fix my hair here."

"Me, too." Jessie pushed through the doorway and untangled her hair with her fingers. Papaw took off in the direction of the sanctuary. She and Mamaw moved to the large adult Sunday school class where they would get ready. Mamaw hung her dress in the corner. "I'm going to run Papaw his suit," she said as Millie burst into the room.

"Oh, good. You didn't back out." She hurried to Jessie's side. "Is that the standing chair? How does it work?"

"Like this." Jessie adjusted the straps, then raised herself slowly to stand. "Isn't it amazing?"

"I can't believe it." Millie reached over and embraced Jessie, then stepped back. "Are you ready?"

"As ready as I can be." She glanced toward a window. "I wish the weather would settle down though."

"Me too." Millie plopped into a chair and kicked off her shoes, pulling a pair of scruffy house slippers from her oversized purse. "When Deidre gets here, I might need her to work on *my* hair too."

Mamaw walked back in and scooted into a chair. "Homer asked Ben to watch the weather reports. I'm afraid we're now under a tornado watch. We should've had the radio on while we were driving over."

Jessie closed her eyes. A "watch" meant a possible tornado, or a thunderstorm with hail.

But possible didn't *mean* it would happen. Not today.

She twisted around to look out the small window. What if her guests stayed away? She so wanted to share this day with her friends and family. "Mamaw, what if no one comes?"

"Now don't worry. This church has a good-sized basement, so people will know they'll be fine if the worst happens. You may even have a few extra people who live around here drop in. I don't know." Mamaw stood again. "I better go to the reception area and see if everything's ready. Matt says the cake is beautiful. Do you want to come?"

Jessie hesitated, then shook her head. "I don't want to run into Matt."

Millie walked to the doorway. "I'll send Sarah and Amy to make sure the hallway stays clear. It will give them something to do until time to get dressed."

A few minutes later, Amy hollered from the hallway. "All clear."

Jessie pushed to the kitchen and gasped. The wedding cake was even more beautiful than she'd imagined. It towered above the table, dripping with sunflowers, brown ribbon and greenery. The four-stack cake had columns which led to two decorated sheet cakes on each side.

"What do you think?" Angeline waved from the corner where she sat tying ribbons.

"It's even prettier than I thought it would be." Jessie moved toward Matt's table. The chocolate cake looked scrumptious, covered with chocolate-dipped strawberries and the Crimson Tide logo on one side. Other team memorabilia surrounded the table.

"Oh, I love the cakes." Mamaw clapped her hands to her cheeks. "I can't believe Ms. Marston did such a wonderful job on such short notice."

"Oh, Mamaw. It's wonderful." Jessie fought the urge to dip a finger into the decadent chocolate icing.

"Martha." Millie's voice floated from somewhere outside the fellowship hall. "I need you."

As she retreated, Jessie joined Angeline. "How are you doing?"

"I'm okay." Angeline twisted another ribbon with green wire. "Ben apologized. And Millie did too. I don't understand why. I probably deserved what I got and so much more. I mean, look at the way I ruined things."

"I'm glad I don't always get what I deserve." Jessie lifted her eyebrows. "I mean, it all worked out, didn't it?"

"I guess. But you still need to have it all together to be a Christian, don't you? I could never do that, so what's the use?" Angeline placed the ribbon on the table and turned to Jessie. "I mean, why even try?"

Jessie drew a full breath. She'd found freedom and now she could share. "It's not that we're perfect in the sense of doing everything right. But we *can* go to God and apologize and start new. God has new mercy every day for His children."

"Children?"

"God considers us His children when we accept Him as Father." She shifted in her chair. How could she put this? "I like to think I'm God's precious daughter."

Angeline's lips pursed as a look of contemplation came over her. "My dad used to call me precious. When he was *actually* home ..." Her voice choked. "But would God think about *me* that way?"

"He does," Jessie said. "You can talk to Him and ask Him into your heart."

"Here?" Angeline looked around the empty room.

"Sure." She clutched Angeline's hand. "Go ahead."

Angeline looked toward the doorway again, then closed her eyes. "God, if I'm really precious to You, show me. I'm sorry for the way I've lived. I want to change, but I'm not sure how." She looked up, eyes shining. "Was that okay?"

Jessie reached for Angeline's hand and squeezed. "More than okay."

Angeline breathed out. "You know ... I don't feel *changed*, but somehow I do feel *better*."

"Change isn't always sudden, though it can be. Some things we have to work out—"

"Jessie." Millie's voice echoed from the other room. "Deidre's ready to fix your hair."

She released Angeline's hand. "I better go. I'm being paged."

Angeline stood. "When I finish these ribbons, I'll join y'all."

Jessie pushed into the hallway. With one simple prayer, her wedding day turned extra special. *Thank you, God. You go above and beyond all I could ask for.*

***

Jessie wheeled back through the doorway and into the classroom. Her soul calmed and most of her fear vanished. She was ready to get married.

Mamaw sat still as Deidre flipped the curling iron to produce the last curl before using a hair pick to lift the dark gray hair and spray it into place.

"Hey, Jessie. Doesn't your grandmother look divine?" Deidre glanced into a hand mirror and fingered her own red spiked hair before handing the mirror to Mamaw.

Jessie nodded. "Your hair is beautiful, Mamaw."

"You think so, darling?" She took the mirror from Deidre. "My, my. It does look nice."

Deidre motioned Jessie over to her makeshift station. "Now, you wanted something simple." She held up a magazine and pointed to a photo. "Half up, half down, like we practiced last week. Right?"

"Sounds perfect." Jessie turned to her grandmother. "Have you heard anything else from Ben about the weather?"

"The rain's stopped and the sun is out. But we're still under a tornado watch—sunshine isn't good on a stormy day." Mamaw glanced at her watch. "I'd better step to the bathroom and change. Too many people in and out of here." She exited the room with her dress.

Jessie's jaw tensed. Sunshine would heat things up and add to instability in the air. Why was it now that her life was becoming more stable the weather wasn't cooperating?

She waited while Deidre combed, curled, pinned, and sprayed her hair into a replica of the photo. Millie then started Jessie's makeup.

Angeline strolled into the room. "Estelle just drove up. Oh, and I love your hair." She handed Millie a tube of lipstick. "Here's the perfect color. Pink Honey."

"Thanks, Angeline." Millie applied the lipstick, covered it with a touch of lip-gloss and stepped back to survey her work. She then handed Jessie the mirror.

Jessie gasped. Was the woman in the mirror really her?

"Well, what do you think?" Deidre leaned forward and tucked a stray hair.

"Oh, my hair is gorgeous." She reached up to touch it, then stopped. "I can't believe it's me."

"You should be on the cover of a bride magazine." Angeline poked her head out the door and shouted. "Estelle. Come on."

A moment later, Estelle hurried into the room. "Oh, Jessie," she sighed. "You look so beautiful."

"Lovely." Angeline unpacked the orange covers they'd made for the wheelchair. "Is it time to put on your gown? I can put these covers on while you get ready."

Jessie glanced at her phone. Five 'til two. "I better go ahead as long as it'll take me. Papaw told me this morning he wanted to talk to me before the ceremony."

Mamaw re-entered the room and shut the door as Estelle unveiled the dress. The strapless gown was fitted and flared at the bottom. So different from the other.

But it had been her mother's.

Angeline covered the wheelchair and attached the veil to its back. Mamaw and Estelle helped Jessie slip into the champagne gown. Millie added tea-stained slippers to her feet for the final touch. Using the handles on her chair, she pushed herself to her feet.

"Oh, Jessie." Mamaw wiped a tear.

"Now, what do you think?" Millie spun the full-length mirror toward her.

Jessie recalled her mother's photo in her journal and her breath caught. The gown fit so well and the veil extended past her shoulders. The second veil, attached to the wheelchair, created a flow, a train of delicate tulle descending to the floor. She couldn't wait to see Matt *and* his expression.

"Can you hold the mirror behind me so I can see the back?"

Millie moved behind her and Jessie twisted to see. From behind, the train covered much of the chair, giving her a momentary illusion of being without it.

"It's wonderful," she whispered.

Mamaw reached over and hugged her long and hard, being careful not to mess up Jessie's hair or makeup. "I love you, darling. Is it okay if I go get your papaw?"

"Please do. But I'm going to lower the chair first. Oh, and hand me a tissue."

"Try not to smudge your makeup." Millie scolded, though her tone was light. "I've got more to do than reapply it. I have a dress to get into."

Jessie released the chair back to its regular position. "I'll be careful."

Millie clutched Deidre's arm. "Are you sure you can direct the wedding after I take my place?"

"We went over this at rehearsal, girlfriend. I got it." She dragged Millie along through the open door. "Let's go get you ready."

Jessie waited alone. What would Papaw say on this extra-special day?

***

Homer slipped the orange tie around his neck. He fumbled with it for several minutes. Aggravating contraptions. Only good for weddings and funerals.

Martha bustled in the small classroom. "Here. Let me."

She smoothed out the mess he'd made into a passable knot. "Now. Jessie's ready for you."

He reached into his coat pocket and wrapped his hand around the small box. It was time.

In a few moments, he knocked at the door, tugging at the tie. "Jessie?"

"Come on in."

He stepped in and stared at her for several seconds, then moved to her side. How could anyone look so beautiful and still shred his heart? So many memories swirled, making him short of breath. He finally spoke. "You look like your mother."

Tears pooled in Jessie's eyes. "Do I?"

"So much." He sank into a nearby chair. This was so hard. "I wish Elizabeth could be here. I remember the joy in her heart, the way she'd make everyone feel like they were the most special person in the world. Do you remember that?"

She reached over and took his hand. "Kinda. My memory isn't too good when it comes to the times before the wreck, but the images I do have are wonderful."

Her hand seemed so tiny in his. "You're every bit as beautiful as I remember her being on her wedding day. I didn't think anyone could ever mend those broken parts of me left by her passing. But you did. From the day we brought you home from the hospital, you've been a joy and delight to me and Martha. Raising you has been like having another daughter."

Jessie dabbed at her eyes with a tissue.

"I don't know if I really ever said it out loud, but I—I love you." He reached into his pocket and removed the box. "I saved this to give to you on your wedding day and now here it is."

She opened the small box and pulled out a delicate silver chain with a small cross on it. She rubbed her finger over the small diamond in the cross's center. "It's beautiful, Papaw. Where did you get it?"

"I'd bought this for Elizabeth to give her on her thirtieth birthday."

His voice cracked. He pulled a handkerchief from his pocket and rubbed his nose. He had to settle down. "But she died a few weeks before, as you know. I put it away for all these years."

Jessie clutched the necklace to her. "I could never ask for a better father than you. You've made up for all I might've missed. I'm sorry I didn't always see it like that. Instead, I chased a dream that's always been right before me." She reached over and hugged him. "I love you, too."

"Now you'll have to get Millie to put that necklace on you. I'm no good at that sort of thing." Homer stood. He'd made it over one more hurdle. "I guess I best get back to Matt. He was seeming a little nervous for some rea—"

A siren's whine split the air in the distance. Homer turned as Jessie's head whipped toward the window. That sound meant only one thing.

Tornado.

Chapter Twenty-Five

Homer stepped outside the room; the piercing blast echoed throughout the church. This couldn't be happening. Not on his baby girl's day. Though the siren stood sentinel a half-mile away, he wanted to cover his ears. He peeked back in the room. "Wait here. I'll see what they're saying."

Several people stepped into the hallway from various rooms, including Martha who joined him. Ben trotted down the hall in their direction.

Homer met him halfway. "What are they saying?"

"A circulation's been spotted less than twenty miles to the east, over near Topton. Hail and high winds could whirl right up into a tornado. They're advising everyone to take cover. What do you want to do?"

"Oh, Homer." Martha clutched his arm. "The wedding."

"It's all right." He patted her arm to reassure her, knowing he had to act fast. "Let's get everyone in the basement. The stairs are over there near the fellowship hall. Ben, can you take Jessie and Martha downstairs please? I'll send Stu so you can carry her chair down the steps."

Martha followed Ben into the classroom as Millie ran down the aisle toward them. She stopped beside Homer. "I'll get a head count when we get there and make sure no one is missing."

"Good. I'll find Stu and Matt." Homer glanced at the small crowd. Angelina and Estelle came from the direction of the fellowship hall, Jessie with them. He couldn't let anything happen to all these people who were so dear to him.

Angeline hung onto Estelle's arm. "I hate storms." Her face had lost all color.

Homer crossed the hallway, lowering his voice to Ben. "Angeline's terrified. Might get hysterical."

"Come on, ladies. Nothing to fear. It's a precautionary warning." Ben put his arm around Angeline's shoulders. "I'm here. We'll be fine in the basement."

"But what about my mother?" Her voice came out as a sob. "She's alone."

"Does she have a storm shelter?" Ben steered her away, out of the range of Homer's hearing.

Homer sped toward the sanctuary, faster than he'd remembered moving in a long time. Tornado warnings were often more of a threat that didn't turn into anything but wind and rain. He couldn't take a chance though. The storms of '74 had carried death and destruction with them, an awfulness even the years couldn't erase.

As he crossed the hallway into the main sanctuary, Matt and Stu herded several people toward him. Matt stopped when he reached Homer. "Did you get Jessie downstairs?"

Homer nodded. "Ben's seeing to it, but he'll need Stu to help with the chair."

"I'm on it." Stu took off with Amy and Sarah following.

"I checked the parking lot, but didn't see anyone else," Matt said. "It's looking rough outside. Surely anyone who gets here later will know to come to the basement."

Homer looked out a nearby window. "They will." He then moved in the direction of the basement, checking each classroom. No one. He turned into the main area where the children met on Sundays. Empty. By now, he reckoned, everyone had heard the alarm and headed downstairs. He reached the basement door.

Pastor Allen emerged. "Homer. Just got my family here. Is everyone downstairs?"

"As far as I know. I've checked the classrooms and Matt looked outside."

They moved downstairs. Pastor Allen's wife Margaret and their two children were standing at the bottom of the stairs, talking to Martha. Matt's family gathered in a corner. A good twenty or so stood or sat in the large area to his right. But no Jessie.

He interrupted. "Martha, where's Jessie?"

"She and Millie and the bridesmaids are in that room over there. Jessie insisted she wasn't going to see Matt until she walked down the aisle. Storm or no storm."

Homer couldn't help but smile. Ah, Jessie …

He and Pastor Allen then joined Ben, Angeline still clutching his arm. At least her color had improved. Ben showed him a radar picture of the county on his iPhone. "They're saying no damage so far, except a few trees down. The problem is there's another outbreak of storms less than an hour behind this one. I doubt they'll lift the warning for quite some time. It says here it could be nightfall before the atmosphere loses this instability."

Pastor Allen grimaced, then shook his head. "Quite a dilemma. You need to talk with your family and Matt's and decide what you want to do. I'm willing to wait it out or even postpone it if necessary. Your call."

Martha stepped to Homer's side and grabbed his hand. "What should we do?"

"I'm not sure. We'll have to ask Jessie." Homer breathed another prayer. *God, help us.*

Angeline jumped as another rumble of thunder sounded. Matt and his dad crossed the room and joined them.

Ben started toward the stairs, but Angeline clung to him.

"Where are you going?"

"I need to make sure no one else has come in. They might not know there's a basement." He gently pulled from her grasp. "I'll be fine. Wait here for me."

Angeline sat in a nearby chair, fixing her eyes on the basement door.

Matt stepped closer to Homer and lowered his voice. "The storm should be here in a few minutes according to the radar. The weatherman said it has lessened in intensity, but they're going to keep the warning up." His brow rose slowly. "Have you told Jessie?"

Homer shook his head. "I was just going to see what she wants to do. What do you think?"

Millie stepped from the other room, followed by the bridesmaids. "Jessie wants Matt to come in there."

"Are you sure?" Matt said. "She was adamant about not seeing me."

Millie frowned. "Well, I guess tornados trump tradition."

Matt crossed to the room as thunder rolled overhead. Homer glanced at the friends and family around him. It would be all right. It had to be.

A door closed above, and Ben trotted down the steps followed by two more people.

Wayne and Shay. Would the storms of this day ever end?

Matt turned. Paused. Martha lifted her fingertips to her lips as Shay flounced down the stairs, her smocked blue dress damp from rain.

Wayne straightened in front of Homer. "Please. I need to see Jessie."

But Homer didn't move.

"Follow me," Matt finally said, then pushed through the kitchen door.

"Stay with me, Shay." Martha reached for the child's hand and led the girl to a chair.

Another crash of thunder and a gust of wind rattled the door leading to the basement. Heavy rain pounded on the building above them. But Homer's focus was on the kitchen door. *God, help Jessie.*

***

Jessie shivered as thunder rattled Mason jars on a nearby shelf. Millie told her earlier it looked like no change in the forecast for several hours, which meant she had a decision to make. Tradition or no, Jessie wouldn't make a decision without Matt.

She glanced up as Matt entered the room, then stiffened.

Her father.

Matt moved behind her, resting his hands on her shoulders. Wayne stopped a few feet away, his eyes glistening as he looked down at her.

Did he recognize the dress?

He cleared his throat. His hands flexed into fists. And then … he shifted his weight until he knelt, balanced on one foot, forearms resting on his knee. "I know I'm the last person you expected to see here. I've done so much wrong in my life, Jessie. For once, I wanted to do the right thing." He glanced toward the door behind him, then back at her. "We drove back today because—because I want to watch my daughter get married." His brow went up. "And hopefully begin to fix things between us."

Matt's grip tightened on her. The man she loved stood behind her, and the one whose blood flowed through her veins but wasn't part of her life knelt in front. The time had come—the time to be real, but not the time to be cruel. "I don't know if we can make things *right* between us. I still have anger and resentment over you abandoning me. I *do* forgive you, but I haven't quite worked through it all. My heart was shattered in a thousand pieces when Mama died. And then you—you just left. It was like you trampled on those pieces as they lay on the hospital floor." She swiped at a tear, only vaguely aware of how crying would mess with her makeup. No more hiding or pretending.

"Jessie—I—"

She held up her hand. "I'm not finished. I lost my faith in a father that day. But Papaw made up for what you didn't give me. He's been the man that for whatever reason you couldn't or wouldn't be." She reached for Matt's hand. "And Matt. He's filled places in my heart by his kindness, his acceptance of me as I am. I might not be whole in body but God has used these men to piece my heart back together. And I know He'll continue to do so."

Wayne nodded. "That's good then. And you're right. I did do all those things. I'm only telling you how sorry I am and that I hope you'll give me one more chance."

Jessie took a minute before she voiced her decision. "Stay for the wedding. I don't know what tomorrow will bring. But I do hope you find the peace you're looking for, whether I'm in your life or not."

With those words, she reached a new place of contentment. Only

God could lavish so much grace in this moment, grace to truly forgive her father and accept her past. She extended her free hand to Wayne.

He stood, took a small step forward and gripped her fingers for a moment. The tears that had glistened before now threatened to spill over. Without another word, he turned and left.

Matt released her shoulders and moved in front of her. "You are amazing, Jessie." Only then did his eyes move over her. "And so beautiful."

She hugged herself. "I could use a little less drama about now."

Matt knelt beside her and grasped her hands. "It's crazy everything's turning out like it is. I don't know if the weather will let up for a while."

"Millie saw the report on her phone." Jessie shrugged. "You know, I told you how I prayed for God to take control the other day? Well, I guess I tried to take it back with this wedding. But you see how well that worked. I can't do this without Him."

"Me neither. And I can't change the weather. Or your father being here."

Jessie leaned forward and kissed his cheek. "I'm peaceful about it all now. Maybe God is beginning that healing I asked for."

"You're one special lady, you know that? But what do you want to do? I don't think the storm will be as bad as we thought. But with another storm right behind it, the warning could stay up for hours. We can't go upstairs for a wedding with a possible tornado around."

"Of course not." Jessie straightened her shoulders. "Get everyone to set up the chairs, and we'll get married down here. Right now. In the midst of the storm. I figure if this is the worst thing that happens to us, our life together will be more than wonderful."

"It will." Matt kissed her again, then stood. "I'll send Sarah and Amy back in case you need anything while we set this place up for a wedding."

After he left and as Jessie waited, a whisper of hope nestled in her soul. Though so much had happened in her life, God had seen her through it all. Another rumble of thunder sounded nearby, but it didn't matter. Her God and her family stood with her.

***

Homer hurried over to Matt as he reentered the room. "Well, son?"

"Jessie and I are ready to have a wedding. Right here." Matt motioned to Millie. "Can you get the basement in shape for the ceremony?"

"Uh." Millie glanced around the white-walled room. "S—sure. Give me a few minutes."

She cupped her hands around her mouth. "Attention, people. We're going to have a wedding." Applause broke out among the crowd. "We need to get those Christmas play props over there placed in the storage room along with anything else in the way. Let's line those chairs on both sides to make an aisle."

Stu and Ben moved chairs. Homer removed his jacket and handed it to Martha as Wayne walked up to him. "I've made a mess of things, Mr. Smith."

Homer crossed his arms. "You did. And being sorry about it won't change the past."

Wayne studied a spot on the floor. "No, it won't."

"I *know* it won't, because it didn't work for me." Homer's voice softened. "No. I've made lots of mistakes, but Jessie forgave me."

"I've missed so much," Wayne said. "Days I can never get back."

"No." Homer shook his head. "You can't. Jessie's a wonderful girl and you didn't get to see her grow up. Even in a wheelchair, she has courage I've rarely seen in adults."

"It's my loss, I know." Wayne shifted. "I think the hardest part of recovery is regret. I can't go back. My counselor, Mike, tells me to focus on going forward."

"Sounds like you have a wise man helping you." Homer smiled as Shay skipped toward them. "And you have a lot to look forward to. Now let's help Millie move these Christmas decorations."

In less than ten minutes, the basement had been transformed into a makeshift wedding chapel complete with leftover Valentine flowers and an arch from the couple's banquet. The photographer and videographer set up their equipment.

"What about music?" Martha turned to Matt.

Matt pointed to Estelle, fumbling with an instrument. "Millie found a small keyboard in the storage room and Estelle plays the organ at her church. And she knows the wedding march."

"Matt, you need to take your place by Pastor Allen," Millie prodded. "It's time to get married."

Chapter Twenty-Six

Jessie grasped Papaw's hand while they waited with the rest of the wedding party in the back room. Millie had touched up her makeup, but she scarcely noticed. Soft, tinny notes of an unknown song drifted to them, a heavenly choir to her ears.

Nothing would stop her marriage to Matt. This day would be unforgettable, but not only because of the storm. Something had shifted in her life. She was no longer Jessie Smith, the poor crippled girl. She had friends, family who would back her to the end, a man who loved her unconditionally, and a God who would love her for all eternity. She was ready to move forward.

The flower girl, on cue, dripped chrysanthemum petals on the basement floor, followed by Amy, Sarah, and Millie. The groomsmen came next, and through the open doorway, Jessie could see Matt, so handsome in his brown suit. Everyone stood on the first notes of the wedding march.

"It's time." She smiled up at her papaw, releasing his hand. She then pushed the wheels, while he walked beside her. Her eyes remained fixed on Matt as if he were the only one in the room. Jessie couldn't help but smile.

The love shining in his eyes erased any lingering doubts. They were prepared to re-enter life as one. She and Papaw stopped a hairsbreadth short of where he and Pastor Allen stood. Mamaw joined them.

"Who gives this woman to be married to this man?" Pastor Allen asked.

"Her grandmother and I." Papaw placed her hands into Matt's then found his spot beside Mamaw on the front row. Jessie carefully pumped the chair until she stood fully facing Matt. Murmurs of approval sounded behind her as she again clasped Matt's hands.

Pastor Allen cleared his throat, then went over the biblical account of Ruth and Boaz and how they were brought together to become one and eventually be in the lineage of Christ. Chris, the church's music minister, followed his words with an inspiring rendition of "I Will Be Here." Each word in the *a capella* song pulled Jessie closer to Matt, knowing he would be there for her.

"Now." Pastor Allen turned to the audience as Matt and Jessie faced each other. "This special couple has something to say to each other."

Matt turned to her. "Jessie, you are the love and joy of my life. Through all of the uncertainties and trials now and forever, I promise to be faithful to you and love you. I will protect and defend you, pledging my everlasting love to you always."

Tears trickled down Jessie's cheeks. "Matt, I love you. You truly are the only one for me in this journey God began twenty years ago. I give you my heart, my life, and a pledge to be ever faithful and loving until death parts us. No matter what lies ahead, God has joined us together and given me an overflow of love for you."

"May I have the rings?" Pastor Allen accepted them from Millie and Matt's father. "The ring is the symbol of the commitment which binds these two together. They symbolize two people, each making a contribution to the life of the other and their new life together. Let us pray. Bless, O Lord, the giving of these rings that they who wear them may abide together in Your peace and love."

Matt slipped the ring on her finger. "I give you this ring, as I give you myself, with love and affection."

Jessie's hand trembled as she slipped the ring on his finger. He now belonged to her. "I give you this ring, as I give you myself, with love and affection."

A sob escaped from someone behind her. Jessie knew without looking that it had come from Mamaw.

The pastor said, "What God has joined together let no man put asunder. I now pronounce you man and wife." He smiled at Matt. "Matt, you may kiss your bride."

Matt reached to Jessie as she wrapped her arms around his neck, caressing his lips with hers for a long moment. Laughter sounded behind them … not that she cared.

With the kiss over, Matt helped maneuver her chair toward their family and friends.

"It is now my privilege to introduce to you for the first time, Mr. and Mrs. Matt Jansen."

Applause and cheers broke out. Matt kissed Jessie again, and in the midst of another rumble of thunder.

***

Homer stood behind Martha in line for food, the wedding party now in full swing. The tornado warning had ended, and everyone moved upstairs to the fellowship hall. Now three o'clock, Millie and the other ladies had hurried to put the food out. A call to the caterer informed them that too many trees were down around Central City for a return trip. No matter. Jessie was married.

Homer snagged some strawberries and broccoli from the fruit and vegetable trays adorning the table, then added a few cheese straws and some chicken tenders, deciding that a little barbeque sauce would be good on them.

He moved to one of the tables and set his plate down by Martha. "I'll get us some cake."

"Good," Martha said. "I would like a piece of both. And one of those chocolate-covered strawberries."

The ladies who'd taken their positions as servers filled two plates with cake, strawberries, and candy. He maneuvered between tables, nodding to Lilac. Martha sure had been surprised to see her cousin.

"Wasn't it a beautiful ceremony? Beside all that thundering," Martha said. "I think I cried through the whole thing."

"I know you did," Homer teased. "And yes. It was nice. I'm relieved the storm's blown over. Ben's father ran home to check out his chicken houses and said the damage around the county wasn't bad. Mostly trees down." He bit into a chicken tender.

"Deidre talked to her sister at the diner." Martha placed her punch cup on the table. "She said they were scared when the siren sounded, but the storm was over before she knew it." She raised her hand to her mouth. "Oh, look at Jessie and Millie over by the fence."

Jessie sat with Millie and the other girls, laughing as the photographer snapped photo after photo. Shay moved by Jessie as another was taken.

"Jessie is doing all right." Homer nodded in their direction.

Martha sighed. "She is. And Shay's a lovely little girl."

Shay left Jessie and ran up to Martha. "Daddy said he thought it would be okay for me to come to your farm sometimes and help feed the animals." She turned fully to Martha. "And Papaw Smith said he would take me fishing."

The child called him Papaw. She reached over and hugged him and another piece of his broken heart slipped back into place. Another child to ease the passing of his Elizabeth. Maybe things did work out sometimes, even if not as we expected.

***

Jessie spooned the last bite of wedding cake into her mouth. The vanilla tinged with a touch of almond was even better than the chocolate cake. The wind still whistled outside, but all apprehension of the storm had passed. Rest and peace nestled inside her soul and for once, she was complete.

Matt smiled. "Happy?"

She nodded. "Very."

He took her plate and tossed it in the nearby garbage can. "I have a surprise."

She reached up and grasped her new necklace. "It's been a day full of surprises already."

"Hey, Ben." His voice rose over the chattering guests. "Are you ready?"

Ben lifted a CD player from under the counter and plugged it in.

Soon, strains of a country love song filled the fellowship hall.

Matt held out his hands. "I think we need a dance to celebrate, don't you?"

Her dance? She swallowed hard. "I don't think this chair can do that."

"Allow me." He lifted her with no effort from the chair and held her close. "This is your wedding and you should be able to dance."

She placed her hands around his neck and leaned into his chest as they began to sway with the music. What could she say? The completeness she felt before went to a new level. She closed her eyes. An image of her and Matt, standing and dancing to the music overrode reality. She dipped and twirled in perfect harmony as the music grew.

Matt whispered in her ear. "You're all I'll ever need."

She opened her eyes. "You are more than I ever hoped for, Matt Jansen. You complete me."

He leaned over and kissed her gently as applause broke around them. "For always and ever."

***

Angeline perched on an oversized child's chair while Ben sat on the floor beside her. What a day. The main room in the children's building glowed with neon paint: green, pink, yellow, and orange. Chairs and tables were scattered around with an interactive toy section in the corner. She scooped the icing off her piece of cake and nibbled on it. The storm was over and Mother was okay. Now sugar seemed to hit the spot.

"Can I tell you something?" She set her plate on a nearby table. "I've wrestled with this whole Christian thing. But today I think I'm starting to understand a little."

"Great." Ben popped a whole chocolate strawberry in his mouth.

"Before the service, I said a prayer and told God I wanted to change. What do I do now?"

"Pray, read the Bible, go to church, get baptized. That's what most people do."

She frowned. His answer seemed too rehearsed. "What did you do?"

"Honestly? I got baptized and went to church." He shrugged. "But I don't pray unless I'm in trouble or read the Bible except in church. I guess my relationship with God has been kind of distant."

"How's that working for you?"

He rolled his eyes. "What happened to me at Slider's was a real wake-up call. I need to commit to acting right. Man, if Stu hadn't stopped me, I'd have driven home. Maybe killed myself or someone else."

She shook her head. Did guys ever learn? "You did make a fool of yourself."

"Do you have to keep reminding me? Tomorrow I'm going to church. Going to recommit to living better." He looked at her directly. "Do you want to come?"

"I thought you'd never ask." Angeline stood, plate in hand. "We'd better join the party. I have a lot of birdseed that needs tossing." She started toward the reception area, Ben right behind her.

"Did you see Matt's truck yet? Stu and I did a nice job *decorating* it while they were taking wedding pictures."

Angeline flashed a smile. "Why don't you show me?"

His hand brushed against hers and she gripped it. He opened the door and they stepped out into the bright sunshine together. Ben wasn't perfect, but neither was she. Maybe she could take a baby step in the direction of trusting a guy.

***

Homer rubbed his arms. The chilled wind bit through his thin dress coat. They needed to hurry with the bouquet-tossing. A small crowd still hung around in the parking lot. Jessie had changed into something warm and waited for Matt on the church's porch.

Matt pulled his truck to the front and hopped out. Someone had scrawled *JUST MARRIED* across the back windshield. Cans and old tennis shoes were tied to the back bumper.

"Are you sure the weather's not stormy where they're going?" Martha tugged at Homer's arm. "They could stay around here for one night."

"It's fine." Homer grunted. "They're driving away from the bad weather. I think it's about over anyway."

"I'm glad. When they get back, we'll help them move the rest of their things into the trailer," Martha said. "Oh, look. They're starting."

Matt took the garter and did the traditional "flip" into the crowd of young men. No one seemed to want it. It landed at Ben's feet and he bent to retrieve it.

Tony turned to him. "Man, what are you thinking? You do not want this."

Millie punched his arm. "Watch it."

"I didn't *try* to catch it."

Jessie wheeled around, hugging her light blue pea coat tightly to her. "Here it goes." She tossed the bouquet behind her. It landed in Angeline's arms.

"Whoa." She blushed as she held it out. "Someone take it."

"Too late," Estelle said. "It's yours now."

Homer chuckled. Matt reached down and swung Jessie from the chair with a quick swoop.

"Now, on to the Smoky Mountains." He carried his red-faced bride to the truck. Ben opened the door and Matt placed her inside. He ran around the truck, got in, and revved the motor.

They waved through open windows and pulled out of the parking lot. They were on their own. His Jessie ... her Matt.

Homer rubbed his eyes with his handkerchief before depositing it back in his pocket. Life was full now instead of empty, and he was grateful. His family had grown with the addition of Matt and Shay. New friends added to the mix, and the life he once thought of as old and stale had been given new energy. Maybe the new normal wouldn't be so bad.

Epilogue

The large oak separated the vivid sunshine into fingers of light behind the old house. Homer removed the lid from the tote nearest him. Today would be freeing, the perfect day to bring darkness to light. Jessie and Matt were back from their honeymoon and they were tackling the process of cleaning out the shed. Matt brought the first load to the back yard and left for another.

Homer handed Jessie a ceramic horse. As she cradled it in her arms, he glanced at the number of filled totes circling them in the backyard. He picked up Elizabeth's cheerleading pompoms. A heavy weight settled in his stomach with each discovery. How could he continue? Jessie grew stronger somehow with each item she held. He could do this for her. She was worth the pain.

"Martha, what you got there?" Homer asked.

Martha stood, a crocheted afghan draped in her arms.

"It was the baby blanket I crocheted for Jessie when Elizabeth first found out she was pregnant. We were all so excited."

Jessie patted Mamaw's arm. "I'm sorry this is hurting you."

"It's healing, not hurting They're real good memories."

Martha placed the afghan with the other crocheted items from the box. Jessie set the horse in a blue tote, which held items she would save. A large box was filled with things to sell. They would use that money to buy what they still needed for Jessie and Matt's new home. He wiped his brow. He'd been able to provide for his family. Maybe it was okay to ask for a little help sometimes.

Homer stacked the empty totes, one inside the other, and placed the lids in a pile. Only three totes left. Yep. He could do this.

He could finish.

Martha lifted another lid. "Oh, look."

"What is it?" Jessie moved beside Mamaw.

"Photos." Martha picked up the top album and placed it in Jessie's lap. Page after page of Jessie as a newborn smiled up from the book. The faces of Elizabeth and Wayne also filled the album.

"Wayne wasn't drinking then." Martha shook her head. "I wish you could have known him, how he was before."

"I do, too. But we can't go back and now it's time to make new memories." Jessie closed the album. "Let's put these in my closet so I can look at them later."

Homer and Martha grabbed each side of the tote and moved up the back steps into the house. They rounded the table in the kitchen, crossed the living room, then Homer pushed open the door into Jessie's bedroom. He sighed.

"I know this is hard for you, too." Martha helped lift each album from the box onto the low shelf in the closet. It's a good thing you've done. A really good thing."

He gave a weak smile. Martha and Jessie still loved him. Maybe God did too. "I'm glad you put up with me. Most people wouldn't, I reckon."

"Probably not." The corners of her mouth crawled to a grin. "But I'm not most people." She grasped his hand.

He planted a kiss on her cheek. Time to show her he could change. "I don't mean to be so ornery. I'm thinking about going to church with you again. Sometime. When I'm not too busy."

Martha's eyes shone. "There's nothing I'd like better."

"And when we finish cleaning out the shed, I'm going to try and sell that land."

"Why?"

"It has too many bad memories."

Martha put her arm through his as they walked back through the house. "But one day, your great-grandchildren might need a place to marry and live and create new memories."

He'd not thought of that. His Jessie with a baby? He couldn't help but smile. "You're right. I might better keep it."

They stepped out into the gentle sunshine. Martha moved to where Jessie was and together they looked through the last container. He leaned against the house, taking a glance up. He said he'd never forgive God. Maybe he'd spoken too soon.

When Elizabeth died, part of him died with her. God was nowhere to be found in his pain. How could anyone understand the death of one's child? Parents weren't supposed to outlive their children, especially if they had only one child. But he and Martha made it through. His one consolation: knowing Elizabeth loved God and was in heaven and they still had Jessie.

This new beginning was for him as much as for Jessie and Matt. Who would have thought at his age he could start over?

And Martha? He'd promised her no more lies. Maybe going to church could be the first step back to a part of his life he thought he'd lost forever.

Life, which had often been tasteless and flat since Elizabeth's death, had taken on new meaning. He'd grabbed hold of the life preserver of grace offered to him, and it held strong.

Martha's remark about not selling his uncle's place made him grin. Great-grandchildren. It would be good to hear the squeals and laughter of little ones around the house again. Real good.

***

The heat of an unusually mellow winter day warmed Homer. He, Martha, and Jessie lounged on the front porch and waited for Matt. The young'un had been married near three months and he'd never seen her happier. Jessie pulled the thick woolen scarf Martha had crocheted closer to her face.

"Are you warm enough?" Martha stood. "You're not going to get another headache in this sunshine, are you? Maybe you should go inside."

"I'm fine. This sunshine feels wonderful."

It bothered Homer that Jessie had started having headaches again after doing so well since the wedding. She'd made an appointment with Dr. Dixon and as soon as Matt got in from work, they'd take her. And he'd treat them all to supper at the diner afterward. Maybe Jessie could eat. She complained of feeling sick and she sure didn't need to lose weight.

The roar of the engine announced Matt's arrival. As he bounded up the steps, Jessie grinned and accepted his kiss. "Hey, honey," she said.

"Feeling better today? Give me a minute to wash up and we'll go." He pushed through the door.

Homer gazed into the nearby woods, close to Jessie's home. The trees were still bare, but early buttercups had begun to push through and color the ground in many places. He'd plowed and readied his corn patch, and his cows grazed in the small pasture. Wayne brought Shay over a week ago and let her stay all day. Life was good … except for Jessie's headaches.

Matt stepped back onto the porch. "Are we ready to go? We've got thirty minutes until your appointment."

Jessie glanced at her phone. "We have plenty of time."

Homer stood. "I know one thing. If the doc doesn't give us a good answer as to why you've had migraines lately we're going to a specialist."

They all moved toward Martha's car.

"That's right," Martha said, as she opened the car door. "There's one in Central City near the hospital."

Jessie shrugged. "Okay. I can tell when I'm outnumbered."

They made the short drive to the Riverview Clinic. After a brief wait, Dr. Dixon's nurse called Jessie back. Matt went along.

Homer thumbed through two farming magazines and a recent edition of a sporting magazine. What was taking so long? He looked at Martha. "Do you think something's wrong?"

***

Jessie shifted in her chair. Why were examination rooms always so cold?

She'd already been to the lab for blood work and a urine sample. When they made it back to the room, the nurse took Jessie's temperature and a blood pressure reading. All normal.

"Wait here and the doctor will talk to you." The nurse picked up the chart and left.

"You look pale." Matt sat in a chair by her, gripping her hand. "Are you sure you're okay?"

"You know I hate to have my blood drawn." Jessie shook her head. "And it seems my whole life I've given away most of it."

After a long wait, Dr. Dixon finally arrived. "I'm so sorry I'm late." She held a chart in her hand and glanced over it as she pushed back her graying hair. "I was waiting for the lab work before I examined you."

"Everything look good?" Matt asked.

Dr. Dixon glanced up. "It depends on what you consider good. Everything checks out normal ..." She smiled. " ... for a woman who's going to have a baby."

Matt's mouth dropped open. He turned to Jessie. "A baby?"

Everything inside Jessie suddenly came together in the knowing. The nausea, headaches, the odd feeling deep inside ... all of it spoke of a human life beginning inside her womb. She would be a mother. "I'm going to have a baby." She smiled at Matt. "And you're going to be a daddy."

Matt hugged her, then the doctor. "I'm going to be a daddy," he repeated.

"Now," Dr. Dixon said. "I figure you're about five weeks along. I'll set up an appointment with an obstetrician in Central City who specializes in high-risk pregnancies, though you'll eventually wind up going to Huntsville. Not that I anticipate problems but that's what you'll want to do. As far as the headaches, I believe as you move along in the pregnancy, they'll decrease. For most women, pregnancy is good for migraines. I'll give you something for the nausea. Try to eat and I think you'll feel better."

After a quick exam, Jessie dressed. She was going to be a mother. What would Mamaw and Papaw think?

They waited for the nurse to return with her paperwork. "Matt, what do you want? A girl or a boy?"

"A princess or a football player?" Matt hadn't been able to sit still since the doctor gave them the news. "Either would be great. We'll have to turn the extra bedroom into a nursery. And after supper, we'll go by my folks' house He chuckled. "They'll be in shock."

"They will. Oh, I can't wait to decorate the nursery. And the smaller bedroom can be a toy room."

Jessie hugged herself. The abandoned girl, loved by God and her grandparents, had come full circle. She was now giving life to another. God had redeemed what others viewed as impossible and brought restoration. Hope against all odds.

Jessie's hope.

Her life had been a journey, not one she'd always savored. However, God was in control. Today and always.

In her heart, she sang a song of joy and praise as she relaxed in the rest of God, so sweet and precious. Like dancing with Matt, God picked her up, whirled and twirled her as she moved through life. She owed it all to the Him who had begun a healing in her soul, guiding, leading, wooing, loving, and forgiving. What more could she ask? Something she'd known in her head moved to her heart. The healing truly had begun.

***

Another ten minutes passed. Homer stood and approached the receptionist, determined to find out what was the matter with his Jessie. As he reached the sliding glass window, the door beside him opened. He jumped slightly as Matt wheeled Jessie out.

He stopped. "Y'all have been back there forever. Is something wrong?"

"No, Papaw. I'm healthy."

"That's good to hear," Martha said, gathering her purse. They followed Jessie and Matt out the door and to the parking lot.

Homer paused by the car. "Now, what did the doctor say?"

Jessie smiled at Matt before answering. She looked so beautiful in the fading sunshine. "She said in thirty-six weeks we're all going to be very busy." She laid her hand over her stomach. "Taking care of a baby."

Homer gaped. "A what?"

"You're going to be a mother?" Martha laughed, hugging Jessie, then Matt. "A baby. I just can't believe it."

Jessie grasped her grandparent's hands. "You know, I'd always dreamed of being a wife and mother but wondered if it would be possible with this wheelchair. When Matt proposed, it was half my dream answered. And today I see the beginning of the rest of it. How special is that?"

Homer had no words. His Jessie was going to be a mother. After the accident, he'd thought she'd never really recover, that they would always care for her. As she grew stronger and more independent, he scarcely hoped that one day she would graduate and go to college or get a job. Until Matt came along, he never dreamed she'd marry.

And he sure wouldn't allow himself to hope for a great-grandbaby. But there she was, talking to Martha about a baby's room with Matt looking as proud—as proud as he did—when he'd found out Martha was pregnant with Elizabeth.

"Did you hear me, Papaw?" Jessie tugged at his arm. "Do you want a girl or a boy? And don't give me the 'I just want the baby to be healthy' answer."

A boy or girl? "Well, darling, as much as I love my girls, it might be nice to have a little boy around. You know, we could buy him some overalls and a baseball cap. Fix him up right."

"And play football." Matt opened the car door. "Let's go. We've got to get Jessie to the diner. She's eating for two, you know."

They loaded the car. As Homer turned onto the highway, he couldn't help but chuckle. Yep. That's what they'd do. Tomorrow he and Martha would go to the clothes section of the farm supply store. His little farmer would need some tiny overalls, a little blue shirt, and of course, a John Deere cap. And when he got a little older, he'd need some good work boots. Heck, a little girl could wear that outfit also. He might oughta get a pink shirt too.

Just in case.

Made in the USA
Lexington, KY
16 July 2019